Praise for previous Justice Inc. books

"One of romantic intrigue's best, M.J. Rodgers pens another keeper with *Beauty vs. the Beast.*"
—Debbie Richardson
Romantic Times

"The talented M.J. Rodgers sparkles once again with a wonderful array of characters and thoroughly innovative storytelling in *Baby vs. the Bar.*"
—Debbie Richardson
Romantic Times

Praise for other M.J. Rodgers books

Who is Jane Williams?
"M.J. Rodgers has written a very tightly paced, very suspenseful story... Just when we think we have the mystery solved, a new and interesting development happens."
—Hollie Domiano
Affaire de Coeur

"This absorbing romantic mystery will challenge readers who enjoy sorting red herrings from the bait and catch."
—Sue Wright
Gothic Journal

On the Scent
"Ms. Rodger's imaginative trip through the provocative world of fragrance is spellbinding."
—Barbara Kelly
Affaire de Coeur

Dear Reader,

Open the gilded doors and step into the world of
M.J. Rodgers's JUSTICE INC. A world where
principle courts passion. In this Seattle law firm,
legal eagles battle headline-stealing cases...and
find heart-stealing romance in the bargain.

M.J. Rodgers has become synonymous with the
best in romantic mystery. Having written her very
first book for Intrigue seven years ago, she has
gone on to become one of the bestselling and most
popular Intrigue authors. Her books are
perennial Reviewers Choice Award winners, and
she is the recipient of the Career Achievement
Award for Romantic Mystery from *Romantic Times*.

So turn the page and enter the world of
JUSTICE INC.

Regards,

Debra Matteucci
Senior Editor & Editorial Coodinator
Harlequin Books
300 East 42nd Street
New York, NY 10017

M.J. Rodgers

HEART VS. HUMBUG

Harlequin Books

TORONTO • NEW YORK • LONDON
AMSTERDAM • PARIS • SYDNEY • HAMBURG
STOCKHOLM • ATHENS • TOKYO • MILAN
MADRID • WARSAW • BUDAPEST • AUCKLAND

SPECIAL ACKNOWLEDGMENT

My thanks to a very special friend, T. Lorraine Vassalo, of
Ottawa, Ontario, for her wonderful recipes for Loin of Veal
and Grand Marnier French Toast, both of which appear
briefly in this story and everlastingly on my hips.

ISBN 0-373-22350-1

HEART VS. HUMBUG

WASHINGTON

Columbia Beach

Port Ludlow

Puget Sound

Everett

Mukilteo

South Point

Lofall

Edmonds

OLYMPIC PENINSULA

Poulsbo

Winslow

Bremerton

Seattle

KITSAP PENINSULA

Hoodsport

Gig Harbor

Tahlequah

Shelton

Tacoma

Olympia

Justice Inc.
Law Offices

CAST OF CHARACTERS

Octavia Osborne—A top-notch lawyer who is not afraid to let her heart lead the way to justice.

Brett Merlin—An infamous lawyer known as "the Magician," a man who believes the law cannot afford to have a heart.

Mab Osborne—Octavia's grandmother; a lady who breaks all the stereotypes.

Dole Scroogen—His nickname is "the Scrooge." He lives up to it—and then some.

Nancy Scroogen—Scroogen's wife; a lady who suffers in silence.

John Winslow—He has a key to the crucial locked door and maybe a key to grandmother's heart.

Douglas Twitch—He is a genius at engineering, and maybe at murder, too.

Constance Kope—She has a knack for design and maybe a need for revenge.

Ronald Scroogen—His relationship with his father is full of conflict and confusion.

ABOUT THE AUTHOR

Heart Vs. Humbug is the third book in the JUSTICE INC. courtroom series by bestselling author M.J. Rodgers. In the months to come she will continue to bring you the stories of these dedicated attorneys known as Seattle's legal sleuths.

M.J. is the winner of the *Romantic Times* Career Achievement Award for Romantic Mysteries, twice the winner of their Reviewer's Choice Award for Best Intrigue, and is also the winner of B. Dalton Bookseller's top-selling Intrigue Award. She loves to hear from readers and will autograph a sticker for placement inside your copy of *Heart Vs. Humbug* if you send a self-addressed stamped envelope to her at P.O. Box 284, Seabeck, WA 98380-0284.

Books by M.J. Rodgers

HARLEQUIN INTRIGUE
102—FOR LOVE OR MONEY
128—A TASTE OF DEATH
140—BLOODSTONE
157—DEAD RINGER
176—BONES OF CONTENTION
185—RISKY BUSINESS
202—ALL THE EVIDENCE
214—TO DIE FOR
254—SANTA CLAUS IS COMING
271—ON THE SCENT
290—WHO IS JANE WILLIAMS?
335—BEAUTY VS. THE BEAST
342—BABY VS. THE BAR

HARLEQUIN
AMERICAN ROMANCE
492—FIRE MAGIC
520—THE ADVENTURESS
563—THE GIFT-WRAPPED GROOM

Prologue

The intruder crept silently beneath the shadowy wings of the December overcast that blacked out the moon like a swooping bird of prey.

Not much farther now. Just a few more steps.

A few more *careful* steps.

Perceptions in daylight took so many subtle visual cues for granted. Beneath the absolute black of this inky night, without even a horizontal reference, a sense of balance could falter and a sense of direction could quickly become disoriented.

Still, the intruder welcomed the absence of the light. The weak might gather around their paltry incandescents and fluorescents trying to push the darkness aside, but the strong sought the night's cloak to open new doors to opportunity.

One such door lay just ahead. The intruder grasped its knob and slipped quietly inside the greenhouse.

The relative spacing of the rows of plants to either side of the center path had been memorized, even the exact number of steps to the storeroom at its back paced out. Nothing had been left to chance. Nothing.

The intruder started boldly forward...only to instantly trip and fall heavily to the ground, letting out a startled oath.

Luckily, the earthen path was cushioned with moss, and the intruder's thick clothing and gloves prevented abraded skin.

But the intruder didn't feel lucky. The intruder felt angry. How could this happen after all this planning!

Muffled curses spat through the intruder's teeth, all the more angry because they had to be muffled. Nothing was worse than having to keep silent while the rage seethed inside.

The intruder sat back on the heels of black running shoes and dug into the deep pockets of black sweatpants to draw out a small penlight. The flashlight beam bobbed along the mossy path as the intruder searched for the obstruction.

There it was. An electric cord strung loosely across the path, connecting a string of Christmas tree lights draped over the miniature fir trees on either side. Some fool had stopped in the middle of decorating the trees, leaving the cord swinging ankle-high over the path, marked with strings of gold tinsel and a large orange plastic caution cone.

Lot of help those markers were in the dark. Better make sure there weren't any more such surprises.

The intruder pointed the thin stream of the flashlight ahead. No more gold tinsel and orange caution cones stood in the way.

The intruder rose and began to resume the interrupted journey forward when suddenly the sounds of heavy boots crunched on the frozen gravel outside of the greenhouse.

The watchman!

The intruder quickly switched off the penlight, pulled up the hood of the black sweatshirt, dropped to the rich earth beside the path, jackknifed between the trunks of miniature fir trees, and lay concealed beneath the cover of their thick green branches.

The pungent odor of the dark, rich compost burned the intruder's nose. But that discomfort was of far less concern than the question now burning in the intruder's mind. Would the carefully selected dark clothing blend into the black earth?

The telltale sounds of the watchman's boots stopped at the edge of the window-lined structure. The intruder remained stock-still as a strong beam of light flashed into the greenhouse.

"Somebody in there?" the watchman called, his voice thick and raspy with age.

The intruder knew about this watchman. His name was Hank. Hank had been given this job to keep him going after his wife died. Both Hank's eyesight and hearing had seen better days. These were all things the intruder had considered before selecting this night to enter the greenhouse.

The intruder lay facedown, absolutely still, as Hank's flashlight swept over the plants and then the path. Once. Twice. A third time. The intruder's hands began to sweat within the heavy gloves.

Hank switched off his flashlight. He muttered beneath his breath as he shuffled back to the warm shed at the rear of the community center. The intruder knew Hank would now return to watching the old movies on his small TV set and carrying on conversations with his dead wife.

The intruder exhaled in relief. Whatever Hank might have seen or heard, he had satisfied himself nothing had gotten into the greenhouse. He would not be back.

As soon as the watchman's footsteps faded into a soft, spongy echo, the intruder rose to hands and knees and crawled carefully forward.

No more obstructions blocked the path. All would now go according to plan.

And it was a brilliant plan. Getting into the locked storeroom at the back of this greenhouse had been the only risky part. As soon as it was accomplished, everything else should be easy.

But success hinged on no one knowing the intruder had been here this night. No one.

No one would. And when it all started to hit the fan, no one would ever suspect who was *really* behind it. The intruder smiled.

Yes, a truly brilliant plan.

Chapter One

"Romantic men don't have penises," seventy-six-year-old Mab Osborne announced distinctly over the FM radio waves to her devoted listeners of KRIS's "Senior-Sex-Talk" program.

From her spectator position in the corner of the control room, Octavia Osborne nearly choked trying to subdue the resultant chuckle that rumbled in her throat as she listened to her grandmother's outrageous pronouncement.

Seventy-two-year-old Constance Kope did not try to stifle her response. "Mab Osborne, we cannot discuss this... topic, and it is totally unnecessary for you to use that... that... word," Constance said, her fusty Pekingese-like face spread open in prescient horror as she barked her loud protest. She shoved her glasses farther back on her button nose and leaned forward to poke the radio program hostess in the arm with a reprimanding index finger.

Mab took the interruption and poking with inherent good humor. "Precisely, Constance. A penis is totally unnecessary. Would you like to explain why to the radio audience?"

Mab's direct challenge to her would-be critic worked like a dropped stitch in the knitting of Constance Kope's thoughts. The tiny woman's faded brown eyes began to water behind her glasses.

"Heavens, no! I don't wish to discuss—"

"Yes, you're quite right, Constance," Mab interrupted. "This is a topic that I can best do justice to, I believe."

Constance's breath got caught in her throat and came out in a muffled sneeze through her tiny nostrils. She looked like she still wanted to bark but wasn't sure at what.

Octavia stifled another chuckle. There was no telling what the feisty, frank and fun Mab Osborne might say next. Octavia's grandmother was a sturdy five-eight with silver-streaked red hair, bright blue eyes, an even brighter pantsuit and a sense for the dramatic that never failed to delight Octavia and daunt the myriad guests who had appeared with Mab during her forty-year radio career.

Seventy-three-year-old John Winslow, another one of those guests who was currently sitting right next to Octavia in the tiny control room, leaned slightly forward. "Mab, I admit we agreed there were no holds barred in this discussion of 'What Makes Good Sex in One's Seventies,' but don't you think that eliminating a man's penis is a trifle severe?"

Mab's resultant laugh lifted the volume needle to the middle decibels on her radio station's control board.

Octavia swung her attention to John Winslow's neat presence and prescient smile. From his perfect diction to the white silk ascot tucked into his open-throat blue dress shirt, John reminded Octavia of one of those fast-disappearing, refined elderly gentlemen who actually knew what courtly dress and manners really meant.

"John, I'm not suggesting that a man's penis needs to be surgically removed," Mab said. "What I'm saying is that each one of us—whether we're twenty-five or ninety-five—must first embrace the right word images in order to receive full enjoyment from any act."

Seventy-five-year-old Douglas Twitch, Mab's third and final guest on her "Senior-Sex-Talk" panel, leaned forward to grab the microphone.

"Word images? What in the hell are you talking about?"

Octavia watched Mab gaze calmly at the bushy-headed, rawboned man in the worn, faded jeans and gray-and-white checkered shirt. While Mab's confident smile and bearing conjured up images of a thoroughbred charging confidently over a racetrack, Douglas Twitch's beleaguered scowl bore far more resemblance to a plow horse chaffing under the weight of the harness.

"I'm referring to the full spectrum of human sexuality, Douglas," Mab replied. "All of the important books on the subject never describe men as having penises. And quite correctly, I might add."

Octavia watched as Constance Kope's punched-in, Pekingese face colored to match the red Christmas bow that adorned the desk beneath the control panel. John Winslow's hand covered the smirk spreading over his mouth as he bent his full white head of impeccably groomed hair. Douglas Twitch crossed his arms over his barrel chest as his long, horsey brow dug a deep trough.

Mab's eyes were resting on Douglas's long face as the breath shot out of his flared nostrils in short, snorting whinnies.

"Something you wanted to say, Douglas?" she asked.

He grabbed the microphone once again.

"You bet there is. I admit I'm not much of a reader and I never actually got through all the words in my high school biology text, but the pictures were clear enough and nothing on the male human's torso was left out, woman." He sent a meaningful glance around the room. "I repeat, nothing."

He dropped the microphone back onto the control board table as his exclamation point and gave a final satisfied snort of vented spleen.

Mab shrugged her straight shoulders. "But then that was *only* a biology book, wasn't it, Douglas?"

Constance's brow puckered in confusion. "Only a biology book, Mab? What books are you talking about?"

Mab caught Octavia's eye and winked. That was when Octavia knew that Constance had asked her grandmother the right question.

"Why, romance books, of course, Constance," Mab replied. "They are the only books that really explore the profound and rich universe of human emotions."

John leaned forward slightly. "Mab, do I understand you right? Are you saying that in romance books, romantic men don't engage in intercourse?"

"On the contrary, John. In romance novels, romantic men engage in intercourse quite frequently. And enjoy it tremendously, too, I might add."

Octavia felt certain Douglas Twitch's resultant sharp snort registered on some Richter scale as he did his best to scoot his chair away from Mab in the tiny control room. Constance's sigh dissembled into a reprobation.

John's smile spread big enough to hurt. "Okay, Mab. I admit I'm stumped. If these romantic men engage in intercourse frequently and enjoy it tremendously and they don't have penises, *what* do they use?"

"Why, their pulsing manhoods or hardened desire or—"

"Oh, you're saying that it's the word *penis* that isn't used in connection with these romantic men?"

Mab's mischievous eyes twinkled. "Exactly, John. I'm so glad you finally understand."

John let out an amused chortle at being so intellectually reprimanded. "Well, I do and I don't, Mab. Aren't we just dealing with semantics here?"

"Yeah," Douglas said. "You tell her, John. They're the same thing."

Mab shook her head. "No, they are not. Every act in life can be made ordinary or special, depending on how we approach it. The essential part of our approach involves the words we use. Words create the important messages that define our thoughts and feelings for everything."

John arched a sliver of silver eyebrow. "Care to provide an example of what you mean, Mab?"

"Certainly, John. If I tell you I'm hungry and I'm going to grab something to eat, what image comes to mind?"

"You're looking for something quick, whatever is handy."

"Yes, quick and handy. Not very exciting words, are they? But, if, on the other hand, I asked you to dine with me this evening, what images would then come to your mind?"

"Well, I suppose a white tablecloth, candlelight, something special to eat, probably carefully selected."

"Precisely, John—a beautifully set table offering something carefully selected. Words have lifted the ordinary act of eating into the stimulation of feelings that go beyond the mere satiation of hunger. In place of quick we now have special. In place of handy we now have carefully selected. The act of eating has been transcended into an act of caring and sharing appealing to all the senses. That's why romantic men never have sex. They make love."

Douglas squirmed in his chair, his big bony knee slamming into the edge of the control desk in the tiny room. "What in the hell does eating have to do with sex?"

Mab let out a little puff of impatience. "Words, Douglas, images of emotion—where true sensuality and romance come from. Sex is quick and handy. Insignificant. Making love is special and carefully selected. Important. The words we use so clearly create the emotion we anticipate and receive from the act."

Constance nodded. "Oh, I see. You're saying that the right words stimulate feelings that go beyond a mere sexual gratification?"

"Exactly, Constance. It's the stimulation of those other feelings that makes us romantic, transforms an act of physical need into one of emotional fulfillment, and brings out the truly human part of ourselves. The feelings that lead up to and result from doing it are what make the sexual act, or any act, worthwhile."

Douglas rubbed his stiff, grayish beard in apparent irritation. "Yeah, well I still don't see what that has to do with using *hardened desire* in place of *penis.*"

Mab let out the frustrated sigh of a teacher trying to get through to her backward pupil.

"Douglas, when you describe a man using his penis in sexual intercourse, you're talking biology, and clinical images come to mind. But when a man joins a woman to him with his hardened desire within the pages of a romance novel, he's mated with her on an emotional plane, as well. It's that emotional joining that causes the act to transcend the mere elimination of hunger and makes it become a feast at life's most tasty and tantalizing banquet.''

Octavia smiled, thoroughly delighted with Mab's triumphant crossing of her finish line. Her grandmother pointed meaningfully to the two incoming lines lit up on her console and announced that it was time for the panel to take calls from their listeners.

As the seniors chatted with the first caller, Octavia leaned back and let her mind wander. It had been years since she'd last been here. Yet in a way, it felt just like yesterday.

Some of her fondest memories with her grandmother were garnered in this tiny control room. Every day after school, she'd stop by. Hour after hour, she'd sit and watch and listen as Mab's fingers reached out to connect with the switches on the control board and her voice reached out to connect with her listeners—sometimes offering them an interesting new thought about the world, sometimes just an irreverent spate of her own special brand of humor, but always with an honest compassion that came from her heart.

Octavia smiled as she looked up to see the colorful tinsel and the many, many Christmas cards from Mab's devoted listeners taped across the top of the room's walls.

Christmas time had always been the best time to sit in on Mab's broadcasts. It was during the holiday season that Octavia and Mab had laughed the most in this room. And probably cried the most, too. Octavia knew she was who she was today because of what she had learned about life from her grandmother, right here.

And, after witnessing this morning's program, Octavia was delighted to find Mab still as fun and fresh and feisty as ever.

"Ladies and gentlemen, I see our time is up," Mab was saying. "I'd like to thank my guests from the executive committee of the Silver Power League for being with us this morning. Constance Kope, Douglas Twitch and Dr. John Winslow.

"Coming up now is some beautiful Christmas music to keep you company. I'll return at two with our community's news. Until then, this is Mab Osborne and KRIS, Bremerton's senior citizens' radio, reminding you to keep calling and writing the chamber of commerce and the Department of Community Development. Your action is needed to save our community center. Bye for now."

Mab flipped the switch on the main control board to cut in the prerecorded Christmas music.

Octavia sat forward in concern at Mab's final message to her listeners. This was the first she had heard that the community center was in jeopardy. Was that the reason for Mab's call and urgent request for Octavia to come by this morning?

Mab seemed to read the concern in Octavia's eyes. She shook her head at her granddaughter. Octavia understood that was Mab's way of saying that any questions Octavia had would have to wait.

Octavia rose and reached for Constance's hand as she started the rounds of giving each of the seniors a warm handshake and smile. "It was a stimulating show. Thanks for letting me sit in."

As Constance rose to her feet to take Octavia's hand, she gave her comfortably round, five-foot frame a small shake, like the miniature dog she so resembled.

"It had its moments," she agreed.

Douglas scratched irritably at his stiff salt-and-pepper beard after he released Octavia's hand.

"Personally, I could do without Mab always having to sensationalize everything. No penises on men! What a ridiculous thing to say. Isn't that right, Constance?"

Constance's head bent back as she squinted up at the much taller man.

"Now, Douglas, Mab had a commendable point, once she got to it. Although, I do believe the use of that word really wasn't—"

Douglas swung away from Constance to face John. "Don't you agree Mab should be muzzled?"

John's palms came up, a humorous gleam in his eyes. "Doctors, even ophthalmologists, always stay neutral in fights, Douglas. We have to be available later to patch up the combatants."

Mab turned to position herself squarely in front of the horsey, six-foot Douglas Twitch.

"Stop looking for support to gang up on me, Douglas. You never got it when we were in grade school together and you're not getting it now. Muzzle me, indeed! I'm not surprised my point eluded you. I wouldn't be surprised to learn the subtleties of 'Sesame Street' elude you."

Douglas's sallow face colored. He grabbed the pipe hanging out of his checkered shirt pocket and took it like a bit between his prominent teeth, spluttering incoherently.

Mab turned away from his reddened face and calmly slipped her arm through Octavia's.

"I'm glad you arrived in time to hear some of the show. Your being here takes me back, Octavia. Let's go home and I'll fix us both something nice and hot to drink and we can talk."

Octavia nodded. But as they turned to leave the control room, she saw Mab suddenly halt and stiffen.

Octavia followed the direction of her grandmother's fixed gaze. On the other side of the glass barrier that separated the radio control room from the visitors' lounge, two men stood staring.

Octavia noted and dismissed the slouching, sour-pussed shorter man with the squinty dark eyes, thin ashen hair, baggy olive pants and green-and-black-checkered suspenders. But the taller man caught and completely held her attention.

He was at least six-four with bark-brown hair and broad, imposing shoulders in an expensive custom suit of charcoal gray, discreetly trimmed with a dove-gray tie and pocket handkerchief. He looked remarkably formal and forbidding, from the tight laces of his highly polished black shoes to the obdurate shine in his black-rimmed, silver-sprinkled eyes.

Octavia knew instantly that this was a man who had made his mark in the world and would continue to do so.

Those arresting eyes held hers in an intense scrutiny. Their silver shine was stronger than confidence, deeper than desire. For no reason that made any sense, she suddenly felt the rush of blood through her heart and a tingling in her fingertips.

"Who is he, Mab?" she asked.

She could feel her grandmother's eyes dart to her face and then back to the men.

"I don't know who the tall one is you're fixating on, but the short, slimy one is Dole Scroogen. We call him the Scrooge around here."

"And as long as the other one is with the Scrooge, he's not worth your wondering about," Constance announced in what sounded to Octavia like a definite warning.

"What does that damn Scrooge want besides our blood?" Douglas grumbled with more vehemence than Octavia had yet heard from the man.

"He only shows up in person when he can gloat over something," the normally cool, suave John said with surprising heat. "We'd better go see what it is this time."

Their collective comments told Octavia that despite the seniors' previous differences over the content and conduct of the radio show, the appearance of Dole Scroogen had united them instantly in animosity against the man.

They left the tiny control room single file, Mab in the lead, Octavia right behind her, the rest following. Octavia could still feel the stranger's eyes. They had not left her once since the moment she first felt them.

As Octavia and the seniors approached the two men in the waiting room, Dole Scroogen raised his arm to point at Mab.

"That's her. That's Mab Osborne."

The impoliteness of the man's pointing finger and his whiny, condescending tone immediately irritated Octavia.

She knew at that precise moment that she was going to thoroughly dislike Dole Scroogen.

Scroogen's tall companion shifted his eyes from Octavia to her grandmother. He took a step toward Mab. His deep, rich voice vibrated through the small waiting room like an ominous drumroll.

"Mrs. Osborne, I'm Brett Merlin."

Brett Merlin? Octavia felt a small jolt of surprise as she instantly recognized his name. Could this really be the *Magician* of corporate law standing before her? The one whose name every attorney whispered in polite reverence? Well, well. No wonder the guy exuded the aura of the anointed.

Octavia watched, her initial interest heightened even more, as Brett Merlin slipped a sheet of folded paper from his pocket. He held it out to Mab.

"What's this?" Mab asked as she took the paper from his hand.

"It's a copy of a cover letter I faxed to the FCC this morning, Mrs. Osborne. I've also sent by Federal Express a two-hour tape of recorded highlights from your 'Senior-Sex-Talk' programs. I'm demanding the FCC revoke your radio license on the grounds of lewd and immoral content."

Octavia couldn't have been more surprised at Brett Merlin's words than if the man had suddenly announced he was from Mars. He was bringing her grandmother up on a morals charge before the FCC? She didn't know whether to laugh or have this obviously overrated fool of an attorney committed.

Before she could respond to either impulse, a photographer suddenly jumped out from where he had been hidden on the other side of a partition and snapped several photos of Mab. The unexpected flashes from his camera also blinded Octavia, who was standing just behind her grandmother.

By the time Octavia could see and think straight again, it was too late to do anything. The Magician, the Scrooge and the photographer had all vanished—right out the door of her grandmother's radio station.

"OCTAVIA, I'M NOT standing still for this FCC threat."

Octavia smiled. That sounded just like the fearless, independently competent Mab that she had been admiring all her life.

She poured her grandmother's homemade hot apple cider into both their cups and slipped in a cinnamon stick. The spicy fragrance filled the room and Octavia's senses with the sweet, nostalgic past of other cold, overcast December days spent in this bright, cozy kitchen, baking Christmas goodies and stringing popcorn for the tree.

Octavia gathered up all the marvelous memories spilling out of her mind and set them firmly aside as she focused her attention on her grandmother's perky head of silver-and-red curls.

"Before we talk about this FCC thing, Mab, tell me why you called last night and asked me to take the ferry over from Seattle this morning."

Mab shook her straight shoulders, as though trying to disengage some annoying burden clinging to them.

"Because of the Scrooge, Octavia. All the trouble began with him."

"What trouble?"

"When a group of us formed the Silver Power League five years ago, we did so in order to organize senior citizens and show them the kind of power we could wield if united against unfavorable legislation. One of our members gave us a ninety-nine-year lease to some land and an old barn that sat on it to use as our community center."

"Yes, I remember visiting you there a couple of times when you first opened. You had cleaned and painted that old barn and made it very presentable. Now, what has this to do with Dole Scroogen?"

"He's our new landlord."

"And?"

"Remember those documents I asked you to look over nearly a year ago? The ones about the Silver Power League's ninety-nine-year land lease?"

"Yes. You were worried about any loopholes. But the previous owner's lawyer did a very good job drafting that protection clause against your eviction by a subsequent owner."

"Except she didn't anticipate that the Scrooge would levy a ridiculous rent on us."

"Mab, he can't do that. Remember my telling you? There are protection provisions in your lease that prohibit any rent being charged that is not commensurate with property value. The three acres of land your community center sits on has some value, but that old barn isn't worth much."

"You've been away too long, Octavia. We have a new Silver Power League community center."

Yes, she had been away too long—too busy rushing through the arteries of her life to find the time to spend with this special person who had first put Octavia's hand on life's true pulse.

Octavia paused in the middle of her self-recrimination to let her grandmother's last words register. "Wait a minute. Did you just say the *new* center?"

Her grandmother nodded.

"I kept looking at all this talent our members had just going to waste—retired architects, carpenters, plumbers, electricians, landscapers, decorators. Our members may be over sixty, but most are still vital and strong and possess a lifetime of experience and expertise. So a couple of years ago I decided to get them off their duffs and put them to work on some renovations."

"But, Mab—"

Mab raised her hand to halt Octavia's interruption.

"Yes, I know. Any improvements on leased land become the property of the landowner. But you have to understand, Octavia, at that time the landowner was one of our members and a good friend. She was charging us only fifty dollars a month in rent. We knew that on her death everything in her estate was to go to her only surviving blood relative—her great-nephew, Dole Scroogen. She told us that she had spoken to him and he understood her wishes. Plus which, we had the ninety-nine-year lease and we never thought...well, we never thought he would do what he did."

"Go on, Mab."

"When she died, we'd already torn down that old barn and broken ground on the new Silver Power League Community Center and the extensive greenhouse that goes with it. Everyone was so involved by then, so excited at what we were creating."

"And Scroogen?"

"Months went by and he never even contacted us. We thought that like his great aunt, he supported us. We went blissfully on with our plans. The buildings are magnificent. We've all been so proud. We held an open house two months ago. Invited everyone in the community."

Octavia was certain she knew what was coming. "Let me guess. Scroogen showed up then with an appraiser?"

Mab nodded. "Because of our improvements, the property is now worth far more than it was before. He and the appraiser spent hours evaluating every inch before he presented us with an astronomical monthly rent and a six-month deposit demand, all payable by December 1. We barely managed to scrape together December's rent and half of the deposit demand. It cleaned out our savings. He served us immediately with a thirty-day eviction notice. If we don't come up with with the rest of the deposit and January's rent by January 1, we're out."

Octavia sipped her cider. It would be so easy to get upset. But getting upset was not going to help her grandmother's predicament. Only clear thinking could do that. Besides, Octavia had never been one to waste time wringing her hands over what was already done.

"Scroogen must have plans for that land to be so bent on forcing you seniors out."

"About two and a half weeks ago, the bulldozers arrived and started leveling the houses on the rest of the block adjacent to our center. I checked the county assessor's office and found that the Scrooge owns all the property. What's more, he began buying it right after he acquired his great aunt's land and we started building the new Silver Power League Community Center. A public notice went in the newspaper yesterday. He's building a condominium complex."

"Right next to your community center?"

"Right *over* our community center. We invited the workers driving the bulldozers in for tea and cookies and pumped them. Their foreman is Keneth George, a native American of the Suquamish Tribe, and a real nice young man. He told us the Scrooge has approval to build a very exclusive, high-priced condominium complex on all the land he owns."

"So he's been planning on evicting you all along."

"Absolutely. The far-end parcel connects to the water. He's going to build a private ferry system to Seattle for the owners of the condos. Keneth said he's going to use our new community center as a clubhouse and our greenhouse as an indoor garden for the people who purchase the units."

Octavia shook her head. "And he let you build them for him. This guy is a real piece of work. Your Scrooge label fits him only too well. Is the site zoned for multiple-family dwelling?"

"Yes. There was a small four-unit complex in the middle that was inhabited by seniors before he bought them out and tore it down. Octavia, he's setting up the whole block to be a new bedroom community for Seattle."

"And concentrated residences such as this condominium complex mean lots more people. Demands for water, electricity, gas stations, fast-food restaurants, shopping centers, everything rises. That will change the whole atmosphere of your quiet little community."

"That's precisely what I've been telling my radio listeners this last week. The Scrooge's plan to push out the Silver Power League is only the start of the breakup of our community. It isn't just our community center's one block that will be affected. Our whole neighborhood for miles will be changed. With the influx of the affluent commuters, property values and taxes will skyrocket until the seniors on social security will be forced out from homes they've lived in all their lives. Unless he's stopped."

"Are you getting much response to your radio broadcasts?"

"The station has been deluged with callers—of all ages, I'm happy to say—all asking what they can do. I tell them to write letters and make phone calls to the mayor, the chamber of commerce and Bremerton's Community Development Department. Still, every morning the bulldozers arrive at eight sharp."

"Since the condominium complex is already allowed outright by the zoning code, even if these officials were sympathetic, they have no legal recourse to stop it."

"I know. When I called the mayor's office, I was told his hands are tied."

"This complex would be thoroughly welcomed in other Bremerton neighborhoods, inasmuch as it would bring the promise of jobs and new industry. But your neighborhood is such a poor place to put it. Have you mentioned that fact to the Scrooge?"

"I called him as soon as I heard about the condo complex. But he wouldn't listen. He hung up on me."

"Feeling secure in his legal rights, no doubt."

"I don't care about legal rights, Octavia, only what is right. I'm going to raise the money to meet the Scrooge's rent demand. Our little corner of Bremerton is made up mostly of seniors. We know one another. We help one another. We're holding on to our life-style and our neighborhood. We're not letting ourselves be shoved aside."

Octavia rested her hand on her grandmother's arm and gave it a supportive squeeze.

"You say you've been running your broadcasts against Scroogen this last week?"

"Once, sometimes twice, a day, I plead for a call to arms—phone-calling and letter-writing ones, of course. The radio station is our communicator, the only immediate information and entertainment line I have to many nonambulatory seniors. They count on me, Octavia. That's why this business about an FCC complaint is so disturbing. I originally called you hoping you could suggest a legal way to fight the Scrooge's astronomical rent demand. But this FCC complaint is more serious. I can't lose my radio license. The seniors' communication lifeline can't be cut off. What can I do?''

Octavia sent her grandmother a reassuring smile.

''Mab, don't worry about losing your license. This FCC complaint is a joke. Merlin never really thought there was anything lewd or improper about your 'Senior-Sex-Talk' programs. Nor does he expect the FCC to take the complaint seriously, much less revoke your license.''

''Then why did he do and say what he did?''

''My educated guess is that he staged that scene this morning for the sole purpose of getting the photographer to shoot some pictures to go along with a local newspaper story.''

''How do you know that photographer was from the newspaper?''

''Because this ridiculous, trumped-up charge is just the kind of sensational story a newspaper will eat up. Think about it, Mab. A seventy-six-year-old gal is being reported to the FCC because her 'Senior-Sex-Talk' show is alleged to violate a morality clause. Could you ask for better?''

Mab laughed suddenly, relief rampant in the happy sound. ''You're right, Octavia! I don't know why I didn't see it. Even I would run a news brief on that storyline. It's bound to give people a good laugh.''

''Yes, Mab. People are going to laugh,'' Octavia said, not a vestige of humor in her voice. ''And that's the part I'm worried about.''

''What do you mean?''

''Your radio campaign against Scroogen is being taken seriously. People are making calls and writing letters. What better way to draw attention away from the seriousness of what you have to say then by making you and your radio station into a joke?''

"I see. So the Scrooge had Merlin file that complaint with the FCC to make people laugh at me!"

"I doubt Scroogen thought of it. It's too smooth and slick. I think this was the brainchild of the Magician."

"The Magician?"

"It's what Scroogen's attorney, Brett Merlin, is called in legal circles, because he makes his clients' problems just disappear. Merlin's big time. He only takes on the momentous corporate cases that are considered worthy of his mettle. Scroogen is small fry. I can't understand why Merlin is representing him."

"You think that's an important question?"

"If there is one thing I've learned in my legal career, Mab, it's that the players in any battle are what determine how big that battle is going to be. Today's Tuesday. Since the Sunday edition of the Bremerton newspaper is the one with the highest circulation, more than likely that's the edition in which Merlin has arranged for this foolish FCC story to be run."

"What can I do to stop the story?"

"Trying to stop it would be a waste of time. We have to think of a way to cut it down and shove it to an obscure back page. Mab, do you know where Scroogen got all this money to buy up the land adjacent to your community center?"

"He owns a septic installation and servicing company that ministers to much of Kitsap County."

Octavia rose to her feet and snatched up her shoulder bag. "And now he's into land development. That raises one or two questions right there."

"Where are you going?"

Octavia paused on her way to the door to swing around and answer her grandmother's question.

"To call A.J. She's the head of a detective firm that my legal firm uses. I think it might be a good idea for her to do a background check on Scroogen."

"You can use my phone to call her, Octavia."

"No, I'll use my car phone on the way to the Community Development Department. It'll save some time. I want to do a little checking of my own on Scroogen's construction permits for this condominium complex."

"Then you'll be back in plenty of time for dinner."

"I'd better call you later and let you know."

"You expect to spend all day at the Building Department?"

"No, but I don't know how long it's going to take me to discover why this magician has suddenly materialized on the scene."

BRETT ANSWERED THE KNOCK on his hotel room door, impressed that room service had responded so quickly. When instead the gorgeous redhead who had been dancing in and out of his imaginings all day appeared on the other side, he blinked a few times to assure himself his eyes weren't playing tricks.

"Good evening, Mr. Merlin. I'm Octavia Osborne," she announced with a thick, liquid voice as smooth and sweet as cherry brandy. "I want to talk to you."

She glided by him into the room—not waiting for an invitation—treating him to a tantalizing whiff of a subtle, sophisticated scent that reminded him of warm sands and seductive tropical breezes. Brett stayed where he was, holding the door purposely open.

"How did you know I was here, Ms. Osborne? I'm not registered under my name."

"Yes, that was most inconsiderate of you. It took me several hours to track you down."

Brett assessed the situation. The lady's bearing, speech and dress all exuded a classy, cultivated air. But it was seven o'clock at night, she had walked uninvited into his hotel room, and this could very well be an attempt at entrapment.

It wouldn't be the first time a woman had tried to get him into a compromising position for a little legal blackmail.

"Relax, Mr. Merlin. I promise I will not attack you," she said as though reading his thoughts. "Unless seriously provoked, of course."

She had turned to deliver those final words with the challenge of a smile playing around her full lips.

Every legally encoded cell in Brett's brain flashed alarm, exhorting him to immediately escort this woman out of his room.

But her smile spoke to every red-blooded male cell in his body, overriding even his well-developed sense of circumspection. Brett closed the door and stood silently contemplating his unexpected guest.

Octavia Osborne was stunning. He could think of no other word to describe her. She was over six feet in her high heels, with long, flowing flame-red hair, a glowing, golden complexion, and eyes so deep and startling a blue that he had only seen their like in the heart of the fabulous blue-white diamond he had fought so hard to possess.

The moment he'd seen her at the KRIS radio station that morning, he hadn't been able to take his eyes off her. Brett kept her in his peripheral vision now as he walked over to where he had left his drink on the coffee table.

Yes, she possessed that kind of dazzling sparkle that would always draw his eye, but he'd learned the hard way to pass up the breathtaking beauties of the flesh and make do with the plainer and saner—if less exciting—specimens of the female sex.

He would not offer her a drink. He would do nothing to prolong her stay. He would hear what she had to say and then show her the door.

She whirled gracefully out of her cape, the color of a flambéed peach, slipped off her matching gloves, then proceeded to commandeer the most comfortable chair in the room.

He picked up his glass of Scotch from the coffee table, took a swig and sat across the room opposite her on the bench seat beneath the window.

"How may I help you?" he asked.

"I'm Mab Osborne's granddaughter."

Yes, Brett had already noted they shared the same last name. And despite the more than forty years separating the two women, the same flame of Octavia's hair was buried beneath the silver of Mab's. Both women also possessed an elegant air in poise and carriage that marked the familial tie.

"Why did you come here, Ms. Osborne?"

"To stop you from making trouble for Mab, of course."

Brett wondered how. Would Octavia be like the many who had treated him to a bout of unsavory pleading and tears? Or like the few who had offered their bodies? He immediately pushed the tempting thoughts of the latter aside and decided to try to stave off whatever stratagem she had in mind.

"Ms. Osborne, your concern for your grandmother is understandable. But coming here tonight to try to sway me to drop my complaint to the FCC is not the proper way to go about helping her."

"I don't care about your complaint to the FCC. But I do care that you're having the newspaper carry the story about this ridiculous FCC morals charge in order to bring ridicule to my grandmother."

Brett was a little surprised at Octavia's words. He hadn't expected her to figure out that it was the sensational attention of a news story he was after.

"Ms. Osborne, I'm certain the newspaper will be happy to print your grandmother's side of the story. All she has to do is call them."

"Yes, you would like that, wouldn't you. The more space they give to this ridiculous morals charge the better, right?"

"I don't know what you mean."

"Mr. Merlin, let's deal with each other honestly, please. You're Dole Scroogen's attorney. You've deliberately set up this trumped-up morals charge to detract from my grandmother's campaign against Scroogen's building plans— plans that will seriously endanger the life-style of many elderly citizens."

So, Octavia Osborne knew he was a lawyer and that the FCC charge was merely a smokescreen to help Scroogen get on with his development plans.

Was it Scroogen's presence that morning in the radio station that had given the game away? Must have been. He'd told Dole to stay home and let him handle it. Fool should have listened to him. Now he had to deal with the damage control.

Brett swallowed some Scotch and continued to maintain his civilized tone of polite distance, so important in these matters.

"Ms. Osborne, I realize that change is always difficult to accept for those embedded in comfortable grooves."

"A community made up of people who know and care for one another is more than just a comfortable groove."

"Nevertheless, the law is on Mr. Scroogen's side, and the law must prevail if progress is to be made."

"Progress? You call ripping apart the seniors' simple and gentle way of life and replacing it with overpopulation and pollution *progress?* Scroogen's great-aunt wanted the seniors to have use of her land. That's why she gave them a ninety-nine-year lease. What Scroogen is doing circumvents his great aunt's wishes. He is wrong. I urge you to rethink where your loyalties lie."

"Ms. Osborne, according to the law, it is your grandmother who is wrong. Mr. Scroogen received his great-aunt's property without entanglements on her death. He has every right to do with his property as he pleases. And, as for my loyalties, they lie with my client. It is my sworn duty to fight for Dole Scroogen."

She surprised him completely then by laughing, full and luscious, a sound that filled the room with music and inexplicably tightened the muscles at the back of his neck and down his spine.

"Your sworn duty," she repeated, amusement still in her tone after she had gotten her laughter under control. "You say that as though you had no choice. Why are you, of all people, representing a man like Dole Scroogen?"

"What do you mean 'of all people'?"

"I've approached you with candor and honesty, Mr. Merlin. I am disappointed that you do not choose to return them."

"And I am disappointed that you refuse to accept that Mr. Scroogen is within his legal rights to proceed with the building of the condominium complex and evicting the Silver Power League for nonpayment of what is clearly reasonable rent for the facilities they are inhabiting."

She was up and out of her chair in a flash. She crossed the distance between them with a deliberate, determined stride. She stopped directly in front of him. She stood hands on hips, feet planted. Combative blue eyes bore into him. Yet her voice remained warmly mellow and richly resonant.

"Scroogen is trying to evict the seniors from the land that is rightfully theirs to use and from buildings that they built with their own money and moxie. He is determined to turn their sweet and sane neighborhood into yet another crowded, crime-filled Seattle suburb. And you dare talk to me about his legal rights? Where is your heart?"

"The law has no room for a heart, Ms. Osborne. If human beings decided their fate based on their emotions instead of their minds, our civilization would descend into chaos."

"And if human beings decided their fate based only on their minds, they might as well be manikins. Mr. Merlin, the law came into being for the sole purpose of sustaining justice between human beings. But like everything else, unless the law is administered by people with hearts—as well as heads—even its great and lofty goal can be corrupted. What you are trying to do for Scroogen will not achieve justice. The man is both beneath contempt and certainly beneath your legal expertise."

Brett had to admit she spoke well. And he admired the fact that despite the considerable physical arsenal at her disposal, it was her words she wielded at him and not her feminine wiles.

He turned away from the stunning beauty and fire of the lady to down the rest of his drink.

"Who I choose to represent and why is my business."

"No, Mr. Merlin. By attacking my grandmother you have made it mine."

His eyes were drawn back to her face. The liquid richness of her voice had not altered. But both the toss of her fiery hair and the sudden blue sparks in her eyes conveyed pure threat. So far this conversation had been full of confrontation and totally lacking in the kind of feminine cajoling he had expected.

Octavia Osborne had a strong will, and it was that will on which she relied. He found himself as stunned by her inner core as he had been by her outer packaging.

Far too stunned.

In a move that he knew to be both prudent and absolutely necessary, he got to his feet and started toward the door.

"Let me show you out, Ms. Osborne. I'm certain your time is valuable and you don't want to waste it here in a futile attempt to get me to drop my client."

She joined him at the door a moment later, hurtling her cape expertly across her shoulders and fitting her gloves to her fingers in quick, competent clasps.

"You are making a very grave error representing that man, Mr. Merlin. You will be sorry."

"The law is on Mr. Scroogen's side, and I am never sorry to represent the law. Nothing personal, Ms. Osborne."

She moved closer and looked him straight in the eye, a bold body position reserved only for the fiercest of fighters—or lovers. Her warmth and scent struck him like a blow below the belt, leaving him momentarily both mentally and physically winded.

"If you do not leave my grandmother alone, I will go after your Scrooge of a client and grind him down until the size of his wallet makes even *his* heart look huge."

She leaned closer, her sweet breath blowing tantalizingly against his lips. "And everything about it will be personal, believe me."

She turned then and swept out of his hotel room on that subtle, sophisticated scent that swam in his head until his senses started to spin.

By the time the blaring telephone registered in his ears, Brett realized it had probably gone through several ringing cycles.

He forced himself out of his mental and physical fog, enormously irritated that he had let the woman affect him so strongly. He closed the hotel room door on the now empty hallway. Then he strode toward the phone, grabbed the receiver and said hello.

"It's Dole," Scroogen announced on the other end of the line. "I just hung up on a damn irate anonymous caller on my home telephone number!"

"Settle down, Dole. What did the caller say?"

"That *they* were going to get me. I'm sure it was Mab Osborne's voice, although she was trying to disguise it. I tell you, Merlin, this morals charge thing is not threatening enough. I want Mab Osborne off the air. She has to be silenced. Forever."

"What are you talking about?"

"You heard me. I'm going to do whatever it takes to put an end to that woman. Whatever it takes."

Chapter Two

Octavia strode down the dark hallway of the Seattle law offices of Justice Inc., heading for the one door under which the light still burned. She knocked.

The voice on the other side responded instantly, crisply. She opened the door and stepped inside.

Octavia's senior partner, Adam Justice, sat behind his desk, his black hair still scrupulously in place, his white shirt unwrinkled, despite the fact that it was nearly midnight and Octavia knew he'd been here since dawn.

"What brings you by so late?" Adam asked, putting down his pen and shifting his paperwork aside.

Octavia had always liked that about Adam. No matter how busy or involved he was on a case, he never failed to stop what he was doing and give her his complete attention.

She swung into a utilitarian steel-and-leather chair in front of his black metal desk. Like the man who inhabited it, this office had been stripped of all but necessary business essentials.

"An attorney is causing some legal problems for my grandmother, and I need to spend time across the Sound in Bremerton to straighten it out."

"This attorney anyone we know?"

"Brett Merlin. He's representing a real Scrooge of a small businessman who has it in for my grandmother."

Adam was silent for a moment before responding.

"Taking on the Magician won't be easy," he said.

"I know," Octavia agreed, thinking about her earlier meeting with Brett in his hotel room. She had hoped to reach him, but he had shown neither compassion nor compromise—a real letter-of-the-law kind of attorney.

The law has no room for a heart. What a perfectly imbecilic thing to say!

Octavia lifted her chin. "He's about to find out that taking me on won't be easy, either."

Her senior partner almost smiled. Almost.

"I... see. But what I don't see is why Brett Merlin would represent a small businessman against your grandmother. Not more than three weeks ago he was responsible for getting a record $55.5 million jury verdict favoring one of his big corporate clients here in Seattle."

"It's a question that's been on my mind, too, Adam. I'm going to have to rely on A.J. and her detective team to sleuth out the answer."

"I'm sure she'll be happy to oblige. If you need my legal assistance or that of any of your fellow partners, you know you only have to ask."

"I appreciate that. But this is family and that makes it a very personal fight for me."

"You know how long you'll be away?"

"Probably through Christmas."

"Any cases you're working on that need to be picked up by someone else?"

"Just one. My associate can handle it. I've written a few notes to her and left the complete case file on her desk, along with a request to keep you informed of the progress."

Adam leaned back in his chair as she paused. Octavia knew he was waiting for her to tell him why she was here in person. They both knew there was more, that Octavia could have settled all this with a few telephone calls. She took a deep breath, knowing there was never going to be a "right" moment to broach the subject.

"I want to retain you as my personal counsel, Adam."

A small frown creased Adam's brow. "You want me to become your attorney? Officially?"

"As of this moment." Octavia pulled out a standard Justice Inc. office contract she had already signed and had notarized and passed it across the desk to him along with a check.

Adam scanned the paperwork and check and leaned his forearms on his desk. His light eyes stared into hers.

"This is a bit formal, isn't it? What's the story?"

Octavia knew if either Kay Kellogg or Marc Truesdale, her other partners at Justice Inc., had asked her that question, she wouldn't have told them. She certainly wasn't about to tell Adam Justice, their firm's senior partner—not after watching Adam turn from man to legal machine during the last six years.

She sent him a large, charming smile, the kind that she knew he didn't know how to take. She hoped it might just make him uncomfortable enough to back off the question.

"Insurance," she said.

The light eyes before her now pointed like two blue lasers. "What do you mean, *insurance?*"

The smile hadn't worked. Octavia knew there was only one sure way to effectively distract the legal mind that was now so firmly fixed on what she had no intention of revealing. She was the only partner at Justice Inc. who both knew Adam Justice's Achilles heel and had the guts to aim for it.

"Six years ago, Adam, you and I were involved in something that neither of us wish to share with anyone else. I want to ensure that neither of us will be forced to speak of it."

Unconsciously, Adam's fingers found and stroked the long white scar that disappeared down his neck into his starched white collar.

"You anticipate that someone might try to force answers from you or me about that...time? Why?"

"Anything is possible when it comes to an attorney of Brett Merlin's ability. I intend to be thorough and aggressive in representing my grandmother. I have no doubt that the Magician will be equally as thorough and aggressive in representing his client. As we both know, his trademark is an uncanny knack for pulling obscure facts and laws out of his legal hat and combining the two to effect his adversary's demise. I prefer to limit the facts he finds."

"So by putting our relationship under a formal legal umbrella, you have placed our knowledge of each other and our communications under the attorney-client privilege."

"Exactly."

Octavia waited. Nothing showed on Adam Justice's stone face in the long moment that passed. Only Octavia's knowledge and sensitivity to the situation allowed her to see the fleeting, tiny flicker of light behind his pale blue eyes.

"All right," he said finally.

Octavia didn't show the relief that poured through her. She didn't dare. Her senior partner was far too observant. He would have immediately suspected her "other" agenda.

Everything had to be done by the book with Adam Justice. Like Brett Merlin, he lived by the letter of the law.

But Octavia was not that kind of lawyer. She used her knowledge of the law to support what she knew to be its true code of justice. And now that the letters in some dusty law book were getting in the way of the spirit with which they were originally formed, Octavia knew it was time to get creative and find a footnote somewhere.

Or pencil one in.

Adam had been the only weak link in the bold plan that she had formulated today. Now that weak link had been braced. Now she could go ahead and fight for justice *her* way.

"BRETT, YOU REALLY SHOULD stay here. We've plenty of room. It will be no trouble," Nancy Scroogen insisted as she dished out blueberry pancakes onto Brett's breakfast plate.

Brett looked up at his aunt, still unsettled to see the deep lines that had dug themselves around her eyes and mouth, seemingly overnight.

Nancy Scroogen was his mother's youngest sister, a mere ten years older than Brett. Brett had gotten along well with his aunt, admiring Nancy's tomboy spirit and sense of adventure.

They had corresponded regularly after Nancy had used her journalism degree to land herself a job as a foreign correspondent. Over the years he had enjoyed her light, breezy postcards from exotic ports of call.

Then, seven years before, Nancy had surprised him completely by suddenly giving up her profession and spirit of wanderlust to settle down and marry Dole Scroogen. Brett had barely heard from or seen her since. Until a week ago.

Now, as he looked at her across the dining-room table in Dole Scroogen's East Bremerton home, he was sad to note how tired she appeared. Despite her assurances to the contrary, he was certain she didn't need someone else in the house to look after. Not when she already had her hands full, he thought, as he noted the scowling faces of Dole and his son Ronald.

"Thanks, Nancy, but I'm comfortable at the hotel. This matter I'm handling for Dole is very simple and should be settled soon. Then I'll be on my way to tackle Rainier. I've climbed it in summer, but I'm told the real test is in winter."

"You want to spend Christmas climbing a mountain, Cousin Brett?" six-year-old Katlyn asked.

Brett smiled at Nancy's little girl sitting beside him. Fortunately for Katlyn, she had inherited her mother's peachy complexion—and attitude.

"The sunlight sparkling on the snow and trees beats any artificial string of lights, Katlyn."

"But don't you want to be home Christmas morning to open all your presents under the Christmas tree?"

Brett stared into his little cousin's eyes, so obviously full of delighted anticipation for that highlight of the season. Sometimes he wondered what it would have been like to have been brought up believing in fantasy instead of staunchly facing reality.

"Your cousin Brett has never been a big fan of Christmas," Nancy told her daughter. "Probably because my sister and her husband didn't believe in decorating or exchanging gifts."

"You didn't get Christmas presents when you were a kid?" Katlyn asked in obvious dismay.

"I was given what I needed at other times of the year," Brett explained.

"Even Santa Claus forgot you at Christmas?"

Brett prided himself on never lying, for any reason. But he also knew from the warning look on Nancy's face that his answer to Katlyn's last question had better be the right one.

"What did you ask Santa for this year?" Brett asked, trying to both deflect his inquisitive cousin and to maintain his integrity.

"I sent Santa a whole list. I sure hope he reads it. Why don't you ask Santa to bring you a mountain so you don't have to go away?"

"Katlyn," Nancy intervened, "leave your cousin alone now so he can eat his breakfast in peace."

"I'm out of syrup," Ronald Scroogen complained in his typically too loud and too sour tone.

Nancy immediately rushed to her feet to get more from the kitchen. Brett flashed Ronald a disapproving look. The young man could have easily gone to the kitchen and gotten it himself.

Ronald was Dole Scroogen's twenty-two-year-old son from a previous marriage. He resembled his father physically, right down to the sour puss and whiny tone of voice. He also had that insecure, young man's way of making everything that came out of his mouth sound like a challenge or a complaint.

Nancy returned to the table with the syrup. Ronald took it out of her hand without a word of thanks.

Brett caught Nancy's eye over the beautiful handmade wreath of fragrant bay leaves adorning the table's center. He sent her an appreciative smile.

"Everything smells, looks and tastes wonderful."

The surprise and gratitude of her returning smile confirmed Brett's suspicion that his aunt wasn't accustomed to getting any appreciation from the two other males sitting at this table. He took a sip of her excellent coffee and worked on controlling his growing irritation.

Brett was only here because of Nancy's call for help. If it hadn't been for Nancy and her little girl, he'd be long gone on his postponed climb. Seeing how her husband and stepson treated her, Brett was surprised that the full-spirited Nancy he once knew wasn't long gone, too. What was keeping her here?

Love, he supposed. Brett stabbed his pancake and shoved it into his mouth, knowing it did no good to wonder how anyone could love Dole Scroogen.

Love was an incredibly imbecilic malady that struck even the sanest of souls and overnight turned clear reasoning power into gooey rubber cement. He remembered the affliction well.

He also remembered what it felt like to wake up the next morning only to realize he'd fallen for a fantasy.

Thank God that nonsense was all behind him.

"I don't suppose you came over this morning just for pancakes, Merlin," Dole said in his usual sour tone. "What's on your mind?"

Brett swallowed and took another sip of coffee, trying not to let his uncle's naturally abrasive manner get to him.

"What you said last night on the telephone disturbed me. It also disturbed me that you hung up afterward when I asked you to wait while I let in room service with my dinner."

"I'm not a man accustomed to waiting, Merlin. And I meant what I said about that Osborne woman."

"Look, Dole, we've already gone over all the reasons for handling this matter my way. Mab Osborne is popular. Insisting on a head-to-head confrontation would just generate more sympathy for her cause. Getting people to laugh at her instead of listen to her is the proper approach."

"The Community Development Department is uneasy about all the mail and telephone calls they've received," Dole said. "I'm getting heat from the chamber of commerce, too."

"They are reacting to the public opinion Mab Osborne has stirred up. But the chamber can't stop you, and I'm not letting Community Development withdraw your building permits. They were legally filed and approved and I'm making sure they abide by them."

"But it's getting worse every day. I even received a threatening letter from the old fools."

"I wish you didn't have to force the seniors out of their center, dear," Nancy interjected.

Dole turned to his wife, his sour puss and whiny voice in full evidence. "Whose side are you on?" he demanded.

"Yours, of course, dear," Nancy said, sounding immediately conciliatory. "I just wish there was another way."

"Was the threatening letter signed?" Brett asked.

"No. But I'm certain it's on Silver Power League stationery and Mab Osborne sent it."

"Hand it over to the police. Let them investigate."

"I've already done that. They say it could be weeks before they know," Scroogen grumbled.

"All these irritations are temporary," Brett assured him. "Once Mab Osborne has been defused, so will that public opinion."

"What if your plan doesn't work? What if she continues to whip up public sentiment against me?"

"After the initial article in this Sunday's paper, I have three follow-up articles scheduled to be released over the next week with selected excerpts from her 'Senior-Sex-Talk' programs."

"What good will that do?"

"Mab Osborne likes to say shocking things to get her listeners' attention. Each excerpt I've selected is taken out of context and is more sensational than the last. She'll be so busy defending herself, she'll have no time to whip up anything. Be patient. These things take time to work, but they do work.''

"And if they don't?"

"Then I will take the next appropriate step. Mab Osborne is like a fly on your wall, Dole. Its buzzing may be annoying, but we don't need a shotgun blast to get rid of it. A flyswatter should do the trick."

"It had better, Merlin."

Brett didn't take that kind of sour tone and threatening language from his paying clients, much less from a man he was only representing for the sake of his aunt. Enough was enough. He put down his fork.

"Dole, if you don't like what I'm doing, then you can go—"

"No!" Nancy interrupted, obviously reading the look on Brett's face and eager to stop what he would say. She leaned across the table to rest her hand on his.

"No, Brett," she said in a calmer tone. "Dole is grateful, as I am, for all your help. He's worked so hard to make this condominium complex happen. It's the dream of a lifetime. We need you to stand by us to see this dream come true. Isn't that right, dear?"

Dole deigned to look up from his breakfast.

"Yeah. You do your thing, Merlin, so I can do mine. I need more coffee here, Nancy."

For once Nancy didn't obediently jump up. Her hand remained on Brett's arm, her pleading eyes on his face, waiting for his response. "Brett?"

Brett exhaled a frustrated breath as he nodded.

"The coffee?" Dole's irritated voice reminded.

Nancy smiled as she rose to her feet. "Coming, dear."

Brett shook his head as he witnessed the domestic scene. Whoever said someone could become a slave to love knew what he was talking about.

"The city water and sewer lines were connected a day ago," Scroogen said, sounding pleased for once. "The land should be completely dug out for the underground garage in the next few days. In a week or so, the concrete guys can come in and start on the foundation. Tami, my secretary, is arranging for a ribbon-cutting ceremony. The mayor, the city council, the chamber—everyone who is anyone is being invited."

"Can I cut the ribbon?" Ronald asked his father, the eagerness and excitement clear in his voice.

"Don't talk nonsense," Scroogen said. "Someone important, like the mayor, has to cut the ribbon."

Brett saw what might have been anger or disappointment or both flare through Ronald's eyes as he rose to his feet and stalked silently away from the breakfast table.

Dole didn't even look up from his refilled coffee cup. Although not a fan of Dole's son, Brett felt sorry for him at that moment. No doubt about it, Scroogen could be pretty damn insensitive.

"So, did you ever find out who the redhead was with those old fogys?" Scroogen asked.

The lady's stunning face and figure flashed through Brett's mind and with it a very annoying automatic tightening of the muscles down his back.

"She's Octavia Osborne," he said, concentrating his eyes on the swirling coffee in his cup. "Mab's granddaughter."

"How did you find out?"

"She came to see me last night just before you called."

"*Why* did she come to see you?"

Brett looked up at the suspicious tone that had entered Dole's voice. Did this guy trust anybody?

"To try to warn me away," Brett answered. "Her threats were dramatic, but empty. Neither Mab Osborne nor her granddaughter can stop progress, no matter how much they might want to."

"So you're sure this granddaughter can't cause any trouble?"

"I'm sure," Brett said, his words replete with confidence. "Octavia Osborne is no one to worry about. The law is on your side, and I'm here to see it's enforced."

The telephone blared at the instant Brett had finished giving his client that positive and unwavering assurance.

Nancy got up to answer it and brought the cordless receiver to the table to hand to her husband.

"It's the foreman at the construction site, dear."

Dole took the phone. "Yeah?"

Brett watched his uncle's greenish-tinged face turn positively purple. Finally, Dole threw his napkin onto the floor and flew to his feet.

"What?" he yelled into the mouthpiece.

OCTAVIA'S GENUINE appreciation flowed through her voice. "Mab, this new community center of yours is outstanding. Its long rectangular shape, myriad skylights, ribbons of leaded glass windows and spotless white tile floor make it marvelously open and spacious. And the soft upholstered furniture you've selected adds just the right amount of warmth."

Mab beamed. "I admit I had my doubts at first about the simplicity of the center's design, but the natural light and clean lines are effective and efficient. We can cordon off any area with partitions, or open up the whole floor space for a large event, like our annual Christmas party coming up in a couple of weeks. How much better it will be now that we don't have to crowd everyone into that old barn. Constance's design was right, as always."

"Constance Kope designed this center?" Octavia asked. "That little lady who was on your 'Senior-Sex-Talk' program yesterday?"

"Yes, Constance and her husband owned an architectural design firm before he became ill, and they both retired a few years back. She has an infallible eye for what works."

"When I think that your Silver Power League singlehandedly created this building and all its beauty, I am in awe, Mab."

Mab smiled proudly. "Wait until you see the greenhouse. Douglas Twitch engineered its habitat to maintain temperature, moisture and lighting control."

"Douglas is an environmental engineer?" Octavia asked.

"A very fine one, who was put out to pasture only because the big firm he worked at for forty years checked the calendar instead of his contributions."

"I thought you and Douglas didn't get along."

"His mental limitations are irksome. But the greenhouse he designed is an engineering marvel."

Octavia chuckled at her grandmother's unmitigated contradiction on the intellectual credentials of Douglas Twitch.

"Lead the way to this greenhouse, Mab."

"No, first I want you to see what we are doing to raise money for our rent. It's just a stopgap measure, of course. I'm counting on you to put all your legal training to work to come up with something more permanent. But for now, well, our members are busy working on them over in this room."

Octavia gave her watch a quick glance. "Them?" she repeated.

Mab smiled. "Come see for yourself."

Octavia followed her grandmother to the other side of a partition and saw that an assembly line of sorts had been set up. Seniors sat on both sides of a long set of tables drawn close to the windows to receive an optimum of natural light.

Each member of the assembly line had a task. The first attached legs to a stuffed doll's torso. The second affixed arms that crossed over the doll's chest. The third screwed on a head. The fourth, hair. And so on down the line until the finished doll emerged at the end, holding in its fist a white piece of paper filled with scribbles.

Octavia picked up one of the completed dolls, examined its thin, ashen-colored hair, tiny dark eyes, sour puss, baggy olive pants and green-and-black-checkered suspenders, and chuckled.

"This doll looks exactly like Scroogen."

"Squeeze it," Mab urged.

Octavia did. *"Read it and weep, I'm raising your rent."*

Octavia laughed. "It sounds exactly like him, too."

"John Winslow did the voice. He's very good at mimicking."

"When do they go on sale?"

"Today. I'm advertising them on the radio this afternoon. We're calling it the Scroogen Doll."

Octavia shook her head as she set the sour-pussed, eight-inch specimen back on the table. "No, could be a legal problem there. Better call it the Scrooge Doll."

"But we want people to associate it with Scroogen," Mab protested.

"You think someone could mistake it for anyone else?"

"I guess not. The design is ours, a couple of our members got the materials wholesale, and the rest of our members are doing all the assembly. Our profit is nearly eighty-five percent on each doll. If we can just sell enough of them, we can stave off the Scrooge's kicking us out for another two months."

"You're a marvel, Mab."

"But as I said, Octavia, it's only a stopgap measure. We need to find a substantial and consistent money-maker to meet the Scrooge's ridiculous rent. Although, I must tell you, it galls me to think the money we're working so hard to raise is all going to line that man's pockets."

"Yes, it galls me, too," Octavia agreed.

"Have you thought of a way to stop him?"

"Let's just say I'm working on it."

"What is it, Octavia?"

"What's what, Mab?"

"Ever since you arrived at my house this morning with your bags and a promise to stay awhile, you've been deliberately deflecting my every question about what you did yesterday, and you've been purposely vague about how you plan to attack this problem."

"Have I?"

"Octavia, you're only vague when you're involved in something you don't want me to know about. What is it? And why do you keep looking at your watch?"

Octavia refocused her eyes back on Mab's face as she wrapped an arm around her grandmother's shoulders.

"It's just after nine. Let's go see that engineering marvel of a greenhouse now."

"You're not going to tell me what you're up to, are you."

"You are a wise and perceptive lady."

"And you are an exasperating one."

Octavia chuckled.

"Oh, come on," Mab said, her tone resigned. "The greenhouse is this way."

They stepped out of the brightness of the center into a heavy, overcast day and made their way up a rise and along a graveled path to the large and lovely white-and-glass English-style conservatory that spread elegantly over an entire acre.

"Oh, that is marvelous," Octavia said in appreciation at the classical, elegant lines of the structure. "When you said greenhouse, I was thinking utilitarian. But using the classic design of an English conservatory makes it absolutely charming."

"Yes," Mab agreed mechanically. Her head was turned and she obviously wasn't listening to her granddaughter.

"What's going on over there?" Mab asked finally, pointing to the adjacent property where a bulldozer lay idle as several workers stood looking down into a muddy pit.

Octavia leisurely turned in the direction of Mab's pointing finger. Then her eyes swung immediately to the brandnew bronze Bentley with the license plate reading LAW MAN pulling up to the side of the curb. She smiled as she watched Brett Merlin get out of the driver's side and Dole Scroogen exit the passenger door.

"The workers seem to have found something," Mab said, her eyes still fixed on the construction crew.

"Have they? Well, why don't we go see what it is?" Octavia suggested as she gently steered Mab into the direction of the workers and the pit.

BRETT SAW OCTAVIA the instant he swung out of the driver's seat of his Bentley. She wore a turquoise suit with gold trim today, as classy and colorful as the lady herself. Her long flowing hair as before was unfettered, her heels as usual were high. Yet despite those high heels, she somehow seemed to glide across the soft earth toward the construction site.

Brett and Dole reached the construction workers as Octavia and her grandmother strolled up over the slight rise.

"Good morning," Octavia said with a vivid graciousness that sprayed out like luminous paint over the canvas of the dull day. She was as stunning and self-composed as she had been in his hotel room the night before. Brett found himself instantly on guard. He returned her gracious greeting with a simple nod of the head.

He watched as the grubby workmen around the pit turned to stare at the beautifully groomed woman with the flame-red hair. They quickly got off their knees and onto their feet.

"Morning, ma'am," they murmured.

Octavia continued to smile as she moved to the edge of the pit and looked over its side at the lone workman at its bottom.

"You seem to have found something there," she said.

"I don't appreciate being called and told to drop everything to come out here, George," Scroogen shouted before the man had a chance to answer Octavia. "What's going on?"

The stocky, black-haired man in the pit lost the smile he had flashed at Octavia the moment he turned to face Scroogen. "We found this."

He pointed to a large black stone sticking up out of the pit.

"Well, what is it?" Dole asked.

"It looks like something's been carved on that stone," Octavia said, peering down. "You don't suppose it's early native American handiwork, do you?"

"I believe it is," the foreman said, his black eyes glowing above his high cheekbones.

"How would you know?" Scroogen challenged.

"I am Suquamish, the tribe of Chief Sealth for whom Seattle was named. My people hunted and fished this land long before the white man came."

"So you found this beautiful and important symbol of early native American culture right here?" Octavia asked, the awe clearly in her voice.

"The rain last night must have washed some of the covering dirt away," the foreman explained. "We only realized it was buried here when we arrived this morning and the jaws of the bulldozer started to lift it out of the mud. I withdrew the machinery immediately when I saw the carving."

Brett moved around Scroogen to get a better look at the gray scars on the dark stone that stuck out of the mud. Out of the corner of his eye he could see a dozen or so seniors emerging from the community center and heading in the direction of the pit. He felt distinctly uneasy with this find and the crowd gathering to view it. And with the less-than-languid smile that played around Octavia's lips.

"This place has nothing to do with Indians," Scroogen protested, irritation making his tone even whinier than usual. "This was all farmland before those rinky-dink houses were put up after World War II."

"Their foundations did not go very deep, Mr. Scroogen," George said. "We have had to dig far deeper to accommodate the foundation for the condominium and underground parking structure. It is at this greater depth that this carved stone has been uncovered."

The curious seniors arrived then and crowded behind Octavia and Mab Osborne, asking what was going on and trying to get a better look.

"Is that what the workmen dug up?" a voice suddenly asked from beside Brett. Brett looked over in surprise to see the young, eager eyes of a man with a reporter's badge on the flap of his windbreaker and a 35-mm camera slung over his shoulder.

"Where did you come from?" Brett asked.

"I'm with the Bremerton newspaper. We got a call that you guys dug up some ancient Indian stuff."

The reporter turned to the workman beside the stone. "What do those markings mean?"

"We do not know," George said.

Brett tried to get the reporter's attention. "Who called you and when?"

"We got an anonymous tip about thirty minutes ago." The reporter turned back toward the foreman. "You the one who found this?"

"Yes. I'm the construction foreman, Keneth George."

The reporter slung his camera around and started to take pictures. "Can you get rid of the rest of the dirt to see if there is more carving farther down the stone?"

"I don't think that would be wise," Octavia said. "If this is a previously unknown site of early native American habitation, professionals need to be called in to excavate properly. It would be best to stop all work here immediately."

"Yes," the foreman said as he nodded toward Octavia. "As I told Mr. Scroogen when I phoned him, we must stop all work."

"The hell you will," Scroogen protested. "I don't have time for this nonsense. This land has to be excavated and graded by next week. Dig that damn thing up and send it to whoever has to decide what it is."

"That is not how the law works, Mr. Scroogen," Octavia said. "Artifacts must be examined at the site of their unearthing by the proper authorities. There may be other precious native American objects buried here. I'm certain your attorney would not advise you to do anything against the law."

She turned to Brett, that elusive smile just lifting the sides of her ample lips. Out of the corner of his eye, Brett could see the reporter stepping back to take a shot of the crowd.

"Isn't that right, Mr. Merlin?" she asked.

"Only if it is a bona fide artifact," Brett said, doubting it more and more by the second. From that smile on Octavia's face and the way he had watched her orchestrating this little scene, Brett was certain that somehow she had to be behind this far too "coincidental" find and the call to the newspaper. He didn't like this. Not at all.

"I will call in my tribe's cultural expert," George said.

"No, you won't," Scroogen protested. "I'm not stopping these bulldozers just because you've dug up some stupid stone."

George's face darkened perceptively. He scrambled up the sloping, five-foot-high muddy pit wall to stand before Scroogen.

"The stone must be examined," George said, anger in his eyes and voice.

Brett stepped between the two men, hearing the click of the news reporter's camera. If he didn't take control of this situation now, it could quickly escalate beyond anyone's control.

"Mr. George, I'm Brett Merlin, Mr. Scroogen's attorney. Mr. Scroogen is merely skeptical about the authenticity of this stone carving, as am I. We'd both appreciate your calling your tribe's professional archaeologist to settle the matter."

"Mr. Merlin, I'm surprised you would suggest such a thing," Octavia said. "Surely you know that is not the proper legal procedure in a case like this."

"Oh?" Brett said, turning to her. "And what would you know of the proper legal procedure?"

"Mr. Scroogen must first report this find to the group issuing the building permit for this site—namely, Bremerton's Community Development Department. They in turn will have to contact the state representative of the Archaeology and Historical Preservation Department in Olympia, who will then contact the professional archaeologists from the tribes so they can visit this site to do a thorough examination."

She knew the proper legal procedure, all right. Too well. It was just as Brett had suspected from the first. She had to be behind this business.

He stepped closer and faced her squarely. "How do you know this?" he challenged.

"Because I'm a lawyer."

She was a lawyer?

Brett watched the satisfied smile on Octavia's face as she delivered that piece of unexpected news. He couldn't be more surprised—or more annoyed—to realize how completely off-guard she had caught him.

But what irritated him most was that he knew she had expected the error. She knew he had not taken her threats seriously. She knew he had been misled and bamboozled by her beauty, just like probably every other poor sap who had met her. She knew it, and she had counted on it.

It seemed he had made a couple of very serious errors when it came to this lady. He gave himself a moment to regroup his thoughts before going on the offensive to save what he could from the situation.

"Why didn't you tell me this before?" he demanded. "Why have you hidden the fact that you are an attorney?"

A single eyebrow arched up her forehead. "You, Brett Merlin, accuse *me* of hiding the fact that I'm an attorney? You, who marched into my grandmother's radio station yesterday and handed her a fallacious complaint you sent to the FCC without mentioning the fact that you were only doing it because you are a high-powered attorney hired by Scroogen to make trouble for her?"

She paused in her ultra-composed—and obviously rehearsed—indignation to turn to the reporter standing just beside her.

"You did get all that, didn't you?" she asked sweetly.

"Every word," he answered as he pointed at the tape recorder that had suddenly materialized in his hand. The young man then turned and shoved the mike into Brett's face.

"Is what Ms. Osborne said true? Is your FCC complaint against Mab Osborne merely an attempt to make trouble for her?"

"Let's not get off the subject here," Brett said quickly. "We are at the future site of an exciting new condominium complex that will bring both jobs and prosperity to this community, a complex that could be delayed by the discovery of this stone carving. The question you should be asking is, who might be responsible for putting the carving on this stone?"

"Are you saying you don't believe this is an Indian relic, Mr. Merlin?" the reporter asked, the inflection in his voice obviously hoping Brett would say just that.

"I'm saying that no one here is qualified to make such a determination," Brett answered cautiously.

"Is the legal procedure that Ms. Osborne delineated accurate, as you understand it?" the reporter pressed.

"Only if this really is an ancient native American artifact," Brett said.

Brett turned back to the foreman. "Mr. George, would you ask your tribe's cultural representative to come over now? If he looks at the carving and says it isn't early native American, it would be a quick and easy solution that would save a lot of time and needless involvement of others."

"I'll use the phone in my truck," George said, and quickly made for his vehicle parked at the curb.

"This carving may originate with another tribe and, therefore, be beyond the expertise of a Suquamish cultural anthropologist," Octavia said. "No, Mr. Merlin. Quick and easy will not suffice. This find must be reported and handled according to the prescribed law for its protection."

Octavia then turned to the reporter. "You appear to be in on the beginning of what could be a major new native American find. This could make an excellent continuing story."

Her words had the effect of redoubling the young man's photographic efforts. With every picture the news reporter snapped, Brett watched Octavia's smile grow.

"Stop this," Scroogen yelled at the reporter, and then waved his arms at the seniors. "Get out of here. You're trespassing. The rest of you construction workers, get back to work."

"Wait, Dole," Brett said, wondering if this wasn't exactly what Octavia Osborne wanted Scroogen to do—right in front of a reporter.

"I can't wait!" Scroogen protested.

Brett grabbed Dole's arm and lowered his voice so the others couldn't hear.

"Legally, you have to wait, Dole."

"I'm under time-sensitive contracts to develop this land. If I renege on those contracts, I'll be ruined!"

"Keep your voice down and slow down. A little delay will not ruin you, Dole, so save the dramatics. I very much doubt this so-called ancient carving is legitimate. Far more likely it is a contemporary artistic endeavor."

Brett paused to look directly at Octavia, who was urging the reporter to take even more pictures.

He returned his attention to his recalcitrant client. "Look, Dole, you have no choice now but to report this as prescribed by law. But if what I suspect is true, it won't take long before this supposed relic is relegated to the trash bin as a phony. At the most, it should only be a few days' delay. A few days won't jeopardize your schedule."

"But—"

Brett poked Dole in the ribs before conveying the rest of his caution beneath his breath. "Would you rather someone serve you with a court order to cease and desist all your building operations, giving the media a chance to turn this so called 'find' and your construction site into a real sideshow?"

"That could happen?"

"I've no doubt that Octavia Osborne would see to it," Brett said. "Dole, don't you get it? This attorney wants you to screw up and turn this into a fight. That's why she made sure that damn reporter is on hand. This has all been carefully orchestrated to cause you trouble."

"I thought you told me less than an hour ago that Octavia Osborne couldn't cause me any trouble?"

"Yes, well, I admit I underestimated the lady and the foolish lengths she'd go to. Still, she'll find she's caused more trouble for herself than you. Now, use the car phone to call the Community Development Department and report this 'find.'"

"Why don't you do it?"

"Because you're the developer. And because I'm going to be having a word with this reckless attorney and put the fear of God into her, so we don't find ourselves facing any more of this kind of foolishness. Go, Dole. The sooner you make the call, the sooner we can put an end to this delay."

As soon as Dole obediently, albeit reluctantly, turned toward the direction of the car, Brett turned toward Octavia. She stood in the middle of the seniors and the workmen and the reporter, jabbering confidently.

He could have understood her taking any legal avenue available to protect her grandmother's interests. But not this flagrant disregard for the law.

Brett Merlin knew how to quell an unscrupulous adversary's slams at his clients. He knew how to make such an unethical attorney quaver and crawl.

And he knew he was about to do all this to Octavia Osborne.

OCTAVIA DIDN'T HAVE to see Brett's eyes to feel them. She wasn't sure why this was so. She suspected it was because of the power behind those eyes, a power that was almost palpable.

He was coming at her from behind. She could feel the change in the air pressure, the spark along her skin, the rush of blood through her heart, the tingle in her fingertips, with every step that drew him closer.

At the precise second he came to a stop behind her, she cut short an answer to the reporter's question and swung around to face him squarely. He was a man to be faced squarely.

"Yes?" she asked.

The sprinkle of light silver in the center of his black eyes had solidified into stone. She sensed his surface anger and something deeper and more dangerous—and much more difficult to control. The tingling in her fingertips increased.

"I want to talk to you," Brett said. "Alone, please. This way."

He bowed in the direction he wished her to go, and then simply waited with the stiff dignity of someone who was accustomed to being obeyed.

Men had made the mistake of trying to order Octavia around. One or two had even tried to take her arm to coerce her. None got a second chance to repeat either mistake.

But Octavia was rather fascinated by the approach Brett Merlin was using to get his way. There was such a polite refinement to it, such an outrageous self-assurance.

What a thoroughly annoying and exciting man. She could barely wait to find out what other emotions this man would engender in her.

But she controlled her curiosity, deliberately making Brett wait, while she turned back to the reporter to conclude their interview. Only then did she deign to accompany Brett to a point some twenty-five feet away from the crowd. She stopped when he did and turned to face him.

He folded his arms across his chest and scowled at her, like a judge about to give a three-time offender a life sentence. The cold anger that solidified the silver in his eyes could have frozen fire.

"You are in serious trouble, Ms. Osborne."

His voice was rigid and stern. He stood before her so marvelously self-assured and self-important. Octavia's laughter bubbled up from her throat and erupted into a short, spontaneous roar.

And all the while she laughed, she watched Brett Merlin's countenance darken until it matched the blackened clouds hanging ominously in the heavy sky overhead.

"What's so funny?" he asked in a voice that thundered as the silver in his eyes shot through with lightning.

"You are an interesting man, Mr. Merlin," she said after she had finally gotten her merriment under control. "Your client's building plans are about to be buried beneath an ancient Indian stone carving and you call me aside to tell me *I'm* in serious trouble?"

He stepped closer and towered over her—deliberately, she knew. She admired the calculated cunning of the move, almost as much as she admired the breadth of his broad shoulders. The guy was a big, imposing hunk who knew how to throw his weight around with class. She stared steadfastly into his incredibly alive quicksilver eyes.

"I'm going to have you investigated, Ms. Osborne. Thoroughly. Until I know about each and every breath you've taken since you were born. And when I connect you with that piece of fakery laying in that pit back there—and I will connect you with it—I am going to see that you are brought up on criminal charges and disbarred."

Octavia could tell that Brett Merlin fully expected his awesome reputation, presence and words to effect fear and trepidation in her.

His unmitigated pomposity was absolutely magnificent. She put aside her admiration of it long enough to stand on her tiptoes, stretching tall until she was at eye level with him. She tossed her head back, waves of flaming-red hair falling off her cheeks.

"If you ever repeat those slanderous allegations to a third party, Mr. Magician, I will see to it that it is you, not I, who disappears from the legal scene in one highly publicized puff of courtroom smoke."

She noted with enormous satisfaction the instant shifting of the silver light in his eyes. She sensed she was witnessing a very rare event. Brett Merlin, the deadly Magician of corporate law, reaching to pull a rabbit out of his hat only to find his hand grasping the ears of a tiger.

Octavia chuckled again, thoroughly enjoying the moment.

But the chuckle died in her throat the instant she heard the cry behind her. Startled, she swung in the direction of the outburst.

She was just in time to see her grandmother falling face-first into the excavation pit.

Chapter Three

Brett turned with Octavia at the sound of the cry. The second he saw Mab Osborne falling, he moved. He reached the rim of the pit and scrambled down its sides, slipping the last few feet to the soft, muddy bottom where the elderly woman lay. He dropped to his knees, gently lifting Mab's head out of the mud and resting her on his knee as he pressed his finger to the pulse point in her neck.

But his fingers were caked in the slippery mud and he couldn't feel her pulse.

"Mrs. Osborne?"

She lay limp and absolutely still in his hands.

A sudden movement beside him drew Brett's eyes. Octavia dropped next to him. His first reaction was surprise at how fast she must have moved to have gotten here so soon after him.

His second was admiration for her coolheaded composure and farsightedness as she calmly dug into her shoulder bag for a compact mirror and immediately placed it beneath her grandmother's nose.

"She's breathing," Octavia said as the mirror fogged.

Octavia raised her head and voice to address the quiet spectators watching from the rim of the pit. "Someone please get an ambulance."

"John Winslow has already gone to call 911," one of the seniors yelled down.

Brett watched Octavia nod solemnly and direct her attention back to her grandmother. She slipped out of her mud-splattered suit coat and draped it over the unconscious woman. She held her grandmother's shoulders firmly as she spoke in a tone of stern sobriety that caught him completely off-guard.

"Listen to me, Mab Osborne, you wake up. You don't have time for this nap. You have a radio broadcast to give this afternoon. You know how important your broadcasts are. There are homebound people out there counting on you."

To Brett's continuing surprise and amazement, Mab Osborne began to stir. Her eyes fluttered open. Octavia stared down into them and smiled.

"Hi."

"Octavia," Mab said. "What was all that about my missing my broadcast?"

"Not to worry. You have plenty of time now. How do you feel?"

Slowly, Mab lifted each arm and each leg in turn. "I think I'm a little bruised is all."

"Any headache?"

"No, but it's cold, isn't it?"

Octavia scooted around in the mud in order to transfer Mab's head from its resting place on Brett's knee to a new resting place on hers. She wrapped her jacket more closely around her grandmother's shoulders.

"We'll have you out of this excavation pit just as soon as the medics get here," she promised.

"Why am I in this pit?" Mab asked.

For the first time, Brett heard a small annotation of anxiety underlying the normally mellow mark of Octavia's voice.

"Mab, don't you remember falling?"

"I didn't fall, Octavia. I was pushed. I want to know why."

"Pushed?" Octavia said as though she must have heard wrong.

"Yes, pushed," Mab repeated.

"Who pushed you?" Octavia asked.

"Let's just say I can make a good guess," Mab replied as she stared up at one particular face looking down at her.

Brett followed the direction of Mab's eyes. He was decidedly uncomfortable, but not surprised, to find himself looking into his uncle's sallow, bitter expression as he peered over the edge of the excavation pit.

"I'll go flag down the medics," Brett said as he got to his feet and climbed out of the pit.

When Brett reached the rim, he grabbed Scroogen and pulled him along toward the street where the medics would arrive. He waited until he and Scroogen were out of hearing distance of the crowd before he confronted him.

"Did you push her, Dole?"

"What?"

"You heard me."

"No, I didn't push the old bag," Scroogen's grating voice said, clearly angry at being asked.

"Where were you when it happened?" Brett asked.

"I was at the car placing that call," Dole said.

"Who did you speak to at the Community Development Department?"

"The line was busy. I was just about to redial when I got distracted by the commotion at the pit. I hung up the phone and went over to see what was happening."

"So you don't have an alibi."

"An alibi? For what? She topples five feet, face-first, into the mud, and she doesn't even break anything."

"Don't sound so disappointed. That's the one piece of good news we've gotten today. No one would have benefited by her being injured."

"What do you mean no one would have benefited? I'm no hypocrite. If the old bag had broken a few bones—or even better her neck—that would have been an end to her and her trouble-making. And that would have been a huge benefit to me."

It rather sickened Brett to see a human being so caught up in himself and the furthering of his own interests that he couldn't find even a little compassion for the pain and suffering of another. He consoled himself that at least no blood tied him to Scroogen.

"You would do well to refrain from expressing those sentiments to anyone else, Dole."

"I'm no fool, Merlin. I know who I can talk to."

"Go on and make that call to Community Development," Brett told him through a tight jaw. "Let's just try to get this mess over with as quickly as possible."

"MRS. OSBORNE, ARE YOU sure someone pushed you?" Detective Sergeant Paul Patterson of the Bremerton Police asked.

"Of course I'm sure," Mab answered.

Octavia could tell by her grandmother's frown that she was clearly disgusted with the question and the stocky detective with the big mustache who had asked it—for the fourth time.

"I questioned everyone at the scene," Sergeant Patterson said, tapping his pen on his notepad, a skeptical look in his grayish eyes. "No one saw anyone push you."

"That's not surprising. Everyone was looking at the carving on the stone in the pit. He would hardly have come up behind me and pushed if someone were watching him."

"You said 'he.' You're sure it was a man who pushed you?"

"I'm sure it was Dole Scroogen."

"Did you see Dole Scroogen push you?"

"No. But he's the only one who would do such a thing."

Octavia read a growing impatience in the sergeant's unconscious tapping of his notepad.

"Mr. Scroogen said he was on the car phone making a call when you fell into the pit."

"Well, what did you expect him to say?" Mab challenged. "That he had crept up behind me and pushed?"

"Mrs. Osborne, you said you were standing on the edge of the pit, trying to get a good look at the carved stone, right?"

"Right."

"Crowded together with the other seniors?"

"Yes."

"Rubbing shoulders?"

"Yes."

"Mrs. Osborne, isn't it possible that the pushing you felt might have been one of your fellow seniors inadvertently bumping you from behind while he or she shifted, trying to get a better look at the carving?"

"If one of my fellow seniors inadvertently bumped me, I am sure he or she would have come forward."

"Not necessarily. If one of your fellow seniors was responsible for knocking you into that excavation pit, he or she might be very embarrassed to admit it."

"I do not believe that is what happened."

Sergeant Patterson cleared his throat as he tapped his notebook some more.

"Think it over. I'll finish this report later. I can see that you are still quite upset by your experience."

Without waiting for confirmation or denial, Sergeant Patterson flipped his notebook closed, turned and trod out of the hospital room.

Octavia watched as Mab crossed her arms over her chest in a dignified anger that most people could not have pulled off covered only in a hospital smock and the single sheet provided with an emergency room bed.

"He doesn't believe me."

"If you had pointed a finger at one of the workmen, he might not have been so hesitant to inquire further. But Scroogen is one of those well-to-do financial pillars of the community that everyone is so fond of admiring these days."

"And I'm seventy-six."

"Yes. Our society's favorable biases toward people of wealth and unfavorable biases toward people of age are still very much with us."

The emergency room doctor sailed into the room then with a big smile on her young, chubby cheeks.

"I have nothing but good news for you, Mrs. Osborne. There's no sign of a concussion and you've no broken bones, which is an absolute wonder."

"Wonder has nothing to do with it, young lady," Mab informed her soberly. "Getting enough calcium and vitamin D, and taking an hour's walk and lifting weights every day is the only way to keep one's bones healthy."

The young doctor dimpled at the lecture. She then referred to the clipboard in her hands.

"All of your lab results have come back perfectly normal. Mrs. Osborne, there are fifty-year-olds who would love to have your blood pressure and lung-capacity readings. You're in great shape."

"Thank you, Doctor. Octavia, hand me my clothes and let's get out of here. I have that radio broadcast to do."

"I'll leave you to get dressed," the doctor said as she twirled out of the room.

"Your clothes are nothing but mud patties, Mab," Octavia said as she picked the once-beautiful, bright blue-and-white flowered silk pantsuit off the chair.

"So are yours and you're wearing them."

"I wish you hadn't reminded me. Look, it won't take but a few minutes for me to drive to your house and get you some fresh clothes and bring them here."

"I'll be late for my broadcast if you do. Octavia, this is radio I'm doing, not TV. I have to tell the seniors about our sale of the Scrooge dolls at the community center this afternoon and tonight. I need to remind them to keep calling and writing. And they need to learn about the carved stone that's been found next door. People are counting on me to tell them what they need to know. I'm not going to let them down, even if I have to wear this hospital sheet to the radio station."

Octavia knew her grandmother meant it, too. At any age, she had always been gutsy. Her all-time heroine. She smiled.

"All right. We'll both go looking bedraggled."

But as she helped Mab on with her mud-caked clothes, Octavia found her smile didn't have much staying power. Despite the cleanup the doctor had attempted, Mab's face and hair still contained streaks of caked dirt, reminding Octavia only too forcibly of those awful first seconds of seeing her lying so deathly still at the bottom of that muddy pit.

And of the hand that had put her there.

Dare she hope Sergeant Patterson was right? Dare she hope that Mab had been accidentally bumped by a fellow senior?

Octavia felt the telltale vibration of her muted beeper, fitted snugly on the waistband of her suit skirt. She drew it out and checked the calling number. It was A.J.

She excused herself and left Mab to finish dressing as she went to find a pay phone. A.J. answered on the first ring.

"Did you know Merlin's legal firm uses the Coltrane Detective Agency?"

"No, A.J. Why do you say that as though it's bad news?"

"Because it is bad news if anyone has anything to hide on your side of this legal fight."

"Coltrane is that good?"

"He's tenacious and will literally leave no stone unturned, and that carved stone on Scroogen's property in particular."

"Well, I didn't expect Merlin to employ a run-of-the-mill investigator. Don't worry, A.J., my back is covered. You learn anything yet about Scroogen?"

"A little. He makes good money on his septic business, because his overhead is low. His only regular employee is his son and he pays him a pittance. All the rest are 'occasional' part-time employees, even his secretary. That way he only has to pay minimum wage and doesn't have to provide any medical coverage, holiday pay, vacations or other fringe benefits."

"In perfect keeping with his Scrooge of a character. Well, I appreciate your calling to let me know about him."

"I didn't call you specifically to tell you about Scroogen, Octavia. Or even Coltrane. It's something about Merlin."

"You've found out something important?" Octavia asked, barely able to keep the eagerness out of her voice.

"Let's just say I think it's going to explain why he's in this fight."

"DID YOU HEAR that woman's radio broadcast this afternoon?"

Brett sat down in the chair next to the phone in his hotel room. He had just walked in when Dole had called.

"No, Dole. After I got cleaned up I was with the Building Department and the State's historical representative all afternoon trying to expedite this rock carving evaluation. *Now* what's the problem?"

"That Osborne woman told her listeners she hoped the stone carving found on my property interfered permanently with my condominium development project!"

"She has a right to her hopes, Dole."

"She doesn't have the right to ridicule me. She described a Christmas Scrooge doll they're selling to raise money and it's me, Merlin! They're selling a damn doll they've made to look like me!"

"Did Mab Osborne say that on the air?"

"She didn't have to. She described it, right down to my checkered suspenders. And when she squeezed the doll it said, 'Read it and weep, I'm raising your rent.'"

"Where are they selling these dolls?"

"At the Silver Power League's community center. They'll be open until ten tonight, selling the dolls and Christmas refreshments. You have to stop them, Merlin."

"I'll swing by and take a look."

"I'll meet you there."

"No, you stay put. Keep away from Mab Osborne."

"But—"

"No buts. If she has any more falls, I don't want you around."

"You heard Sergeant Patterson. He said one of the other seniors probably just bumped her as they jockeyed for position around that pit."

"He also said that Mab Osborne was certain it was you who had pushed her. Dole, use some sense here. Don't set yourself up as a handy scapegoat. I'll take care of this."

Dole cursed in Brett's ear and hung up.

Brett dropped the receiver on the hook, thankful not to have to hear the man's whiny voice anymore. He checked his watch. It was already six. It had been a long, frustrating day arranging for all the important players to be at the site of the stone carving in the morning.

He'd been looking forward to washing up and going out to an early dinner to make up for the lunch he missed. Now it seemed he would have to postpone even that. He picked up his car keys and retraced his steps to the door.

Would Octavia be at the community center with her grandmother? The thought of seeing his flame-haired adversary immediately replaced some of the hungry growling in his stomach with a hungry growling of an entirely different sort.

Brett frowned in irritation.

Thoughts of her and his unwanted reactions to her kept sneaking into his mind. Just more evidence of what a dangerous female she was. When he remembered her laughter and flagrant disregard of his warning that morning, he could barely control his anger.

She was brazenly beautiful and unconscionably unethical. He couldn't think of a worse combination in a woman.

He had underestimated her once. He would not do that again. He had no doubt that Dole's fears about this damn doll were right. Before he stopped at the community center, he was going to swing by the home of his longtime friend, Les Gatton, who also just happened to be a judge of the Kitsap County Superior Court.

Octavia Osborne had succeeded in handing him a few unwanted surprises. It was time for him to return the favor.

OCTAVIA INSTANTLY FELT Brett's eyes. She turned to see him standing near the beautiful twenty-foot Christmas tree gracing the entrance to the the community center. The seniors had transformed it into a magnificent work of art— decorating it with glorious globes and bows of every shape and size and hue and row after row of multicolored twinkling lights and tinsel.

Merlin wasn't looking at the tree, however. He was looking at her.

And that bright silver sparkle in his eyes even eclipsed the lights on the spectacular tree.

He was an unbending, formidable presence, no doubt about it. Octavia wondered fleetingly if perhaps that was the biggest part of his appeal—her inability to bend him.

She dismissed the mental query as soon as it arose. She was a woman of action, not reflection.

And it was time to act.

She had no reasonable explanation for why she did what she did next. It was purely intuitive. Octavia had always been comfortable letting her intuition guide her.

She walked over to Brett Merlin, stopped directly in front of him, rested her hands lightly on his lapels, rose on her tiptoes and then kissed him full on the mouth. Softly. Coolly.

Or at least that was what she had intended. But there was nothing soft about his mouth as his lips came alive beneath hers—or cool about the feel of his hot hands that immediately found their way to the back of her waist and pressed her hungrily to him.

He was returning her kiss. And then some.

His scent was a sophisticated smoky incense, his taste a leaping liquid fire.

Her heart hammered against her rib cage as a delicious wave of sweet heat took over her body. For several brainless, blinding, breathless seconds, she just went with it, melting into the hard body holding hers.

Then she was pulling back, removing her hands from his chest, rocking onto her heels, as the incredible surprise of it all registered.

His hands immediately shifted to grab her shoulders. She could feel the iron strength of his grasp, the heat of his palms. She tried to catch the runaway breath escaping so rapidly from her lungs.

She didn't know whether he had grabbed her shoulders to steady her, prevent her from kissing him again, or pull her into his arms and treat her to some more of that totally unexpected response from those firm lips and that even firmer body.

She stared up into his face, waiting breathlessly. The silver whirled in his eyes, as though it were being spun in a centrifuge. He looked as unsettled and unsure of his motives as she was.

"Why in the hell did you do that?" he demanded after a very long moment in a voice that didn't sound cool or distant at all.

Her unsteady breath still refused to completely fill her lungs in the aftermath of her body's very interesting reaction to his unexpected returning of her kiss. She had a bit of a problem gathering enough air for an answer.

"It's my way of thanking you for going to my grandmother's aid this morning," she managed to say finally.

"A few words would have sufficed."

She smiled, rather tickled at the annoyance in his tone.

"If my kiss bothered you that much, why did you return it?"

He held her in place before him, staring at her as if she were some unfathomable new species he had never encountered before. She was beginning to think he was one, too.

Behind those icy black-and-silver lawyer's eyes was a passion that burned both steel hard and molten hot. She had felt it. She had tasted it. And every female cell in her body was still happily standing at full attention saluting it.

"Good evening, Mr. Merlin. And what are you doing here?" Mab's voice asked from behind Octavia.

Brett's hands released Octavia's shoulders as his eyes switched to her grandmother's face. His voice immediately regained its normally deep, emphatically polite and distant tone.

"Good evening, Ms. Osborne. I hope you are fully recovered from your unfortunate experience this morning?"

"I am, Mr. Merlin. No thanks to your client, of course. But Octavia tells me that you were quick to come to my aid and for that *you* have my sincere thanks. But inquiring about my health isn't what brought you here tonight, is it?"

"I understand that you are selling a very unusual Christmas doll this season. I wonder if I might take a look at it."

"I'm afraid not," Octavia said.

Brett turned back to her, his base-drum voice resounding with an indignant note. "I beg your pardon?"

Octavia smiled. "You can beg all you want, but no one gets a look at the Silver Power League's Scrooge doll until after he's bought it."

"And why is that?"

"Because each one is already Christmas wrapped."

"People are buying this doll not knowing what it looks like?"

"Oh, I gave a description of it during my broadcast early this afternoon," Mab said.

Brett turned back to her. "I missed your broadcast."

Mab smiled. "Looks like you should have continued to tape my show, Mr. Merlin."

"You won't describe the doll to me now?"

"That's right, she won't," Octavia answered.

Brett looked from Octavia to her grandmother and back again. "Are you telling me I'm going to be forced to buy one of these Scrooge dolls in order to see it?"

"Only if you hurry," Mab said. "We're almost sold out of our stock on hand. Even we didn't anticipate how very popular it was going to be. This way."

Octavia tagged along as Brett followed Mab to the table where the last two of the boxed dolls remained. As Brett handed over his money to John Winslow, Octavia moved beside Brett to pat his shoulder. Her body reacted with a distinctly pleasant little jolt when she discovered solid muscle and absolutely no padding on that stalwart shoulder.

"You'll be happy to know your money is going to a good cause," she said.

Brett scowled. "I know where it's going."

"Cheer up. You can always give the doll to your cousin as a Christmas present."

He turned to face her. "You know."

"That Dole Scroogen is your uncle? Yes. How embarrassing that must be for you."

"How did you find out?"

"I hired a good detective."

"So did I. Mine has promised me a full report on you tomorrow, Octavia."

She deliberately smiled into his stern countenance and slipped her arm through his.

"Do you think we know each other well enough to be on a first-name basis?"

His face showed nothing, but she could feel the muscles tensing immediately in his arm. Obviously, his use of her first name had been a slip. Just like his kissing her? A warm wave of feminine power rode through Octavia. Maybe, just maybe, she might be able to move this man, after all. It certainly would be interesting trying.

Actually, quite a bit more than interesting.

"We'll never know each other well," he said, recovering quickly again. "You'll be in jail before that can happen."

She chuckled as she urged him toward the refreshment table.

"I admire a man who's not afraid to get egg all over his face. Let me buy you some eggnog so you can have some on the inside, as well. The seniors make potent stuff. Each cupful contains enough cholesterol to clog several arteries."

"It doesn't sound like you're doing me a favor."

"You expect me to do you a favor?"

"I suppose not."

"Well, suppose again. I'll also buy you one of Mab's cookies, and they are, without a doubt, the best-tasting cookies anywhere. Her specialty at this time of the year is Santa Claus and Scrooge. Normally, her Santa cookie is everyone's favorite, but this year her Scrooge has proven even more popular."

As they approached the table with the refreshments, Octavia smiled as she saw Brett's reaction to the three-inch-round, scowling Scrooge cookie sitting next to the happy countenance of the Santa cookie.

Whereas the Santa cookie was a smiling combination of chocolate and white fudge with a bright red cherry for a nose, the Scrooge cookie was an unhealthy light green with a dull green cherry for a nose.

"So which one would you like to try?" Octavia asked.

"Your grandmother deliberately made that Scrooge cookie's face resemble my uncle's."

"No, you have it all wrong, Brett. Your uncle has deliberately made his face resemble that of a Scrooge. No doubt the result of a lifetime of sour-pussed pettiness."

"You're enjoying this game of mocking my uncle, aren't you?"

"Are you enjoying your game of trying to make my grandmother appear a fool?"

He glared at her long and hard then. Very long and hard. He had a devastating glare—so damn icy, so damn sexy. Octavia's heart bounced around so much, her stomach had to keep volleying it back into her chest.

But she didn't look away. She knew intuitively she must never look away from Brett Merlin. As a lawyer, or as a woman.

He was a man who challenged her too strongly on both levels.

She'd read all about his devastating legal conquests. She could only guess at his personal ones, but she suspected he was just as devastating in them. Maybe A.J. could provide some background there, too. Or maybe that was something she should just find out for herself, firsthand.

He was a formidable adversary. Getting personally involved would be extremely risky. Of course, a healthy risk was why the idea held so much appeal for Octavia.

"What are you doing here, Merlin?"

When she heard the whiny voice behind Brett, at first she thought it was Scroogen's. But as Brett turned and the sour-pussed face belonging to the voice came into view, Octavia realized that she was looking at a much younger version of Dole.

Brett turned around to face the man. "I might ask the same question of you, Ronald."

"I came with my father to see this Scrooge doll they're selling, only they'd just sold the last one. Boy, is he pissed."

Octavia wondered why Ronald sounded so pleased that his father was upset.

"Dole is here?" Brett said, clearly unhappy with the news. "I told him specifically to stay away."

Ronald Scroogen's upper lip curled. His dark eyes squinted. "My father doesn't take orders from you, Merlin," he said. "Nor from anyone else. None of us Scroogens do."

"Give it to me!"

Octavia swung in the direction of the raised voice, just in time to see Dole Scroogen trying to grab a Christmas-wrapped Scrooge doll out of Keneth George's hands.

"Give it to me, I tell you!"

"Take your hands off it, Scroogen," George warned. "It's the last one and I just bought it. You're not the boss here."

Brett moved past her so quickly that Octavia felt the rush of air left in his wake.

"Give it to me or you're fired!" Dole was screaming as Brett reached his side.

Brett grabbed his client's arm and yanked him away from the foreman. The resulting tug-of-war with the box caused the wrapping to tear and the box to spring open. The doll got dumped onto the floor where Scroogen promptly tripped over it. Brett caught his arm and saved him from a fall.

"Read it and weep, I'm raising your rent," the doll whined beneath Scroogen's shoe.

Scroogen angrily shook Brett's steadying hand off his arm and swooped down to scoop up the doll.

"Look at it! It's me!" Scroogen complained as he stared in horror at the doll in his hand. "I knew it! Close them down! Confiscate the dolls!"

Octavia had moved closer to the commotion, as had most of the other people who had gathered in the community center. They formed a circle around Brett, Scroogen and George.

It was Mab who stepped boldly out of that circle to stand face-to-face with Scroogen.

"Your behavior as usual is reprehensible. You are not welcome here," she said. "You had best leave before I'm forced to call the police and have you physically removed."

The greenish tinge to Scroogen's complexion began to turn purple. "How dare you tell me to leave! This is my property, my building! You get out!"

Octavia stepped beside her grandmother, circling an arm protectively around her shoulders. She did not like the color on Scroogen's face, nor the look in his eyes.

"You'd best explain the law to your client, Mr. Merlin. The members of the Silver Power League are in legal possession of this property. They have every right to ask this man to vacate the premises, and if he doesn't, I will have formal trespassing charges filed against him."

Brett laid his hand on Scroogen's arm. "Come on, Dole."

"Give me the doll," George demanded.

Dole threw the doll at his foreman before twisting angrily out of Brett's hold and stomping toward the entrance. Ronald followed his father, a smile of amusement on his face.

Brett did not immediately follow Dole and Ronald Scroogen. He drew a folded piece of paper from his pocket and handed it to Octavia.

"I'll be in touch," his somber voice said. He pivoted on his highly polished shoes and followed his client out the door.

"What is it?" Mab asked as Octavia unfolded the paper.

Octavia quickly scanned the document, a small frown spreading onto her forehead.

"It's a restraining order, prohibiting the Silver Power League from making and selling any more Scrooge dolls, Mab. Merlin's claiming they're both libelous and slanderous to Scroogen. He's forcing the matter into court for resolution."

"I don't understand," Mab said. "How did Merlin get a court order so fast? The dolls only went on sale today, and he hadn't even seen one until he got here."

Octavia refolded the paper. "Obviously one of the Magician's tricks is pulling powerful people out of his hat."

"Can he prove this is libel or slander?"

"I think he just wants this restraining order to halt your sale of the dolls until it's too late."

"Octavia, we're already in the process of making a new batch of Scrooge dolls for sale tomorrow. We have to have the money from those sales. There must be something you can do."

"I can try to get an early hearing."

"What is early?"

"If I'm lucky, maybe next week."

"Next *week?* Octavia, we can't lose even one day of sales if we hope to raise enough money by January 1."

Octavia nodded. "Yes, I know."

"You can't suggest anything else?"

Octavia's mind had been busy considering the possibilities. Before she shared a promising one, she checked to be sure that no one else was close enough to overhear.

"Mab, please understand that as an attorney it would be totally improper of me to suggest you continue to make and sell these dolls on the black market."

"The black market?"

"Yes, if you keep selling these Scrooge dolls in violation of this court order, you would no longer be able to advertise them on radio," Octavia said. "Instead, you would have to use a discreet word of mouth to let prospective buyers know that they are available. And like everything else that is labeled illegal, the demand for them quite naturally would become even greater."

Mab leaned closer, her interest obviously engaged. "How would production and distribution be handled in such a black market operation?"

"Individual members would make and sell the dolls outside of your official facility and without the official sanction of the Silver Power League. These individual members would donate the money they collected on the dolls to go toward the rental demand Scroogen has made on you. Since the Silver Power League doesn't officially know about the black market operation, it can accept the money as it would any other donation."

Mab's lips lifted into a risible smirk. "And this black market selling of the Scrooge doll is something you are *not* suggesting we do?"

"That's right, Mab. I would never suggest you do it. It would be a clear violation of this restraining order that Merlin legally obtained from some judge he probably golfs with on the weekends."

"What would happen if I were involved in this black market operation and got caught?"

"You would have to explain that you were doing the only thing you could think of to save the community center from a greedy landowner. I can see it now. There you would stand with tears in your eyes, a sweet little seventy-six-year-old lady with her hair in a bun, walking with a cane and wearing an old-fashioned pink-and-white lace dress, with a faded sweater draped around your slumped shoulders. I have a very strong feeling the judge would dismiss any charges."

Mab ran a hand through her head of bold, bouncy curls. "I never wear a bun, my shoulders are straight, I don't walk with a cane, and I do not have an old-fashioned pink-and-white lace dress or a faded sweater."

"Still, a few bobby pins, a trip to the neighborhood thrift shop and a little practice hunching over would probably rectify those minor details."

Mab's smile circled to her ears. "Yes, I see."

"Now, as an officer of the court, Mab, I must insist you not even entertain the idea of running this black market operation, much less getting it started right away so as not to lose any valuable time."

Mab gave her granddaughter a quick hug. "Thank you, dear. I'm so glad to see all this lawyering you've been doing hasn't corrupted your heart."

Mab turned and walked over to Constance, who was sitting behind the refreshment table. "Come, Constance. We must find John and Douglas. We have some new... ah... organizing to do."

Octavia smiled as she watched them hurry away.

So much for Brett Merlin and his restraining order. He probably expected her to dissipate all her energy on fighting it through the mess of a legal maze such a suit would create. He was in for a surprise.

Octavia knew better than to enter a fight begun on her adversary's soil and according to her adversary's terms. Particularly this adversary.

Besides, she had better things to do with her time—like continuing the fight she had begun on her own turf under her own terms.

And speaking of time... She checked her watch. Yes, he should have reached his hotel by now. She looked forward to talking with him again. It had been a long time.

Brett Merlin wasn't the only attorney with a friend or two in the right places.

Chapter Four

"Your Honor," Brett began, "I appreciate your hearing this matter on such short notice."

Judge Les Gatton's drawn face and droopy eyes nodded at Brett. Brett knew that Les was one of those morning people who faded fast—both mentally and physically—by afternoon. Which was why, when they went mountain climbing together, Brett always insisted they begin at dawn and call it a day by noon. He wanted Les at his best when he was on the other end of what could literally be his lifeline.

But Brett was intent on getting this matter settled before the weekend; and, since he was appearing before Les unopposed, he saw no problem. However, in deference to Les's diminished capacity, Brett intended to take it slow and make it simple.

Gatton took several long moments to read Brett's quickly prepared brief. Brett waited patiently.

"This is a motion for summary judgment to remove what might be an early Indian artifact from a construction site, is that correct?" Judge Gatton finally asked.

"Yes, Your Honor," Brett said. "While preparing the future site for a condominium complex, the construction crew of my client, Mr. Dole Scroogen, uncovered a stone with carving on it. The carving could be of early native American origins. Mr. Ned Nordix of the State's Archaeology and Historical Preservation Department in Olympia immediately and graciously responded to provide technical support in this matter. I would like to call Mr. Nordix to the stand so that he can tell you himself what was done and why this motion is being made."

"Fine," Gatton said, trying to stifle a yawn. "Bring Mr. Nordix to the stand."

Ned Nordix, a tall, slim, vigorous-looking man with neat pepper curls hugging his scalp, rose from his position beside Dole Scroogen and approached the witness box. He took an oath to tell the truth and explained the duties of his position in the Archaeology and Historical Preservation Department.

"This court recognizes Mr. Nordix as an expert in his field," Judge Gatton said.

"Mr. Nordix, what action have you taken regarding the stone carving found at Mr. Scroogen's construction site?" Brett asked.

"I arranged for cultural anthropologists from two Indian tribes, whose ancestors were known to have inhabited the area around Puget Sound, to meet me at the site early this morning to study the stone carving."

"And what were the results of their study, Mr. Nordix?"

"Indeterminate. Neither of the tribes' cultural anthropologists recognized the carvings as belonging to a known native American culture."

"And what, in your expert opinion, would be the proper way to go about studying the carvings on this stone in order to arrive at the proper determination?"

"My suggestion is that the stone be made available to a team of experts who can devote the time and effort necessary to properly evaluate its authenticity, origin and age."

"Who would comprise this team of experts?"

"I believe a multidisciplinary team should be assembled comprised of experts in native American cultures of Washington State, general archaeologists, and scientists involved in radiocarbon and thermoremanent magnetism."

"Do you believe it is necessary to bring this team of experts to the stone where it currently rests at Mr. Scroogen's construction site?"

"No. It will take time to select and assemble this team of experts and even more time for them to study the stone and make their determination. That delay would seriously jeopardize Mr. Scroogen's building plans. I believe it would be best for all concerned to remove the stone and store it until this team of experts can be identified and brought together."

"Can the carved stone be safely removed, Mr. Nordix?"

"From the examination that I and the native American cultural anthropologists made of the carved stone this morning, none of us felt it would be damaged if moved."

"How would such a move be accomplished?"

"Mr. Scroogen is generously making his crew available tomorrow morning to lift the stone and wrap it under my direction and supervision. He is also providing a truck to transport it to Olympia where I will take custody of the stone until such time as the proper scientific team can be assembled to study it and make the determination as to its origin and antiquity."

"Have all concerned parties agreed to this procedure?"

"Yes, Mr. Merlin. The cultural anthropologists from the tribes I consulted and Mr. Scroogen agreed to this disposition. We believe it will best serve all interests."

"Thank you, Mr. Nordix."

Brett addressed the bench. "Your Honor, I move that this summary judgment be granted."

Gatton cleared his throat. "Since all parties seem to be in agreement I see no—"

"Your Honor!" a voice called from the back of the courtroom.

Brett swung around, his neck and shoulder muscles tensing instantly as he recognized the owner of that voice. Octavia was advancing on the bench with a gliding stride and a challenging gleam in her eyes.

"Your Honor, I'm Octavia Osborne. I ask permission to be heard on this matter before the court."

"How do you qualify as an interested party?"

"In my capacity as a citizen of Washington State, concerned with preserving its history and in support of the legislature's declaration in the Revised Code of Washington, Title 27, paragraph 27.44.030, that all native Indian artifacts are finite, irreplaceable and nonrenewable cultural resources."

"All right. You will be heard as a concerned citizen."

"Thank you, Your Honor. I am against Mr. Merlin's motion to have this carved stone removed from the site at which it was found for the purpose of further study. I believe to do so could result in irreparable harm to the find."

"Ms. Osborne," Judge Gatton said, "Mr. Nordix is an expert in this matter, and he has testified that the stone will not be harmed if moved."

"I respect Mr. Nordix's credentials and position. I would like permission to ask him a few more questions."

"Go ahead, Ms. Osborne."

Brett didn't know what Octavia was trying to pull, but he did know that she better not try any high-handed methods with Ned Nordix. The man was a skilled negotiator and testifier, and he would not allow himself to be bullied.

Her voice retained its thick, liquid quality as she approached the witness. Then, to Brett's surprise, she smiled graciously. Her tone was warm, not confrontational at all.

"Mr. Nordix, is it true that your job is to try to find an accommodation between all interested parties in cases of archaeological finds?"

"Yes."

"So you favor neither the owner of the property on which an artifact is found, nor the native Americans who may subsequently lay claim to such a find?"

"That's right."

"You told this court a moment before that you had met with the cultural representatives of two tribes to examine the carving on the stone, is that correct?"

"Yes."

"Which tribal representatives did you meet with to examine this stone carving?"

"The Suquamish and the Skokomish."

"Are those the only two recognized Indian tribes in Washington State?"

"No. There are twenty-seven different recognized tribes."

"Why then did you meet with only those two?"

"Because the Suquamish and Skokomish tribes were the primary inhabitants of the area where the stone carving was found."

"And yet these tribal experts were unable to determine whether the stone carving was genuine, correct?"

"Yes."

"Why couldn't they say one way or the other?"

"The exact symbols carved in the stone are similar to early Indian carvings, but they are also significantly different in several details."

"If these carvings had been made by ancient members of their tribe, you feel certain they would have recognized them?"

"Yes. They are experts in their own history."

"So if these are genuine Indian carvings on this stone in Mr. Scroogen's building site, they were made by another tribe?"

"That would appear to be a logical assumption, yes."

"If these carvings do belong to another tribe, Mr. Nordix, is it fair to say you have not consulted all possible concerned parties in this matter?"

"Ms. Osborne, the team of experts I plan to assemble will discover if these stone carvings belong to one of the other twenty-five recognized tribes. As soon as we know, the proper authorities within that tribe will be contacted, if they are not already present and part of the scientific team."

"But by then it could be too late."

"What do you mean, too late?"

Octavia turned to the judge. "Your Honor, I would like to answer Mr. Nordix's question by calling my own expert to the stand. If after hearing his testimony Mr. Nordix still wishes to go ahead with his transport of the carved stone, I will withdraw my objection."

"Sounds fair," the judge said. "Mr. Nordix, you are excused for the moment. Call your witness, Ms. Osborne."

Ned Nordix returned to the table to sit beside Brett.

"I call Dr. Watson Pacer to take the stand," Octavia said.

Brett sensed Nordix stiffening at his side in surprise. Nordix obviously recognized the name of Octavia's witness. As eager as Brett was to pump Nordix for the particulars, he was more eager not to be distracted from seeing and hearing this witness for himself. He turned to the back of the courtroom.

A big, lanky man with a dark, leathered face rose from the bench seat at the back and scuffed his way slowly to the front of the courtroom to enter the witness box.

He was somewhere in his sixties. His hair was long, straight and lead-gray. His shoulders were hunched, his head bent. When the court clerk swore him in, he didn't even make the effort to look at her. Brett never trusted a man who would not meet another person's eye.

"Dr. Pacer," Octavia began when her witness had seated himself. "Would you please tell this court what it is you do?"

"I am in charge of the Smithsonian's special project on ancient artifacts from Indian tribes of the Pacific Northwest."

Brett was not pleased to hear he was from the Smithsonian. He hoped this guy would just be some local archaeological talent.

"What credentials caused you to be selected for your position, Dr. Pacer?" Octavia went on.

"I have a Ph.D. in anthropology and in archaeology. Prior to joining the Smithsonian staff, I was chairman of the Department of Anthropology at the University of Washington. I have headed more than a dozen archaeological digs at early Indian sites throughout Washington State. I am the author of twenty-six books on artifacts belonging to tribes of the region, ten of those devoted entirely to petroglyphs and pictographs, which are stone carvings and pictures, respectively. I am also a native American of the Yakima tribe."

"Your Honor," Octavia said. "In view of Dr. Pacer's credentials, I ask that he be judged an expert in ancient Indian artifacts by this court."

"At the very least," Judge Gatton said, obviously impressed by what he had heard. "So ordered."

Octavia turned back to her witness. "Dr. Pacer, did you have occasion to visit Mr. Dole Scroogen's site to view the stone carving that has been discussed in this court this morning?"

"Yes. At your request I went there late this morning."

"And what, if anything, did you conclude from studying that stone carving?"

"It is not just a carving. It is also a painting. So the correct term for it would be pictograph."

"Thank you for the correction. What else can you tell us about this pictograph?"

"It is similar to others that I have seen."

"Where are those others?"

"On a basalt cliff in the Naches River Valley west of Yakima."

"Why is it that Mr. Nordix and the two cultural representatives of the local tribes did not recognize the similarity to these other pictographs of which you are familiar?"

"Possibly because they have not seen the pictographs in the Naches River Valley. They are on my tribe's land."

"Are the pictographs in the Naches River Valley the work of the Yakima people?"

"No. The legends of my tribe say that the pictographs were on the basalt cliff before the Yakimas came to live on the land."

"Dr. Pacer, forgive me for dwelling on this point, but I want to be sure I understand what you're saying. The pictographs on the basalt cliff west of Yakima that resemble the pictograph on the stone sitting on Mr. Scroogen's land are from a people so ancient they predate the Yakimas?"

"Yes."

"What do you know of these ancient people?"

"Very little. We only have their pictographs to study. Whatever else we could find would be immensely important."

"Are you certain that the pictograph on Mr. Scroogen's land was carved and painted by the same ancient people who carved and painted pictographs on the basalt cliff in the Naches valley?"

"Their markings are quite similar, but I cannot say for certain without extensive further study."

"You heard Mr. Nordix say that he plans to move the pictograph off Mr. Scroogen's site in order that it may be studied. What is your opinion about that plan?"

"I am against it."

"Why, Dr. Pacer?"

"Because the pictograph located on Mr. Scroogen's building site contains a sun. Suns often have a connection with death. We know many of them mark graves. If this pictograph marks an ancient grave, that grave may be in the earth below the pictograph. In the process of removing the stone, the grave could be totally demolished and we could lose irreplaceable archaeological evidence."

"How would you recommend this pictograph be studied?"

"By preserving the site where the pictograph was found and bringing the experts to it. If it does prove to be ancient, the ground around and beneath it would then have to be carefully excavated to discover whatever else might have been left by these ancient people."

"How long will it take to study this pictograph?"

"If it is not of ancient Indian origin, this can perhaps be determined in a few days or weeks. If it is of ancient Indian origin, the site around such a pictograph might take many years, even decades, to properly excavate."

"Dr. Pacer, if the pictograph is left in place and experts are brought in to study it as you suggest, are you aware that Mr. Scroogen's plans for a new condominium complex could be jeopardized?"

"Ms. Osborne, the world is full of condominium complexes. It can wait to add another. But we cannot wait, or worse yet, pass up, what may be the only opportunity to find out about these mysterious ancient people and what truths they have to tell us."

"Thank you, Dr. Pacer. That's all I have. I would now like to call Mr. Nordix back to the stand."

Brett quickly rose to his feet. "First, I would like to ask Dr. Pacer a few questions."

"Go ahead, Mr. Merlin," Judge Gatton said, motioning Octavia to the empty table adjacent to where Brett, Scroogen and Ned Nordix sat. As Octavia took her seat, Brett stepped forward.

He knew Pacer's testimony had been detrimental to his motion for summary judgment. Brett was convinced, however, that despite his impressive credentials, Dr. Pacer was hiding something. The man had even refused to meet Octavia's eyes. Why?

Brett strode boldly up to Pacer, stopping just on the other side of the witness stand, getting as close as he could. Pacer's head remained bent. He did not raise his eyes.

"Have you ever met Octavia Osborne before today, Dr. Pacer?"

"Yes."

"Where and under what circumstances?"

"She was a student in a class of mine at UW."

"How long ago was this?"

"Fifteen years."

"Have you kept in touch over the intervening years?"

"Before yesterday, we'd met at two separate social functions since her graduation."

"Have you had or do you currently have any personal or business dealings with Ms. Osborne?"

"No. Octavia and I are merely friendly acquaintances. We have not seen each other frequently enough to foster a friendship."

If true, Brett knew that would rule out collusion between the two. He would let Zane Coltrane decide the truth of that matter later. Now he had other things to address.

"Dr. Pacer, why are you in Washington State?"

"I'm guest lecturing at UW next week."

"How did you come to know of the stone carving on Mr. Scroogen's land?"

"Ms. Osborne called me last evening when I arrived from D.C. to tell me about the pictograph and to ask me to look at it."

"Do you know for certain that the pictograph on Mr. Scroogen's land is authentically ancient Indian?"

"As I said before, no."

"So all of this effort might be for nothing?"

"Yes."

"Have you ever worked outside of the academic or scientific community, Dr. Pacer?"

"No."

"Have you ever had to borrow money or put your financial future on the line to try to build something?"

"No."

"You're not having to give up anything here by insisting that Mr. Scroogen's building plans be delayed, even canceled, so that a group of scientists may find out in a month or two that this artifact is a fake, are you?"

"That is correct. I'm not having to give up anything."

"But Mr. Scroogen will have to. Dr. Pacer, it isn't your money, your time, your life's work, on the line. How can you so easily say the words that will ruin this man's dream?"

"Mr. Merlin, I understand you are representing your client's interests. Please understand I am trying to represent the interests of all the people."

"Then why is it you can't look me in the eye when you say that?"

A moment of quiet descended on the courtroom as Dr. Watson Pacer sifted sideways in the witness chair. His shoulders remained hunched, however, his head bent.

"Mr. Merlin, ten years ago on an archaeological dig, I fell into a deep rock crevice and broke my spine. The medics wanted to lower themselves to me and lift me out. But I couldn't let them. If they descended into that crevice, they could have damaged the delicate pictographs we had discovered there.

"So they lowered ropes instead, and I tied them around my body. They hauled me out. The pictographs were saved.

"Unfortunately, the further damage done to my spine in the process means I will never be able to stand or sit straight again. So, you are right, Mr. Merlin, when you say I cannot look you in the eye. But, I can look myself in the eye. And that has always been more important to me."

Brett had experienced other instances when he wished he had refrained from using a certain phraseology in questioning a witness. But never more so than at this moment with this witness.

Another moment of silence descended on the courtroom, a very uncomfortable moment for Brett.

Octavia Osborne had selected her witness well. Dr. Watson Pacer was an impressive man. And Brett knew that any more questioning of him would do more harm than good for his client.

Brett thanked Dr. Pacer and returned to his seat.

Octavia rose and requested that Mr. Nordix retake the stand. After the judge reminded Ned Nordix he was still under oath, Octavia asked her only question.

"Mr. Nordix, you have heard Dr. Pacer's testimony concerning the pictograph found on Mr. Scroogen's property. What is your recommendation now concerning its further study?"

Ned Nordix looked at Octavia for what seemed like a very long moment without saying anything. She did not prod him, but waited attentively and patiently for his response.

Finally, he shook his head and raised his hands palms up in surrender. "I recommend it stay where it is until a team can be assembled to study it at the site of its find."

"Thank you, Mr. Nordix," Octavia said with a graciousness that brought a smile to Nordix's face.

"No!" Scroogen protested as he jumped to his feet.

Brett pulled Scroogen back into his chair. "I apologize to the court for my client's behavior," he said loudly before whispering an order in Dole's ear to stay seated and shut up.

Judge Les Gatton looked down at the summary judgment motion before him.

"In view of Dr. Pacer's testimony and Mr. Nordix's final recommendation, I have no choice but to deny your motion, Mr. Merlin. The pictograph discovered on Mr. Scroogen's building site will remain where it is until a scientific team is organized to study it. Mr. Nordix, I will leave the assembly of that team in your capable hands. Court is adjourned."

Brett looked over at Octavia's positively beaming face as she flashed him a triumphant grin. Behind her, writing furiously in his notebook, was that same young reporter Brett had last seen at the construction site. No doubt Octavia had given him another call to make sure he'd be on hand.

"Scroogen and I are going to use the phone and call off the trucks and crew tomorrow morning while we still have a chance of reaching them," Ned Nordix said in Brett's ear. "I'm also going to talk with Dr. Pacer and ask him if he'll take a sabbatical from the Smithsonian and his UW speaking commitments to head up the team. We couldn't ask for anyone better."

Brett nodded without saying anything.

He knew when he had been outmaneuvered. She had planned this bogus native American find extremely well, right down to being sure that Dr. Pacer would be on hand to testify today to precisely what she wanted him to say.

Zane had filled Brett in about Octavia's partnership at the small but highly respected Seattle law firm of Justice Inc. He suspected that the reason he hadn't heard about her before was that she had gone to trial on only a few cases, preferring to arrange for out-of-court settlements for her clients whenever possible. Word was that she more than excelled at this behind-the-scenes work.

Brett knew he had been treated to a ringside seat at just how well she excelled. She had known exactly what was going to happen in this courtroom before she had even walked into it. She was good all right. Too damn good.

Nothing about her background had connected her with ancient Indian artifacts. Yet. Brett had told Zane to dig further. He knew it was there. He knew it was just a matter of time.

But she wasn't giving him much time. She was executing her well-thought-out plan with swift precision. Not even the cease-and-desist order on the Scrooge dolls had deflected her path or slowed her pace. She had just dissociated herself from the issue entirely. She was smart as hell, and she moved like lightning.

And she was heading right toward a cliff...and a very big fall.

He reminded himself that she was bringing it on herself and that she would deserve everything she got. But when she turned and their eyes locked, the muscles across Brett's neck and back tightened as he remembered the mind-bending feel and taste of those full lips, of that exciting body pressed so closely to his.

He knew then that despite what she had done, he would not be happy to see her take that inevitable fall.

She walked toward him, bold, brazen and beautiful. She stopped just in front of him. Her scent once again reminded him of heady tropical flowers heated by the sun.

He had no idea what she was going to do or say. He never did. The muscles across his shoulders and into his arms tightened.

"Whenever your client decides to reconsider kicking the seniors out of their community center and destroying their neighborhood with that condominium monstrosity, I have an alternative suggestion for his land use that he may find far easier to implement," she said.

"So, you admit you can stop all this ancient Indian artifact nonsense?"

"Me? Stop what could be history in the making? Now,
how could I do that?"

She looked and sounded so wonderfully innocent—for all
of a second—before the sparkle in her eyes betrayed her.

"Actually, Brett, what I was thinking is that your client's
land adjacent to the Silver Power League's community center would make an excellent museum for the preservation of
native American artifacts, don't you think?"

She was blatantly taunting him. Brett felt his fury toward
her and his attraction for her both increasing far too fast for
control. His hands balled into fists by his side.

"I'm not interested in hearing about your ideas for my
client's property, only about how you faked that artifact. If
you come clean now, I will move for clemency on your behalf."

"What a Mr. Santa Claus," she said, her thick, liquid
voice full of amusement.

He took a step toward her, frustrated and furious at how
glib she could be in such a serious situation.

"No, Octavia, there is no Santa Claus. Once I have the
facts in hand, as an officer of the court, I will be forced to
turn you in. I'm not going to be able to save you."

An inquisitive eyebrow arched up her forehead. "I'm
surprised the idea of saving me would even occur to you,
Brett, or that you would consider turning me in to be something you were *forced* to do. Can it be that you do have a
heart, after all?"

"Octavia, this is not a joke. Your flagrant violation of the
law is something I take very seriously. The law is what I live
by. As a lawyer, it should be what you live by, too."

"The law is a creation of human beings, Brett. It's important, yes. But to place it above the importance of the
human being is to miss its whole point, don't you think?"

His hands had suddenly found her arms. "No, I don't
think that by exalting the law we give it greater importance
than human beings. On the contrary. I think that when we

exalt the law, we bring out what is best and worth exalting in us as human beings."

"What is best and worth exalting," she repeated. "Beautiful thought. And when heart as well as head is used to administer the law, I do believe that what we get reflects the best of the human being and is well worth exalting."

Brett knew her equivocation was foolish. But somehow she didn't look or sound foolish expressing it. Her eyes sparkled like the hard blue center of the diamond he so loved to look at. The feel of her within his hands had his heart beginning to race.

"Octavia, your flagrant disregard for the law is going to make you lose your license to practice your profession, not to mention land you in jail. Is this stupid condominium matter so important that you are prepared to pay such a dear price?"

She smiled at him then, the blue in her eyes dancing like a warm rain. "For my dear of a grandmother? In a second."

"But you're being impossibly reckless! I don't understand."

She touched his cheek as her eyes rested fully on his for the space of a heartbeat. Brett's whole body seemed to ignite at the light in her eyes and the lightness of her touch.

"Yes, I can see you don't understand. I'm sorry you don't have anyone in your life who makes you do impossibly reckless things, Brett."

He moved closer, not in response to a mental signal, but to a sudden, overpowering physical one. But she withdrew her hand, stepped back out of his arms and turned to walk away.

As he watched her glide down the courtroom aisle, her words still revolved in his mind.

What was so damn wonderful about doing impossibly reckless things? They only led to trouble. Good sense and good judgment were the key to success. They had certainly led to his success.

But, damn, he wished that it could be someone else who would have to bring that foolish attorney down. Anyone else.

Brett shrugged aside the wish. He had never gotten anything he wished for, only what he worked for. And first and foremost he worked for the law. He would put her behind bars because it was his duty. And there was no question about his doing his duty. None at all.

"You told me it was going to be all over and done with this morning, Merlin!" Scroogen's annoying voice spat in Brett's ear.

Brett could see his client had returned to the courtroom in the same emotional temperament with which he had left. Brett gathered his legal papers and shoved them into his briefcase.

"Relax, Dole. I predict a few days—a week at the most— is all it will take for a scientific team to find the stone carving is a phony."

"Days? A week? I'll be ruined!"

"You can afford it."

"How do you know?"

"I checked."

Scroogen's voice rose an octave. "You checked? You mean you had *my* finances investigated?"

"An attorney needs to know everything about his client in order to represent his best interests."

"You had no right. I'm not even paying you!"

"Don't remind me."

"What if they find out that stupid thing is real?"

"They won't."

"You still think that attorney orchestrated this?"

"I'm sure of it."

"Well then, get the damn woman."

"I will. But it'll take time."

"More time, time, time. That's all I seem to hear from you. I told you about the telephone calls. I told you about the threatening letter I received."

"Dole, if the Silver Power League is really behind those calls and that letter, they're slitting their own throats. Once the police tie those threats to them, they'll lose their support in the community."

"But the police are dragging their feet! I told them Mab Osborne is behind both the calls and letter."

"They have to investigate properly in order to make any subsequent charges stick."

"She's still making and selling those damn dolls. I swear everywhere I go I see them. They're ignoring your court order. Have her arrested!"

"Dole, she's seventy-six. If I had her arrested because she's trying to raise enough money to save their center, that would just generate more sympathy for her cause and more unfavorable publicity for yours. I'm already worried about what that reporter is going to print about the stone carving and Mab Osborne's plunge down that damn pit of yours."

"Well then, you'll have to do something about keeping that story out of the papers."

"Nothing I can do now except hope that the FCC story eclipses any article on her fall or this phony stone carving. We'll need to wait and see what the Sunday edition brings."

"More waiting. Can't you get that damned attorney arrested at least for being a part of the doll operation?"

"I've had Octavia under surveillance since yesterday. She has nothing to do with the manufacture and sale of the dolls."

"This is insane! My bulldozers have been stopped! I can't even go ahead with the ribbon-cutting ceremony next week!"

"Dole, the moment the scientific team pronounces that stone carving to be a fake and my private investigator ties Octavia Osborne to it, that attorney's misdeeds will be front-page news along with your building progress."

"So what you're telling me is that in the meantime you're just going to sit back and let them get away with it?"

"I didn't say that."

"Then, what in the hell are you going to do?"

"I'll tell you what I'm going to do. I'm putting away the flyswatter and getting out the shotgun," Brett said, snapping his briefcase closed.

Chapter Five

"The story and accompanying pictures of the stone carving take up three-fourths of the Sunday newspaper's front page, Octavia. The other fourth is my fall down that ditch. And all that FCC nonsense about my radio program gets a slim one-column mention on page six!"

Octavia was delighted to hear the burst of enthusiasm from her grandmother as she sat across from her at the breakfast table, inhaling the wonderful smells of a new batch of Christmas cookies sitting on the counter to cool.

"That reporter did a very good job on the pictograph story. But he needs positive reinforcement so he'll keep up the good work. Yearsley is the editor of the newspaper now, isn't he?"

"Yes. Fred Yearsley. His mother is one of our members."

"Remind me to contact him tomorrow morning and give the reporter a commendation."

"With pleasure," Mab said, setting the paper aside.

Octavia poured cream into her coffee and took an appreciative sip. Her grandmother's coffee rivaled the best Seattle had to offer.

"It's still hard for me to believe that you've managed to stop the construction," Mab said.

"Thanks to Dr. Watson Pacer. He was just as impressive as I remembered him, bless his heart."

Mab poured some cream into her coffee and stirred the spoon through it thoughtfully.

"This stone carving has proved a very fortuitous find, especially if it turns out to be an ancient Indian artifact. Almost too fortuitous. I seem to remember that Gordon Twobrook, that young native American chief you met in law school, used to be very interested in ancient tribal rock carving. You two were very close at one time. Octavia, you didn't—"

"Ask me no questions, Mab, and you'll never be forced to testify to something you wished you didn't."

"I . . . see."

Octavia sent her grandmother a sagacious smile. "Yes, you've always been a quick and clever darling."

"Why didn't you ever marry that handsome native American?"

"Why assume that the decision was just mine? It takes two to make a couple, remember."

"Don't give me that, Octavia. No Osborne woman worth her wits couldn't get the man she wanted. No, you held back for some reason. Why?"

"Gordon was and is wonderful, and he's helped me without question on two very sticky occasions now. Truth is, a part of me will always love him. But I need a man who places me before anything and everything else in his life."

"That's asking a lot, isn't it?"

"It's what I'm prepared to give. I can't settle for less."

"Gordon wasn't prepared to do this, I take it?"

"Despite Gordon's love for me, his first duty will always be to his people and their traditions. They still live primitively, as their ancestors did. We spent a season together, long enough to know neither of us could give our all to the other."

"Well, it's for certain that roughing it in the great outdoors has never been your style."

Octavia chuckled as she bit off a small piece of cookie. "Yes, there is quite a bit to be said for indoor plumbing, isn't there. Remind me I need to raid your recipe box for the ingredients to those Scrooge cookies. What gives them that wonderful flavor?''

"Pistachio nuts and Crème de menthe. You won't get into trouble over this artifact business, will you, Octavia?''

"Don't look so worried, Mab. I know what I'm doing.''

Mab sighed. "And to think that I was once afraid your becoming a successful lawyer meant you had turned into one of those staid and stodgy corporate types.''

Octavia laughed. "Not a chance. I spent too many of my formative years with you.''

Mab's small smile told Octavia that her words had pleased her grandmother very much.

"Have you heard that the Scrooge has been receiving some anonymous threatening telephone calls and even a letter?'' Mab asked on a more sober note.

"No, I hadn't,'' Octavia said as she helped herself to another cookie. "What are these threats about?''

"His takeover of the community center. I understand that whoever is doing it has suggested bodily harm against him.''

"How did you find out about the threats?''

"Sergeant Patterson came by the community center last Friday requesting some of our Silver Power League stationery. Scrooge claims we're behind the threats. He wants the police department to compare the stationery used.''

"Is there any possibility that someone in the Silver Power League would call or send threatening letters to Scroogen?''

Mab's shoulders straightened in immediate indignation. "Octavia, I'm surprised at your even suggesting such a thing.''

"Mab, the Silver Power League boasts nearly four hundred members. You've asked them to call and write the people in power to try to stop Scroogen. Would it be so unlikely that one might take it upon him or herself to send a missile Scroogen's way?''

Mab shrugged. "I suppose it's possible. But, Octavia, even if a member vented some anonymous spleen at the

Scrooge, you can hardly blame him. Or her. Besides, it's harmless."

"It won't look harmless if there's a link between that threatening letter and the Silver Power League stationery."

"There won't be. Only the members of the executive committee have access to our stationery. That's me, John, Constance and Douglas. And believe me, if any of us wished that man bodily harm, we'd be happy to tell him right to his face."

"I'm certain *you* would," Octavia said with a smile.

The back doorbell rang.

"Now, who could that be so early on a Sunday morning?" Mab wondered aloud as she got up to answer it.

John Winslow's clean-shaven face poked around the door. "Good morning. Please forgive this early intrusion."

"Come in and have some coffee, John," Mab said.

John stepped inside and Mab closed the door behind him. "I'd love a cup. It's single-digit cold out there this morning."

Octavia thought John's face looked a little frostbitten. He wore a strong-tweed sports jacket with a matching tweed hat, an immaculate dress shirt and tie, and fine leather driving gloves. A parka and wool mittens would probably have kept him warmer, but Octavia was selfishly glad the man insisted on that well-dressed, dapper look that fitted his personality so well.

John immediately removed his hat and bowed his trim body in Octavia's direction.

Every time she saw John, Octavia felt a pang of nostalgia for that refined period of male dress and manners that predated the current coarse trends of butt cracks and beer bellies and calling women bitches.

Why was it that humankind couldn't add new technology and new options for men and women and at the same time still keep all the beautiful clothes and social graces that both sexes once wore so well?

"Mab, I couldn't help noticing that huge madrona tree in the front yard is tipping toward the house," John said. "The dry summer and fall seem to have weakened it. You're going to have to cut it down before it falls on you."

"Yes, I know, John. Octavia already gave me this lecture in the first few minutes of her arrival. But I've watched that tree grow for fifty years and I've been hoping the winter rains might revive it. I'll give it another month. Sit down. I'll get you some coffee and then you can tell me what's wrong."

Octavia hadn't detected anything in John's demeanor to indicate something was wrong. But when John nodded and silently took the chair and coffee Mab offered, she realized that her grandmother's familiarity with her longtime friend had obviously allowed Mab to see something Octavia hadn't.

"Now, what has brought you by?" Mab asked after John had had an opportunity to remove his gloves and sip the coffee that she had poured.

"I heard some disturbing news from a former patient of mine, Mab. He told me you're about to lose your radio station."

"Your friend is mistaken," Mab said. "He was probably misled by that story in today's newspaper about an FCC complaint that could put my radio *license* in jeopardy."

"No, Mab. My source wasn't referring to that story. He hadn't even seen the Sunday paper. And he definitely spoke of you losing your station, not your license."

"How could I lose my radio station?"

"The information reached my friend through a lengthy grapevine that is supposed to lead back to the Scrooge's attorney."

"Brett Merlin?" Octavia said, instantly coming to stiff attention.

"Yes," John confirmed.

Octavia felt her healthy appetite of a moment before leave her. "John, what exactly did your friend say?"

"That Mab was about to lose her station and that the Scrooge's attorney was behind it."

"It's impossible for that attorney to take away my station. I've owned it for forty years. I don't care how good he is. Octavia will tell you I'm right. Won't you, Octavia?"

Octavia wanted to give the reassurance her grandmother was seeking. More than anything. But she couldn't. Not when Brett Merlin was involved.

She had heard every word he said to her in that courtroom the Friday before, and what's more, she had seen his face when he said them. When he confronted her at the construction site, it had been to threaten. But in that courtroom, he wasn't threatening. He was explaining who he was, why he could give her no quarter, why he had to take her down.

And the whole time she had felt the warmth of his hands, the air pulsing between them, charged with the elemental electricity of his mounting desire for her—and hers for him.

It had been the most sensually arousing conversation Octavia had ever had. Here was risk so sharp and so sweet it made her tingle all over.

And shiver, too. Because she knew he meant every word. He was a lawyer first, last, always.

What kind of legal hocus-pocus had his magician's mind conjured up against her grandmother now?

"YOUR HONOR," Brett began, "I represent Voleta Davies Ermasen, the plaintiff in this matter before the court. We are suing Mab Osborne for ownership of the KRIS radio station."

"What is the basis of your suit?" Judge Gatton asked.

"Forty years ago, Voleta Davies Ermasen's parents, Walter and Mildred Davies, died, leaving their radio station to Voleta's younger brother, Joel, then seventeen. A month later, Joel sold the radio station to Mab Osborne, an employee at the station, for five hundred dollars. The original papers recording the transaction are included at the back of my brief."

"One moment," Judge Gatton said as he looked for and found the original bill of sale. He perused it a moment before nodding. "You may continue, Mr. Merlin."

"Your Honor, as Joel Davies was only seventeen when he sold the KRIS radio station to Ms. Osborne, he was a minor under the law and consequently his transfer of ownership of this property to another person was illegal. Mrs. Voleta Davies Ermasen is bringing this suit to invalidate that sale."

Brett saw Octavia rise to her feet.

"Invalidate a sale made more than forty years ago?" her rich voice challenged.

She glared at him. He turned to face her and glared back.

"Whether contracted forty years ago or forty minutes ago, it is still in violation of the law," Brett replied.

He turned back to the bench.

"Your Honor, Joel Davies died without issue six months after the sale in a tragic accident. As the sale of the radio station to Ms. Osborne was illegal, Joel still owned the radio station on his death. Mrs. Davies Ermasen is the sole beneficiary of her brother's estate. The radio station rightfully belongs to her. On her behalf, I am petitioning the court to return the KRIS radio station to her."

Brett knew he was the one prepared this time and Octavia was the one caught off-guard. Still, he could tell from the firm set of her jaw that she was not going down without a fight.

"Your Honor," Octavia said, "the statute of limitations compels the exercise of a right of action within a reasonable period of time to avoid claims made stale through lost or destroyed evidence. That reasonable period of time came and went four decades ago on this matter. It's too old to be reopened."

"This claim is not stale due to lost or destroyed evidence," Brett said. "Your Honor has in his possession the birth certificate of Joel Davies and the original, dated bill of sale between the parties to this illegal, and therefore invalid, contract. Time does not change the facts."

"Nevertheless, Your Honor, the weight of time attests to Mab Osborne's ownership," Octavia said. "For forty years, Mab has nurtured the KRIS radio station, like a mother would a child, struggling to keep it alive and well. Not once in all that time has Mrs. Ermasen come forward to raise an objection to the transfer of her brother's property to Mab. Why now?"

"It's a legitimate question, Mr. Merlin," Judge Gatton said.

"Voleta was only nineteen at the time of this sale," Brett said, "close to a child herself. Until recently, she was unaware of her legal rights in this matter."

Octavia's chin rose as she once again faced Brett. "You mean until you contacted her and convinced her to sue for them."

"You are out of order, Ms. Osborne," the judge admonished.

"I apologize, Your Honor," Octavia said, no real apology in her voice. "However, this sudden push for Mrs. Ermasen's legal 'rights' does not begin to meet the rudimentary requirements of fair play, the basis of all law."

"The basic tenet of fair play insists on the protection of a minor from the machinations of adults intent on taking his property from him at a time when his lack of judgment and experience could be exploited," Brett said.

"How dare you imply I would do such a thing!" Mab shouted as she shot to her feet. "I loved Joel Davies. He had absolutely no interest in that radio station he inherited."

"Ms. Osborne, please sit down," the judge said. "Let your attorney speak on your behalf."

Mab responded to Octavia's coaxing, not the judge's, and retook her seat. Octavia addressed the bench.

"Your Honor, Mab was a dear friend of both Joel and his parents, not just an employee at their radio station. Joel wanted to *give* her the radio station after their death. It was Mab who insisted on paying him five hundred dollars for it."

"Even if true," Brett said, "Joel Davies was a minor and was, therefore, legally incapable of making such a decision and executing such a transaction. The law is clear on this matter."

"The law only becomes clear when sifted through a reasonable mind and heart," Octavia informed Brett directly. "Your Honor, Mab Osborne bought the radio station from Joel Davies in good faith that she was entering a legal transaction. She did not know his age prevented him from transferring the property."

"Ignorance of the law is no defense," Brett interjected. "That radio station could have been helping to support Joel's sister, Voleta, all these years instead of your grandmother."

"You are mistaken," Octavia said. "KRIS hasn't supported my grandmother. She has supported it. The few advertising dollars she's received have seldom covered costs. Through the years she's taken such jobs as schoolteacher, waitress and even bus driver to raise enough money to keep broadcasting."

Octavia redirected her attention to the bench.

"Your Honor, Mab Osborne has devoted her life to serving her community through that local radio station. Every year at this time she spearheads the Supper for Seniors program that delivers hundreds of Christmas dinners to nonambulatory seniors, along with many programs designed to bring them much-needed holiday cheer. In the minds of the elderly citizen community she serves, Mab Osborne *is* KRIS. Surely those facts are more important than some dried ink on some forty-year-old papers?"

Brett watched a frown dig into Les Gatton's brow as his eyes bounced between the lawyer's brief in his hands and the elderly lady sitting at the defense table.

"I will take this matter under advisement," he said finally. "We will reconvene tomorrow at ten. Court is adjourned."

"GATTON LOOKED PRETTY damn uncomfortable up there," Scroogen complained as soon as Brett had exited the courtroom. "Are you sure he's going to take that radio station away from her?"

"Yes," Brett said.

"Because he's your friend?"

"Because it's the law. Gatton agreed to hear the case so quickly because he's my friend. But he puts friendship aside the moment he dons that black robe and takes the bench. Like every judge must."

"Whatever," Scroogen said, impatiently waving his hand as though uninterested in the process, only the outcome. "How soon are we getting her off the air?"

"Gatton will hand down the judgment tomorrow. Ownership will pass to Mrs. Ermasen immediately upon her paying Mab Osborne five hundred dollars, the amount Mab Osborne paid to Joel Davies. Mrs. Ermasen said she would bring the check with her."

"And you feel certain you can count on her?"

"Absolutely. She's excited about owning a radio station. She's been a homemaker for forty years. She was divorced recently, her kids are grown, and she has been wondering what to do with the rest of her life. As soon as I mentioned her getting the radio station and the possibility of her being a deejay, she became ecstatic. I knew then the suit would be a success."

"When did you find out about this illegal sale thing?"

"The private investigation firm I had checking into Mab Osborne's background called me last Friday. And speaking of telephone calls, Nancy said something on the phone this morning about your having received another anonymous threatening letter?"

"Yes. I messengered it to the police as soon as it arrived in the mail. It's even more threatening than the last one. I wish that damn Seattle forensic group would get off their butts and tie it to Mab Osborne so we can get her behind bars."

"From what I've seen of Mab Osborne, she strikes me as far too forthright to resort to anonymous jabs. Are you sure she's the one sending them?"

"Of course I'm sure. She's the one making the calls, too."

"I thought the police department put a tap on your office and home lines days ago. If she's behind the calls, why haven't they caught her?"

"She obviously found out about the tap. The calls have stopped. We're going to have to nail her on the notes."

"By 'we' I trust you're referring to you and the police?"

"What's wrong, Merlin? Did that business with Danette sour you on going after the criminal element?"

Brett kept his temper, but just. He knew Nancy must have been the one to tell Scroogen about Danette. He wished like hell she hadn't. He resented Scroogen knowing about that very personal part of his life.

And he doubly resented him daring to refer to it, as though he had a right, as though they shared something more personal than their nodding acquaintance as in-laws.

"I have to meet with Ned Nordix to try to expedite his putting together a scientific team to study the stone carving. Excuse me," Brett said, turning and walking quickly away.

"OCTAVIA, IS THERE a chance Judge Gatton will let me keep the radio station?"

"The odds are strongly against it, Mab."

"But he didn't rule against me right away. He said he was going to take it under advisement."

"Often a judge only does that to give himself time to prepare a suitable wording for his decision."

Mab slumped back into the cushioned white leather passenger seat of Octavia's 1971 winter-blue Mercedes-Benz Corniche.

"Then we've lost," she said with a sigh.

"Not yet we haven't. What do you know about Voleta Ermasen?"

"I haven't seen or heard from her in forty years, Octavia. I didn't even recognize her in court today."

"What did you know about her forty years ago?"

"Every time I went to dinner at Mildred and Walter's, Voleta seemed to be out on a date. It was Joel and I who talked and got to know each another."

"Who was Joel's legal guardian after his parents died?"

"Voleta. She got married a month later and they took Joel into their home."

"How did Joel die?"

"He fell off a roof into a snowbank, landed wrong and broke his neck. Broke my heart, too, I must tell you. As you know, I had lost your grandfather just months after your mother was born. Joel was like the son I never had."

"And you didn't stay in touch with Voleta?"

"Her husband got a job in Olympia almost right afterward and they moved there. That was the last I heard of them."

"Well, she's here alone. Merlin didn't give me a lot of time to check her out, but I did learn she's registered at a local hotel under her maiden name. That spells divorce to me, and the white circle on her bare ring finger suggests it was recent. She must be feeling lonely. What do you say we invite her over for one of your special dinners tonight?"

Mab's voice rose an octave. "Invite her over for dinner?"

"Yes, and afterward, we could take her by the radio station and give her a good rundown of the operation."

"Octavia, I don't believe you're saying this. You want us to be gracious and hospitable to the woman who is trying to take my radio station away from me?"

"Mab, aren't you the least little bit curious as to why she's trying to take it away?"

"What do you mean, why?"

"You've been running KRIS for so long you've forgotten how much work it is and how little financial reward, if any, you get in return for all that work. Face it, Mab. Unless you do it for love, running a small community radio station is just a monumental pain. Why does Voleta want to do it?''

"Could it be she's forgotten how much trouble it was for her parents when they were running it?'' Mab wondered aloud.

"After forty years, I wouldn't be surprised. Why don't we wine and dine and then remind her?'' Octavia said with a smile.

"WELL, YOU DID IT, Merlin,'' Scroogen said after Judge Gatton handed down his decision the next morning. "I have to tell you, I had my doubts. But the judge ruled just as you said he would.''

Brett ignored the whiny pleasure riding through Scroogen's tone as he looked over at Octavia and Mab.

"Yeah, I did it,'' he said.

"What's wrong?''

"Nothing.''

"Well, how about sounding like it? Mab Osborne's lost her radio station! Soon, the forensic lab's results will be in, and she'll be rotting in a cell where she belongs.''

Brett refocused his attention on Dole's face. The man was staring at Mab, an expression in his eyes that gave Brett more than just a jolt of unease.

"What is it about Mab Osborne, Dole, that pushes your hot button so hard?''

"You have to ask? After those broadcasts of hers?''

"She's just an old woman, hanging on to the past. Your building is still going up. Her interference is going to cost more because of the delay, but you can make that up by charging more for the condos when you sell them. You stand to make millions on the deal. What's the problem here?''

Scroogen turned his face to Brett's then. His pupils had enlarged so much his eyes looked like black holes. Purple blotches whirlpooled beneath his cheeks.

"The problem? I'll tell you what the problem is. For ten years I've been trying to get nominated to the presidency of the chamber of commerce. I should have gotten it long ago.

But my image as the owner of a septic company kept turning them off. So, finally this year they hear about the condo going up and everything changes. I'm given the nomination. Everyone says I'm a shoe-in—until Mab Osborne starts with her broadcasts, whipping up public sentiment against me.

"Suddenly, my name's withdrawn. Too much bad publicity, they say. Can't afford to have me represent them, they say. Nobody on the chamber wants to even know me much less vote for me! She's going to pay, Merlin. For those broadcasts. For the calls. For the letters. I'm going to see she pays!"

Scroogen whirled and walked away, the heat of his angry words still sizzling in the air.

So, this was what it was really all about. The Septic King became the Condominium King in order to enhance his image among his fellow businessmen and snag the presidency of the chamber of commerce.

And Mab Osborne had gotten in the way and spoiled it for him. So now he was after a piece of petty revenge. And Brett was helping him get it.

Great. Just great.

Brett slammed his briefcase closed and looked over at his adversary once again. Octavia was standing behind her grandmother, giving her a reassuring hug as Mab and Voleta bent over the papers that would transfer title of the radio station.

Brett thought about Zane's latest report. About how Mab Osborne had virtually raised Octavia while her cultural anthropologist parents were studying and living with a primitive people. About how strong the bond between grandmother and granddaughter had always been.

He could understand her wanting to do whatever she could to help her grandmother. But he could not understand—would never understand—a lawyer relinquishing her sworn duty to the law.

Everything Brett had just done had been strictly in accordance with the law. He had represented his client well. He had won. He would—could—never do less.

So why did he feel like hell?

She must have felt him looking at her because Octavia suddenly straightened and turned to meet his eye.

She smiled one of those damn secretive smiles that tightened every muscle in his body. Despite everything he knew about her, he wanted her more and more with each passing minute.

He had to stop these dangerous feelings. He had to draw the line. He walked up to her, never once breaking eye contact.

"That was the shot across your bow," he said solemnly.

He expected his words to at least wipe that smile off her face. But that unfathomable smile expanded as she sent him a sparkling blue, mischievous wink.

And that was the instant Brett got his first inkling that somewhere, somehow, something had just gone wrong.

OCTAVIA KEPT THE RADIO on as she drove back to Mab's house after running her late-afternoon errands. She was glad she was just in time for Mab's evening broadcast.

"Ladies and gentlemen," Mab began. "On my earlier segment this afternoon, I told you that there would be some changes here because I have a new partner and co-owner of KRIS. Tonight, I would like to introduce that new partner and co-owner, Voleta Ermasen."

"Hello!" Voleta yelled happily into the mike, probably sending the volume needle off the scale.

Octavia chuckled. Clearly it was going to take some doing to educate Voleta on even the rudimentary points of the broadcasting business.

"As I mentioned this afternoon, listeners," Mab continued, "it is only because of the sweet, understanding nature of Voleta that I am still an owner of KRIS and still broadcasting to you. If Dole Scroogen's attorney had had his way in court this morning, I would have been forced off the airways. And now as I promised earlier, Voleta and I are going to tell you all about Scroogen's plan to try to silence me, aren't we, Voleta?''

Voleta's affirmative blast was softer this time. Octavia suspected that Mab had probably muffled the microphone with a well-placed hand so that the batteries on her listeners' hearing aids didn't all blow at once.

Octavia listened as Voleta told the radio audience about Brett seeking her out and offering to represent her in order to deprive Mab of her radio station.

Although Octavia hadn't been able to convince Voleta to sell full ownership of the radio station to Mab, a half ownership—which gave Mab all decisions regarding program content and editorial direction—wasn't bad, particularly since Voleta would now be paying half the bills.

Of course, the deal had hinged on Mab agreeing to make a broadcaster out of Voleta. Not an easy task. But the lady had a willing, enthusiastic nature, and, considering the alternative, it didn't seem like too high a price to pay.

Besides, after hearing what Scroogen was trying to do to the community center, Voleta was all for fighting him.

Octavia could just see Scroogen pulling out the few remaining ashen hairs from his head as he listened to this broadcast and the one Mab had made earlier that day. The Scrooge was probably turning purple.

And Brett's countenance? Dark and stormy, she'd bet. And those eyes—those incredible, silver-black eyes—how would his eyes have looked? Would that silver in them have solidified as it did when he was angriest? Or would it have liquefied and swirled as it did when surprise or desire caught him?

She would have liked to have seen the reaction in his eyes. She knew the Magician wouldn't give in to this latest defeat. He'd be back on the attack soon enough.

Which meant she had to attack again before he could. And since Brett Merlin's only Achilles heel was the heel he was representing, Octavia had to go after Scroogen. With his penny-pinching attitude, Octavia was certain that A.J.

would soon find some illegally cut corner in the man's business affairs. And then Octavia would use it as leverage to make Scroogen "reconsider" his takeover of the community center.

How she'd do it, she didn't know yet. But she did know that she'd do it. She had complete faith that some plan would occur to her. It always did when her intuition told her she was doing the right thing.

Her intuition also told her she would be facing Brett Merlin again. She was courting danger, but that's what made it so exciting. Remembering the image of his scowling face after she winked at him in court sent a delicious, anticipatory tingle through her chest and arms.

It had been a very long time since she had felt anything like this kind of excitement around a man. It was the risk of him that did it, of course. The delicious challenge that with this man, anything was possible.

She smiled as she pulled off the county road onto the long asphalt driveway to Mab's home. But the smile quickly slid off her face when she applied the brakes and nothing happened.

Octavia froze in disbelief, unable to get her mind to accept the message from her senses. The car was not slowing at all. It was sliding down the driveway like a speeding sled on a sheet of ice.

This couldn't be happening. She stomped on the brake pedal as hard as she could. But the brakes were locked, useless.

And the car continued to race forward. Fast, too fast. And what was worst of all, she could do absolutely nothing about it.

Except grip the steering wheel.

And pray.

Chapter Six

Brett rushed into the emergency room, heart pounding. "Octavia Osborne," he said to the lady at the admitting desk.

"Behind the third drape. You can wait in—"

Brett didn't hear the end of the receptionist's sentence. He was already charging down the aisle, pushing his way clear of the first two drapes. When he pushed past the third, he surged inside, then halted.

Octavia sat on the examining table, fully clothed and composed, as a nurse applied a small dressing to her brow. The painfully tight knot that had gathered in Brett's stomach over the last twenty minutes untied in immediate and thankful relief.

Mab was standing next to her granddaughter, holding her hand, her eyes a bit too bright, her lips a bit too tight. But it was Octavia who was doing the consoling.

"Mab, I'm so sorry. I've already called about the house. I'll get it fixed for you just as soon as humanly possible."

"Octavia, stop worrying. The only important thing is that you're all right."

"It's not the only important thing. I know how much you love your home. You've lived there ever since you married grandfather. You always said you'd never live anywhere else. Fifty years of sweet memories are packed in those walls."

The nurse finished her ministrations and slipped out. Mab gently touched Octavia's bandaged brow. "Walls can be rebuilt. But, you, my sweet, don't come with replaceable parts.''

As Brett watched the two women hug, he began to feel like an intruder and wondered if he shouldn't just leave.

But although Octavia's back was to Brett, she must have felt his presence, because she turned then to meet his eyes. He felt a tug inside him, as though those eyes were pulling him closer, communicating to a part of his body that totally bypassed his brain. The muscles at his neck and down his back tightened.

''I'll be getting back to the center and let everyone know you're all right,'' Mab said as she looked from Octavia's face to Brett's. She flashed Brett a curious look before opening the drape and stepping outside.

Brett slowly approached the examining table, trying to concentrate on the bandage and not on Octavia's eyes, which were watching his every move.

''Sergeant Patterson called to say you had been in an accident,'' he said carefully, his voice purposely cool and distant.

She reached for her suit jacket lying on the end of the examination table and began to put it on.

''Didn't Patterson tell you I was only injured slightly?''

''He said you'd struck your head on the windshield. Head injuries can be serious.''

She looked at him, saying nothing. The intensity of her look tightened the muscles through his arms. ''Did he tell you how the accident happened?''

''He told me your car skidded on black ice.''

She lifted her long, thick hair out of its imprisonment beneath her suit jacket and dropped the cascade of thick waves down her back. Brett tried not to watch the subsequent shifting of her breasts against the silk of her blouse.

A moment later, he realized he had failed and that she was watching him watching her.

He looked quickly back to her face.

''How did it happen?'' he asked.

"The ice was manufactured this afternoon by someone who deliberately hosed down my grandmother's driveway, obviously aware the drop in air temperature would freeze the water."

Octavia's deep resonant tone never displayed even a note of what she might be feeling. It was the rest of her body that did—her eyes, her hands, her shoulders, her chin.

And at the moment Brett could have sworn they all seemed to be cocked and ready to fire. At him.

"Sergeant Patterson believes it was probably just some kids playing around," he said.

Octavia tossed her head, sending waves of flame around her face, her eyes full of deadly, deep-blue sparkle.

"On *just* my grandmother's driveway? I'm surprised Sergeant Patterson didn't credit this 'playing around' to mischievous Christmas elves."

She was mad, all right. Blazing mad. In all his previous experience with angry women, he'd seen them shout, throw things or cry. But not this woman. Brett was fascinated as he watched how her anger unfolded with such clean control and was accompanied by such a warm, thick, brandy-smooth tone.

She turned her head as she looked around for something. Brett saw her stocking feet and made the connection. He located her high heels on the other side of the bed, retrieved them and handed them to her.

"You told Sergeant Patterson that you think your grandmother was the intended target."

Her skirt lifted slightly as she raised each leg in turn to slip on her shoes, treating him to a luscious flash of forbidden flesh. He assiduously kept trying not to look.

"Of course my grandmother was the intended target. It's her driveway. Now, you tell me, Brett. How did your client respond when he found out this afternoon that despite all your efforts to take her radio station away, Mab is still in control of it?"

"Considering what she continues to broadcast on that radio station, I'm sure I don't have to tell you how he responded."

Her eyes locked with his. "No, you don't. He responded by going to my grandmother's home and icing down her driveway, hoping she'd break her neck, just like he hoped she would when he pushed her into that pit."

"Careful," Brett warned. "Those accusations are slanderous."

"Those accusations are the truth."

Octavia scooted forward, trying to ease herself off the raised table, her skirt weaving higher up her thighs. Brett couldn't take any more of that tantalizing sight.

He stepped up to the table and circled his hands around her waist, intending to help her to her feet and end the temptation. But the sudden feel of her warmth hit him simultaneously with the subtle, sweet scent of her skin and hair.

He looked into her face, tilted up to his, into her eyes, darkening into a midnight blue sparkle. Every muscle in his body suddenly coiled tight with desire, every thought in his head suddenly unraveled into thin air.

She wove her hands beneath the lapels of his suit coat as her lips circled into a smile.

"Well, counselor, what's it to be? Are you helping me off this table or am I helping you onto it?"

The challenge in her words and eyes was beyond provocative and spoke directly to everything in him that was male. She was so close, her warmth and scent lapped over his senses. Every red-blooded corpuscle in his body burned like hot sand through his veins. For several seconds his instinct for survival battled with his other instinct, just as old, just as primal.

"Excuse me," the nurse's voice blared suddenly as she shot through the drape. "We're going to be needing this room to... Oh, sorry. Didn't mean to interrupt."

Brett's mind snapped back and with it his self-control. He forced himself to look away from Octavia's eyes.

She turned her head to address the nurse, her voice and composure calm. "I'm just getting helped off the table. It'll be all yours in a minute."

"Right," the nurse said, slipping out through the drape.

Brett took a deep breath and congratulated himself on not accepting Octavia's invitation to jump up on that table. He assured himself his immediate hesitation was only occasioned by his surprise at such an outlandish suggestion.

He wasted no time now in lifting Octavia and setting her on her feet. He felt the flash of heat to his arms and chest as her body brushed his. He tried to ignore it and all those other urgings inside him. He slipped his hands from her waist. He stepped quickly back.

"Thank you." She had the nerve to smile at him before turning toward the chair where her purse lay. She seemed totally unmoved, unaffected.

It was only then that he understood. Her earlier comment had not been an invitation up on that table at all—just a sarcastic dare she was sure he wouldn't accept.

He scowled in irritation to discover that she thought she could so safely taunt him.

"I'll drive you home," he heard himself say.

She started toward the door, slipping the strap of her purse over her shoulder.

"Why?" she asked.

Why, indeed, he wondered. "It occurred to me you might need a ride," he said, keeping the defensiveness out of his tone.

She studied his face for a moment and then smiled. Brett didn't know what that smile meant. He never knew what her smiles meant. He was beginning to think he didn't want to know.

"I do need a ride," she agreed. "Thank you for the offer."

As soon as they were settled in his car, Octavia turned on Brett's stereo and tuned it to KRIS. Christmas music was playing. Between directions, Octavia sang along with every tune. She knew all the words, and her strong contralto voice showed no hesitancy to hit the high notes. She had a pleasant singing voice—deep, mellow, merry.

Brett shook his head, suddenly, unaccountably feeling amused. She was totally alien—an infuriating, foolish, utterly fascinating woman.

She wouldn't fit, refused to fit, into any category he tried to place her. Prior to this business with her grandmother, she had an enviable reputation as an attorney—one could even call it exemplary.

Yet here she was, fabricating a native American find without a wit of concern for the law she had sworn to uphold or for the consequences she would be forced to face once she was caught.

It was he who was worrying about those consequences. For it was he who would be instrumental in making sure she paid them. He had to. He was sworn to uphold the law.

Damn. Why did he have to keep reminding himself of it?

She stopped singing as they approached Mab's house.

"Don't turn into the driveway. Sergeant Patterson said he would see it was sanded tomorrow."

Brett pulled up to the curb and parked. All he could see from that position was a line of fir trees.

"The house is set back about three hundred feet," Octavia explained.

They got out of the car and wove their way through the dense brush and trees. When the house came into view, Brett stopped and stared.

It was an older, neat white house dwarfed by a huge, riotous garden—and the weight of an enormous madrona tree that had fallen and smashed through the living room. Nudging its upended trunk was the demolished front end of a deep blue 1971 Mercedes-Benz with a license plate that read JUST LAW.

A deep frown furrowed Brett's brow. "You're very lucky you only received a cut on the forehead."

"I'm very lucky it wasn't my grandmother who drove down that driveway," Octavia amended.

"Where is she going to stay?"

"With Constance, until I can get things in order here."

"And Constance is?"

"A friend at the Silver Power League. I have a tow truck scheduled to pull my car to a body shop in the morning and a contractor who has agreed to come by and give me an estimate on the damage to the house."

"Where will you stay tonight?"

She started forward. "Right here."

He followed. "You can't. A tree has caved in the roof."

She smiled sweetly at him over her shoulder. "Thank you so much for bringing that to my attention."

"Octavia, it's not safe."

She proceeded boldly forward. "Your client is after my grandmother, not me, remember?"

He ignored the pointed accusation of these words as he looked at the split beam above the smashed living room window.

"The entire structure looks compromised. Get some clothes together, and I'll drive you to a hotel."

Octavia stopped and turned to him, the toss of her head sending the long waves of flame-red hair to dance around her shoulders. A very expressive eyebrow rose up her forehead.

"Mr. Merlin, has anyone ever mentioned to you the possibility that a woman might not appreciate a man presuming to tell her what to do?"

How did she manage to be so damn sarcastic with such a sweet, mellow-sounding voice?

"No, Ms. Osborne," he said with his stiffest upper lip. "No one has mentioned it."

She stared at him a moment longer before breaking out in a sudden laugh, whole and unrestrained.

He realized then how much he liked the sound of her laugh. It had as much music as her singing, and both were rich with a life well-lived.

A life well-lived? Where had that come from?

He frowned to realize he was too tardy to erase such thoughts. He reminded himself he couldn't afford to like anything about her. He shouldn't even be here with her.

"It's all right," she said when her laughter had stopped. "I refused to let Mab drive me to the emergency room until the contractor came by and assured me the kitchen, guest room and bath at the back are still safe. Come on."

As they circled around the house, Brett noticed that the riotous garden was quite overgrown and weedy. One small patch near the back porch had been seen to recently, however. The Christmas berry bushes were in full fruit and scrupulously weeded.

Once up the stairs, through the small porch and inside the house, Octavia made immediately for an old-fashioned wall telephone in the kitchen.

"Who are you going to call?" Brett asked.

"Whoever is making my beeper vibrate."

Brett watched as she pulled the muted beeper off the waistband of her suit skirt. "It's the community center's number," she said. "Must be Mab."

She picked up the receiver and dialed while he surveyed the small, cozy kitchen, smelling so enticingly of cinnamon. Christmas stockings, sewn of rich tapestry fabric and embroidered in gold thread, hung on the walls. A garland of the berry bushes from the outside garden circled the table. There was a comfortable, homey feel to this room. He could picture her as a youngster here, sharing confidences and laughter with her grandmother.

"Hi, Mab. I'm here at—"

Brett turned toward Octavia as her voice stopped in midsentence. He watched with growing unease as Octavia listened to whatever was being communicated on the other end of the telephone, her eyes focused intently out the window but, obviously, seeing something much less pleasant.

"I'll be right over," she said finally and shoved the receiver back onto the wall base.

"What is it? What's wrong?" Brett asked.

Her voice was smooth and calm, but the look in her eyes and the sudden tightness to her lips told a different story.

"A sewer line broke. The community center is flooding."

OCTAVIA'S NOSE TWITCHED as she stood at the entrance to the Silver Power League's community center and gazed inside. The overhead fluorescents illuminated the once-magnificent Christmas tree and decorations, now floating like flotsam and jetsam over the smelly sludge weaving over the tile floor.

All the lovely, graceful furniture was also ruined, soggy and seeped with the stench of raw sewage.

It was an incredibly disheartening scene of decimation.

Octavia turned to Mab, standing quietly by her side. "No one was hurt?"

"Not physically," Mab said.

Her grandmother's phraseology was telling. It was hard for Octavia to view this desecration. She understood it had to be a hundred times harder for the seniors, all silently surveying the smelly blight on their once-beautiful center.

She put her arm around her grandmother's shoulders and hugged her, knowing no words could convey the hot, heavy sadness that sunk inside her own chest.

"It happened so fast," Constance said, her voice trembling.

"The sewage just began to gush in through the open back door," John said, dismay clear in his voice.

"The back door was open," Mab said sadly.

"It was coming in so fast and so hard, I couldn't even get near the door to close it," John added.

"We all concentrated on evacuating everyone as quickly as possible," Mab explained.

"Except Douglas," Constance said. "He ran out the front door. He said he was going to circle around back to try to find out where it was coming from."

"As soon as everyone was out of the community center, we took refuge in the greenhouse," Mab said. "Fortunately, it's on higher ground, so the sewage didn't reach there."

"The firemen must have finally found the break," John said. "The gushing slowed to a trickle a few moments ago."

The rapid-fire explanations ceased and another uncomfortable quiet dropped over those gathered.

Octavia felt Brett's hand lightly grasp her arm in an unexpected gesture of comfort and support. Despite the dispiriting scene in front of her, a warm tingling began in her fingertips and spread into her chest.

"We have to meet here early tomorrow morning, everyone," Mab announced, almost fiercely. "We'll need to organize into teams and committees. There's so much to do to fix things up."

Octavia watched as John's hand slipped around Mab's. His voice was gentle. "I'm not sure we can fix it this time, Mab."

"We have to, John," Mab said. "So many count on us to lead the way. This center has come to represent the strength and vitality of our community. We've all worked so hard to make it something special."

"But, Mab—" Constance began.

"This is a...difficult setback, yes," Mab interrupted, her volume and determination picking up with each word. "But our members need this celebration of Christmas this year more than any other. So many are far away from their families. For some, we are their only family. Now, we've promised them a real dress-up Christmas party here. We're just going to have to work harder to keep that promise."

Mab's indomitable spirit in the face of the unspeakable destruction before them brought a small lump to Octavia's throat and several appreciative mumbles from the seniors behind them. John smiled and sandwiched Mab's hand between both of his.

"Okay, Mab. Tomorrow we begin again."

A chorus of affirmative responses rose up behind them.

"Someone needs to tell Douglas," Constance said. "Why hasn't he come back? He might have fallen out there somewhere in the dark. He might have—"

"Found out what the hell happened," Douglas finished her sentence as he stomped toward the group gathered in front of the entrance to the community center, a look of both triumph and anger across his rough features.

They turned as one toward him.

"What is it, Douglas?" Octavia asked, a question that was immediately echoed by several others.

"The flex-fitting on the sewer pipe running through Scroogen's construction site next door was severed right at the section pointed at the community center. The firemen suspect it was deliberate sabotage. And I'll give you one guess who was behind it."

Sabotage. Scroogen. The two words buzzed concurrently through the seniors like a roar.

From the moment she had met Scroogen, Octavia had disliked him. Now, as she once again looked upon the devastating aftermath of such a wanton act, she wondered if it could be possible that Scroogen was so petty and vindictive as to have purposely planned and executed such a thing.

He was so much in her thoughts that when his distinctive whiny voice suddenly erupted behind her, Octavia was startled into spinning around. Scroogen's hands wove beneath his suit coat to thumb his checkered suspenders as he arrogantly pushed his way through the crowd.

He stopped at the entrance to the center and let out a low grunt as he took in the scene inside. Octavia could have sworn there was a mixture of disgust and glee in his whiny voice.

"Well, this is really quite a mess. You people better clean it up before I take possession of this place next month, or I'll see to it that my lawyer slaps a hefty fine on you."

It was an incredibly hateful remark, even for Scroogen. Octavia was overcome by an almost irresistible urge to punch the man in the mouth.

She might have succumbed to that urge, too, if her grandmother hadn't beaten her to it. Mab stepped right up to Scroogen and smacked him squarely across his sour puss with her purse.

"I'M BLEEDING!" Scroogen whined.

Brett shook his head as he returned the first-aid kit to the glove compartment of his car. He had spirited Scroogen away from the angry seniors as quickly as he could. No telling which one would have taken a swing at him next.

"You've a bloody nose is all, Dole. What in the hell are you doing here?"

"What do you mean what am I doing here? This is my property!"

"And it's eight o'clock at night, not exactly the time when a landlord comes calling."

"I was driving to the store to get some wine when I heard the fire engine. As soon as I saw it heading toward the construction site, I followed."

"You live on the other side of town. Why would you have to drive over here to pick up some wine?"

"Because the vintage I buy is only sold over here. What's with all these questions, anyway?"

"They're a preview of the coming attractions. The police will be asking them soon. Did you have anything to do with severing that main sewer line on your construction site?"

"Don't you try to put me on the defensive! I'm the injured party here, Merlin. I'm filing charges against that woman!"

"It would be a waste of time, Dole. You're not really injured and you were the one who provoked the fight."

"*I* provoked the fight? I did no such thing!"

"The center they have worked on so hard is swamped in sewage and you threaten a stupid fine if they don't clean it up. That was enough to light anyone's fuse. Let it go, Dole. You'll only make a bad situation worse."

"You accuse me of making a bad situation worse? Let me remind you, Merlin, that before you came, work was progressing on my condominium complex! Before you came, no one was selling dolls that poked fun at me! I never should have listened to Nancy when she said I needed your help. I don't need your help. I never did. I can handle this on my own. You're fired!''

Dole jumped out of the passenger seat of Brett's car and stomped away into the dark night.

Brett just sat there staring in surprise at the retreating figure, feeling the icy night air swirl into the car. Finally, he leaned over to grasp the passenger door and pull it closed. His arm squeezed the packaged doll of Scroogen's likeness sitting between the seats, the one he had never bothered to open.

A whiny voice spat out into the car. *Read it and weep, I'm raising your rent.*

Brett straightened as a sudden chuckle erupted in his throat. Damn, if that didn't sound exactly like his ex-client.

Ex-client. The full implications of what had just happened sunk in then. Dole was no longer his client.

Brett could call Zane off the case tonight. He didn't have to stay around, uncover Octavia's wrongdoing and throw her into jail. Tomorrow, he could get his climbing gear together and head for Rainier. He was out of it. Totally out of it.

His lips circled into a smile, a very big smile. What the hell, maybe he'd been wrong all these years. Maybe wishes did come true. Maybe there even was a Santa Claus.

"GOOD MORNING, DOLE," Tami Lammock said as Scroogen pushed through the door into his office. "Another one of those letters came in so I put it . . .''

The rest of his secretary's sentence froze on her lips as her eyes darted over her boss's appearance.

"Geez, Dole, you look like you just got out of a mud bath. What on earth happened?''

"I've been knocked down and attacked." He turned his left side toward her and pointed at his shoulder.

Tami scooted around her desk to get a closer look. Her small hazel eyes widened as they took in the telltale red stain seeping through his shirt.

She reached out a tentative hand to lightly touch his arm, her bottom lip quivering. "My God! You're bleeding!"

"Yes, this time those senile seniors have gone too far."

Tami's eyes shot to his. "Someone from the Silver Power League did this?"

"Attacked me in the parking lot not three minutes ago. From behind, of course. I'll lay you odds it was Mab Osborne, too!"

Tami dropped her hand from Scroogen's shirtsleeve and plopped her forest-green, polyester pant-suited bottom against the edge of her desk.

"But it's so hard to believe that an old woman would—"

Scroogen swung impatiently toward the open door to his inner office, interrupting what he did not want to hear, slinging his words over his shoulder.

"Tell my son I want to see him in my office. Now."

"He's not in yet."

"Forget him. You're witness enough to my condition. Get the chief of police on the phone. I'm pressing charges. And get hold of the newspaper editor, too. They've been so eager to splash stories about that damn stone carving all over the front page. Let's see how eager they are to run this one!"

Scroogen stomped into his enormous paneled office, leaving a trail of muddy footprints on the thick gold carpet. He slammed the solid oak door behind him for added emphasis.

The wound stung. But it was more of an irritation than a jab of real pain.

Still, he would have gladly endured even real pain to have her where he had her now. He would see to it that the police arrested her for attacking him.

As he circled his huge oak desk, he slowed as a peculiar burning sensation spread from his back into his arms and legs.

Damn annoying. What in the hell was causing it, anyway?

He sank heavily into his black leather chair, resting his elbows on its thick-padded arms, being careful not to lean back against his injured shoulder. He immediately recognized the telltale silver envelope Tami had placed on the top of his mail.

The intercom buzzed. He leaned over and pushed the button. "You got him?"

"The chief of police is on vacation, visiting relatives for the holidays. Sergeant Patterson is on line two. Will he do?"

The corners of Scroogen's mouth dropped in disgust as his stomach jumped with irritation. "All right, I'll talk to Patterson."

"Shall I bring in some wet towels and the first-aid kit?"

Scroogen could hardly feel the wound now. Even the odd burning sensation was retreating, leaving a diffuse tingling in its wake.

"No. I'm not cleaning up. I want the police and the newspaper to take pictures of me as I am. Get Yearsley on the line just as soon as I'm finished with Patterson."

Scroogen flipped off the intercom, pressed the button for line two, then activated the speaker phone. He rubbed his palms together, trying to work a peculiar pins-and-needles tingling out of his fingers.

"Dole Scroogen here, Sergeant Patterson. Five minutes ago I was attacked in the parking lot behind my office."

"What happened, exactly, sir?"

"I drove in as usual to my parking space, got out, locked my car, started toward my office. Someone sneaked up behind me, knocked me to the ground and struck me on the left shoulder with some sharp instrument while yelling 'Silver Power.'"

"Can you identify the person who struck you?"

"I told you I was knocked to the ground and struck from behind. But the voice sounded like Mab Osborne's."

"Did this attacker try to take your wallet or valuables?"

Scroogen's stomach turned over in a queasy wave. He gulped down a strong urge to retch and attributed it to the dunce on the other end of the line.

"You fool! This wasn't that kind of attack! Does she have to kill me before you guys do something?"

"How badly are you injured?"

Scroogen took a moment to glance over at the caked blood clinging to the ripped edges of his shirt. Some had even splashed onto his suspenders. Both blurred in front of his eyes. He blinked, trying to refocus.

"My shoulder's bleeding. That good enough for you?"

"Perhaps it would be best if you seek medical attention before coming down to the office to give us your official statement on this matter."

An acrid bile rose in Scroogen's throat. "I don't have time to go traipsing down to your office. I have a business to run."

"I understand you're a very busy man, sir, but we will need you in person in order to—"

Scroogen slammed his palm down on his desk right next to the speakerphone's mike. "Then stop wasting my time and get down here. And make sure you bring a camera!"

Scroogen punched the speakerphone, disconnecting the line. Anger churned at his stomach, quickly transmogrifying into a violent wave of nausea. In some surprise, Scroogen found himself doubled over, retching into the solid oak wastepaper basket.

His head throbbed as he straightened up and a shiver skidded down his back. The room swam like a white blur before his eyes. Sweat dampened his armpits and groin, soaked his socks, collected at the back of his knees. A powerful new wave of nausea doubled him over and he retched again. He shivered and wrapped his sweaty, shaky hands around his middle as an appalling chill swirled into his lungs.

The intercom buzzed. He unwrapped one hand to stretch a finger toward the button.

"Yeah?"

"Shall I get the editor of the newspaper now?"

Scroogen tried to blink away the persistent blurring before his eyes.

"Yeah. We got anything to settle a stomach?"

"I'll run over to the drugstore after I get the editor on the line."

Scroogen released the button on the intercom.

He tried to straighten up, but the effort made him feel even weaker and incredibly dizzy. He slumped back over the side of his chair, hugging his arms to his chest. He shivered again. His face was beginning to go numb. He wished like hell he hadn't left his suit coat in the car.

The intercom buzzed again. The button blurred before his eyes. He whacked at it twice before connecting with numb fingers. He tried to clear his throat, but the collected mucus stuck like a frozen Popsicle to the back of his Adam's apple. He moved his lips, but he could barely feel them.

"Yeah?"

"Dole, you sound awful," Tami said on the other end of the intercom. "I'm on my way to the drugstore. Back soon with some relief. Fred Yearsley from the newspaper is on two."

Scroogen released the intercom button without answering. He shook as an icy sweat climbed up his spine and spread out over his back and down his legs. He couldn't feel his tongue anymore. Or his jaw.

He barely found the button on the speakerphone. He strained to push out his words.

"Yrsy. Got a stuy."

"That you, Scroogen?"

Scroogen concentrated on forcing his increasingly numb mouth to open and close. "I gt a stury f'r yu."

"Did you say a story? Look, you'll have to stop mumbling and speak up."

Scroogen shivered anew as the iciness clutching at his spine spread into his leg muscles.

"Ma . . . Ma—"

"Look, I don't appreciate these kinds of games, who-ever you are. Lose my number."

The dial tone blared out of the speakerphone.

Scroogen quaked. He didn't know how much of it was from anger or cold, but every single cell in his body seemed to be vibrating at once. He tried to reach the speakerphone to turn off that damn blaring noise, but his hand felt so cold and heavy and the effort was so exhausting that he gave up.

He closed his eyes, but the fuzzy, swirling snow still swam behind his lids.

His breath came out in rapid little puffs. His legs con-vulsed beneath the desk. A sharp pain shot through his chest.

Scroogen forgot his anger at the newspaper editor. Scroogen even forgot his anger at Mab Osborne. Along with the bone-chilling cold, a frozen kind of panic clutched at his insides. He was ill. Desperately ill.

He raised his head. Tried to open his eyes. The room swam in sickening waves, everything thick and green-tinged.

He closed his eyes. He didn't even feel the impact when his head fell forward onto the hard oak desktop.

Chapter Seven

"It's going to take the boys some time, but they'll get it pumped out of there," Douglas said in his gruff voice, his large, bony frame leaning against a long tanker truck that had printed on the sides, Sons of a Twitch.

Octavia watched Douglas's *boys*, two hefty men in their fifties, as they attached a suction pump to the back of the large tanker truck. They grinned over scruffy beards and gave thumbs-up signs before dragging the large vacuum-type hose over to the community center to get started on the cleanup job.

"Your *boys* are pretty special, stopping all their own work to come over here to help their dad this way," Octavia said.

Douglas shrugged his big, bony shoulders and kicked at a tire of the truck with the toe of his boot. "I better go help 'em," he mumbled after a moment.

"We'll need a crew to disinfect after the initial cleanup," John said. "I'll start calling this morning for volunteers."

"And we'll need furniture and decorations," Constance added. "Nothing new, but maybe some members can donate a few extra pieces that they don't need."

"I have a lot of old but perfectly good furniture I'd be happy to donate," Voleta said. "Of course, some of the arms are a bit frayed."

"We can knit Christmas slipcovers to cover any imperfections," Constance said. "It will give everything a homey, festive look."

"I'm certain I can talk a few of our members into using their trucks to bring the furniture donations here," John said.

"But only after a new paint job," Mab added as she walked up. "A spanking new paint job!"

Octavia turned toward her grandmother, glad to see her arrive at last. "Is that where you've been this morning, Mab? Arranging for the paint?"

"That and making a quick radio announcement so that all the seniors who are able will join us here to help. I explained what happened and the fact that we only have a few days until the Christmas party. We have an awful lot of work to do."

Octavia was delighted to see and hear the determination in Mab's face and voice as well as in the other seniors this morning. They all wore sloppy sweat clothes and old running shoes and a spirit of hope and can-do that was undeniable and unbeatable.

She was very proud of her gutsy grandmother for leading this charge after they had been dealt such a disheartening defeat. The emotional endurance and energy of Mab—and of all these seniors—was truly inspiring.

"Mrs. Osborne?"

Octavia turned with her grandmother to see Detective Sergeant Patterson approaching.

"Yes, Sergeant," Mab said. "I assume you're here in response to the firemen's report about Scroogen's deliberate sabotage of our center last night."

"No, I'm not here about that matter. I wonder if you would mind coming with me back to the station."

"If this isn't about the sabotage to the community center," Octavia said, "what do you want with my grandmother?"

"Dole Scroogen was attacked this morning."

"By whom?" Mab asked.

"That's what we're trying to determine," Sergeant Patterson said, looking very pointedly at Mab. "Mr. Scroogen said he believed it was you who attacked him."

"Believed?" Octavia challenged. "If someone attacked him, shouldn't he know?"

"He was pushed down and struck from behind, Ms. Osborne. He didn't see his attacker. Now, Mrs. Osborne, if you will come with me—"

"I did not strike that man from behind," Mab said, crossing her arms over her chest. "I refuse to be dragged downtown to answer any such ridiculous charges."

"Mrs. Osborne, I must insist."

"Insist all you like. I'm needed here. If the Scrooge has any complaint against me, bring him here, and I'll be happy to call him a liar to his face."

"I'm sorry, but I can't do that," Sergeant Patterson said.

"Why? Because he's a big businessman and I'm only an old woman?"

"No, ma'am. Because Mr. Scroogen died thirty minutes ago."

"I CAN'T BELIEVE he's gone!" Nancy wailed as she fell back into Brett's arms and broke down into heart-wrenching, sobs.

Brett eased her back on the deep sofa in the Scroogen living room and cradled her head against his shoulder. He didn't say anything to her. He didn't know what to say. He felt as shocked and disoriented by this unexpected turn of events as anyone.

He focused his attention on Dole's son. Ronald paced before them, as solemn and sour-pussed as always. But this time, Brett granted, he had cause for his morose demeanor.

"What happened, Ronald?"

Ronald stopped pacing and came to stand in front of Brett. His tone, for once, lacked its normal belligerence.

"His secretary, Tami, said he was feeling sick to his stomach, so she went out to the drugstore to get him something. When she got back, she found him lying beneath his desk, unconscious. When she couldn't rouse him, she called 911. I got there just while the medics were finishing. They told me they had done everything they could, but that he was . . . gone.''

Nancy turned her face into Brett's shoulder as Ronald's final words faded away. Her body was racked with new sobs.

Ronald stood stiffly, his hands hanging off his arms like dead weights, his eyes blinking like light bulbs going bad.

''The medics couldn't tell you why he died?'' Brett pushed.

Ronald shook his head in jerky little spurts.

''How was his heart?''

Nancy's head rose at Brett's question. ''He had a complete checkup a month ago. Everything was perfect!''

She dabbed a drenched tissue at her red eyes and swollen nose. ''Brett, he was only forty-five! This is not right! He shouldn't have died! You must find out what happened!''

''I'll find out, Nancy,'' Brett assured her, before she once again drowned his shoulder in her wet sobs.

Consoling distraught women had never been Brett's forte. But investigating the mysterious death of his uncle was something he knew he could do for his aunt.

''Where's your sister?'' he asked of Ronald.

Ronald stared down at him, still appearing to be in a daze. Brett doubted whether the reality of his father's death had sunk in yet. He knew that somehow he was going to have to try to help Dole's son through this troubled time, just as he was going to have to help Nancy.

Ronald's answer, when it finally came, was almost mechanical. ''Attending a Christmas party at school.''

Brett didn't want to be the one to tell Katlyn about her father. Maybe it would be best for his cousin to remain in school until Nancy could cope with the task.

Or Ronald? Perhaps that was what the young man needed—to be useful to others to help him work out his own grief. Perhaps a nudge in the right direction would show him the way.

Worth a try.

"Ronald, you're the man of the family now," Brett said. "Nancy and Katlyn are going to need you to be here for them. They are going to need you to be strong."

Ronald looked down at his stepmother, sobbing so inconsolably, his eyes appearing to focus for the first time in many minutes.

"They need you, Ronald. Katlyn and Nancy need you."

Brett angled his head meaningfully toward the other side of the couch. After a moment, Ronald slowly sat next to his stepmother. He shoved his arm awkwardly across her shoulders.

As he disengaged himself from Nancy and got to his feet Brett nodded at Ronald. Ronald shifted his body closer to his stepmother, slipping his arm more securely around her shoulders.

"It's okay," he said a little gruffly. "I'm here. You can lean on me."

When Nancy shifted her head and rested it on his thin chest, his face drew in some color and he patted her shoulder, a little uncertainly at first and then with more confidence. Finally, he secured his arm fully around her and looked up at Brett.

"I'll take care of them," he announced with a stiffness that could have been grief or pride in his new position—or a mixture of both. "I'm the man of the family now."

Brett was gratified that Ronald was responding so well to his minimal coaching. Now he could spend his time finding out how and why Dole had died.

Damn, what a mess. And here he was right back in the middle of it. What in the hell had happened?

"Mrs. Osborne, I understand what kind of man Dole Scroogen was," Sergeant Patterson said as he stood before her, fingering both ends of his drooping mustache.

"And what kind of man was he?" Mab asked as she sat in the straight-backed chair across the table from Octavia in the small interrogation room.

"He slapped that ridiculous rent on you seniors, trying to kick you out of the buildings you had built," Patterson replied. "He was trying to take your radio station away from you. He pushed you into that ditch."

"So now you believe it was Scroogen who pushed me?"

Octavia had not missed the sarcasm in her grandmother's last two questions. Sergeant Patterson couldn't have missed it, either, although he was valiantly trying to overlook it.

"Yes, ma'am, I do believe Scroogen must have pushed you. Which is why I also don't blame you one bit for hitting him when he showed up at your center last night and made that nasty remark about your cleaning up that sewage accident."

"It wasn't an accident, Sergeant," Mab corrected him.

"No, ma'am. It was deliberate sabotage," Patterson agreed.

"So you did get a report from the firemen?"

"Yes, ma'am. And a Mrs. Kope called us last night to report Mr. Scroogen's unwanted remark and appearance after the calamity at your community center. Of course, we both know Scroogen dumped that sewage into your center, don't we?"

"Do you know that?"

The sarcasm in Mab's tone was getting a little too much for the sergeant. A frown drew his eyebrows together.

"Well, naturally we'll be investigating the matter further, but you know he was the one who did it, right?"

"It would not surprise me," Mab admitted, for the first time without sarcasm.

"And that's why it doesn't surprise me that you were still upset enough at Scroogen this morning to seek him out in the parking lot in back of his building and strike him again. Of course, you might have just gone there to give him a piece of your mind. But when you saw him and remembered all the terrible things that he had done, why, you just grabbed whatever was handy and struck out like any of us would. Isn't that the way it happened?"

Octavia was sorely tempted to give the persistent sergeant a proper dressing down. But she didn't because she knew that Mab could not only handle the man, but also wanted to.

"Sergeant, for the umpteenth time, I did not go to the parking lot in back of Mr. Scroogen's building this morning. I did not strike him."

"Mrs. Osborne, there were close to twenty witnesses who saw you smack Dole Scroogen in the face last night with your purse."

"That's right, Sergeant. I whacked him in the face with my purse. He had it coming."

Octavia watched as the sergeant plopped one of his big shoes on the seat of his unoccupied chair and rested an elbow on his bent knee as he loomed over Mab, obviously trying to intimidate her.

"And this morning? He had it coming to him then, too?"

"I did not strike him this morning. I did not even see him this morning."

Patterson straightened and removed his shoe from the chair.

"Where were you from eight to eight-thirty?" he asked, his previously solicitous tone becoming a little frayed around the edges in the face of Mab's continual denials.

"As I told you before, I arrived at the radio station at eight and made the announcement to inform the members of the Silver Power League about the trouble at the center and to ask for volunteers to help out. Then I went over to the paint supply store to see the owner about getting the paint."

"What time did you leave for the paint store?"

"Right after I made the announcement and then put the tape of Christmas music back on to play."

"How long did it take you to do those things?"

"As I explained before, I wasn't looking at the clock."

"Can you estimate it for me? Five minutes? Ten minutes?"

"Sergeant Patterson, we've been over this at least a dozen times."

"And my grandmother's answers aren't going to change," Octavia said.

"Humor me," the sergeant said with an insincere smile directed at them both. "Tell me again, Mrs. Osborne."

"Closer to five minutes than ten."

"How long does it take to drive to the paint supply shop?"

"About ten minutes."

"Well, then I'm confused, Mrs. Osborne. If you left at five after eight and it only takes ten minutes to drive there, why did the owner of the paint supply store say that you didn't speak to him until eight-thirty?"

"Because that's when he arrived to open up his store."

"So where were you between the time you made the announcement to the radio audience and the time you met with the paint store owner?"

"In his parking lot, waiting in my car."

"Why did you drive over so early, just to wait in the parking lot?"

"I thought he opened at seven-thirty. I forgot that during the winter he doesn't open until eight-thirty."

"How long did you sit in your car waiting?"

"Fifteen minutes."

"But no one saw you waiting in this parking lot for fifteen minutes, did they?"

"My grandmother already told you the store wasn't open yet," Octavia said. "No one was around, remember?"

"Please, Ms. Osborne. Let your grandmother answer the questions. Now, Mrs. Osborne, why didn't you just call this paint store owner?"

"I needed to ask a favor. Courtesy demanded that I ask it in person."

"What was this favor?"

"I asked that he extend us credit on the paint we needed for our center. He agreed. Then over the next hour or so, I looked through his swatches. The original color he sold us for the center had been discontinued by the manufacturer.

That's why we got it below cost. I had to make sure he had
a color in stock that would match.''

"Mrs. Osborne, I sent a uniformed officer out to time
how long it takes for someone to drive from your radio station to the back parking lot of Mr. Scroogen's offices and
then to the paint store. What would you say if I told you that
the officer made it in exactly twenty-two minutes?''

"I'd say you were wasting the officer's time and the tax-
payer's money on useless trips.''

Frustration now openly rode in on the sergeant's tone.
"You have no alibi. But you do have a motive. And, as my
officer proved, you also had enough time to drive to Mr.
Scroogen's office, strike him down, and then drive to the
paint store in time to meet with its owner.''

"I'm sure there are quite a few other people who also had
such an opportunity.''

"Ma'am, don't you understand? No one is going to make
a big deal about your hitting the guy. We can make this all
go away if you'll just cooperate.''

"You mean if I just plead guilty to something I didn't
do.''

A knock came at the door. Patterson looked almost re-
lieved at the interruption. He opened the door, stepped
outside the room, and closed the door behind him.

"Octavia, I'm getting tired of going over the same ground
with the same questions,'' Mab said when he had left.
"Maybe I shouldn't have been so willing to cooperate.'' She
picked up her glass of water and took a good, long drink.

Octavia gave her arm a reassuring pat. "I'm sure Sergeant Patterson has had hardened criminals who were easier to intimidate. I'm proud of you, Mab.''

Her grandmother's lips extended into a small smile. "I've
watched enough episodes of 'Murder She Wrote' to know
how to handle a policeman who pretends to be on the suspect's side so she'll confess. I would almost be enjoying this
if it weren't taking so much time. There's so much I need to
be attending to at the community center.''

"Don't worry. John, Constance and Douglas seemed to have everything pretty well in hand when we left."

"Did you notice that when they heard about the Scrooge being dead, they all looked kind of numbed?"

"It's numbing news."

"I can't seem to get used to it, either, Octavia. I keep telling myself I should feel something like sadness or relief, but I can't seem to feel anything but a sense of acute disorientation."

"Yes, the unexpectedness of it makes it seem unreal, doesn't it?"

Mab sighed. "I know he left a wife and a couple of kids. I do feel sad for them. I suppose I should be worried about whether they're going to go ahead with the condominium complex, but I just can't seem to focus on that now."

Patterson opened the door and came back into the room. He wore a different look on his face, a far-too-satisfied look that made Octavia immediately sit up and take careful notice.

What had happened in his out-of-room conference?

Patterson was holding something in his hand, something that swung against his pant leg as he walked toward the table where Mab and Octavia sat. He kept it out of sight until he reached the table. Then he suddenly shoved it right into Mab's face.

"Do you recognize these, ma'am?"

While Mab was pulling her glasses out of her purse, Octavia was quickly studying the objects resting inside the cellophane bag that was swinging from Sergeant Patterson's hand.

The bag contained a pair of soiled brown gardening gloves. It also contained a gardening tool of some sort with three sharp, forklike steel prongs feeding out of a wooden handle.

When Octavia saw the initials M.O. on that handle and the telltale red stains between the dried dirt on the sharp fork edges, a sliver of unease shot through her chest. She grabbed

Mab's arm, rushing into speech before her grandmother could.

"Sergeant Patterson, I'm advising my client not to answer any more questions."

The sergeant smiled. "These are your gloves and gardening tool, aren't they, Mrs. Osborne?"

Octavia's fingers retained their firm, cautionary grasp on Mab's arm. "As I said before, Sergeant. On advice of her counsel, my grandmother is evoking her right to remain silent."

"She can still listen," Patterson said, his smile spreading to show every one of his back teeth. "A couple of detectives just found these items thrown into the trash Dumpster behind Dole Scroogen's office. This gardening tool is called a cultivator, I'm told. Is that right, Mrs. Osborne?"

Mab obediently remained silent.

Patterson leaned closer. "Did you throw them away so you wouldn't be caught with them?"

Octavia could feel the pressure mounting in her grandmother. Mab was not normally the quiet type, and remaining silent in the face of this accusation had to be more than difficult.

Patterson dropped the items in the cellophane bag onto the table with a loud thud—for effect, Octavia was certain. Then he leaned his stocky body across the table until he was almost nose-to-nose with Mab.

"When the experts have a look at the bloodstain on this cultivator, we both know whose blood they will find, don't we?"

Octavia continued to hold firmly on to her grandmother's arm. Mab, bless her, continued to remain silent.

"All right," Patterson said, straightening up after a couple of very long and uncomfortable minutes for them all.

"Now, you're a smart lady, Mrs. Osborne, and your granddaughter here is a smart lawyer, so I don't see any need for us to play games with one another."

Patterson spread his feet, crossed his arms over his barrel chest and looked down his long nose at them.

"So this is how it plays. The medics who examined Mr. Scroogen's body said there are three gashes on the back of his shoulder—gashes that exactly match the steel prongs on this cultivator. Now, we all know you hit him."

Neither Octavia nor Mab said a word.

Patterson uncrossed his arms. "Come on, ladies. It's no big deal. The wounds were superficial, barely broke the skin. I know that in view of Mr. Scroogen's provoking acts and Mrs. Osborne's advanced years the prosecuting attorney will recommend a suspended sentence."

Again Octavia and Mab remained silent.

Patterson was clearly annoyed now. His hands flew into the air. "All the court will do is slap you on the wrist. For God's sake, make it easy on yourself and just admit it. Then we can forget all about it and get on with the rest of our lives."

Octavia stood, bringing Mab with her.

"My grandmother has nothing to say. We're leaving."

"Your grandmother is going nowhere."

"Are you arresting her?"

"If I have to."

"Based on what evidence?"

"What evidence? Haven't you been listening? She has a very strong motive, a history of previous violence against the victim, opportunity, and we found her gloves and gardening tool with the victim's blood on it literally at the scene of the crime."

"Where is your proof that these gloves or this gardening tool belong to my grandmother or that this red coloration is even blood, much less the blood of the victim?"

"Ms. Osborne, you know that's what the forensic experts are going to find. Why are you wasting our time this way?"

"Sergeant Patterson, you know you don't have any evidence with which to hold my grandmother, much less charge her with any crime. So how about you stop wasting our time. Excuse us."

As Octavia turned herself and Mab toward the door, Sergeant Patterson's voice rose.

"This deal I just offered your grandmother for a suspended sentence is null and void the second you take her out that door without her confession. I mean that. Now, play it smart, and let's close the book on this one. Have her plead guilty to simple assault."

Octavia stopped at the door and swung around.

"Sergeant Patterson, this is not a case of simple assault. This is a very serious case of someone deliberately attempting to implicate my grandmother in the attack on Dole Scroogen this morning. Don't allow yourself to be duped into becoming a party to this malicious act."

And with that, Octavia swept her arm around Mab and both of them walked out of the interrogation room.

Brett had been closely watching and listening to Sergeant Patterson's interrogation of Mab Osborne through the two-way mirror in the adjacent observation room. Patterson joined him there a few moments after Octavia and Mab left.

"I told you you wouldn't be able to bully that lawyer into having her grandmother confess."

Patterson shook his head. "She's a fool, Merlin. And so is the old woman. We're going to have all the proof we need soon. They're just prolonging the inevitable."

"I don't know, Sergeant. The image of Mab Osborne creeping up behind Scroogen, striking him with a gardening tool and then knocking him to the ground yelling 'Silver Power' just refuses to materialize in my mind."

"You say that? After being present last night when she smacked Scroogen right in the face with her purse."

"She's a gutsy gal, Sergeant. But she doesn't strike me as the kind of woman who would attack when a man's back is turned."

"You make her sound like Wyatt Earp upholding the code of the Old West. I thought you'd be happy to see I'm not letting her get away with attacking your uncle just because he's dead."

"I do appreciate your diligence, Sergeant. The whole family does. I just want to see that the right person is prosecuted."

Patterson frowned as he crossed his arms over his chest.

"The only reason I let you watch the woman's interrogation is because Judge Gatton called over and asked me to keep you apprised of our progress on Scroogen's case. Don't make me regret my decision to interpret that request so generously."

"I'm not trying to give you a hard time, Sergeant."

"After all the animosity that existed between your uncle and that Osborne woman, I'm surprised you're defending her."

"I tell you, Sergeant, the act is just not in keeping with Mab Osborne's character."

The door to the observation room opened and a plainclothes detective stepped inside.

"Sergeant, I thought you'd want to know. Our local fingerprint guru just compared Mab Osborne's fingerprints off the drinking glass in the interrogation room with the fingerprints on the gardening tool. They're a match. A perfect match. And hers are the only fingerprints on that gardening tool."

Patterson turned to face Brett. His upper lip curled into his mustache.

"Now what do you say about her character, Merlin?"

Chapter Eight

"Like I told you, Octavia, my gardening tool and gloves are locked in our storeroom. Come on, I'll show you."

Octavia followed her grandmother down the mossy path dividing the lush and lovely plants of the Silver Power League's greenhouse. Everywhere she looked was a feast for the eyes as glossy green leaves and healthy shoots shot toward the light. Many of the plants had been adorned with Christmas decorations in keeping with the season. The perfume of the flowers and the freshness of the air combined in a special fragrance.

"Who is raising and looking after all these plants?"

"Our members. So many live in apartments now and don't have room for the gardens they once had. They miss them. So they come here and the league gives them a full bed to plant and tend. The only rule is that they care for what they bring into the greenhouse so that it can remain lovely for us all."

"Mab, you don't have time to tend your garden at home."

"I'm not trying to grow any plants here in our greenhouse. It's for those who have no gardens."

"Then why did you bring in your gloves and gardening tool?"

"One of our members had to have hip replacement surgery a couple of weeks ago. She called me, worried the weeds would overrun her plants while she was recuperating over the next several weeks. I grabbed my cultivator and gardening gloves off the back porch and brought them with me so I could keep her bed tended until she got back.''

They reached the door to the storeroom and Mab pulled a distinctive silver-plated key out of fanny-pack purse. She unlocked the door and Octavia followed her inside.

The storeroom was small and compact. On the left wall were the blinking lights of a computerized panel connected to a monitor and keyboard sitting on a small, postmaster-type desk.

Mounted on the middle wall were neat pale shelves, still giving off the smell of new wood. Light silver envelopes and paper rested on them. On the right side was a large metal cabinet. A black strip with white lettering identified it as containing supplies. When Mab opened the cabinet, she immediately let out a small exclamation.

''My gloves and cultivator are gone. I distinctly remember putting them right there. What happened to them?''

''They're on their way to the forensic lab in Seattle,'' Brett's voice said from behind them.

Octavia swung around. She had felt him there just the instant before he spoke. Her heart quickened its beat and her fingertips began to tingle, just as they always did when she came face-to-face with those arresting eyes.

''Why are you here?'' she asked.

''To tell you that Sergeant Patterson identified Mab's fingerprints on that gardening tool his men dug out of the Dumpster.''

''Where did he get my fingerprints?'' Mab asked.

''The water glass,'' Octavia said, in instant understanding. ''I thought it odd that he brought you water in a glass instead of a plastic cup.''

Brett nodded in confirmation. ''Patterson messengered the gloves and gardening tool to the Seattle forensic lab to check on the blood. The coroner's office has agreed to send a sample of Scroogen's blood along to see if there's a match.''

Octavia had anticipated bad news ever since she had seen Sergeant Patterson dangling those gloves and cultivator in that plastic bag. She was not at all pleased to hear Brett's confirmation of it, however.

"So Sergeant Patterson sent you over with this *good* news?"

She watched the silver in Brett's eyes solidify and was a little surprised to see this signal of anger in him.

"I'm not Sergeant Patterson's messenger," he informed her with that ultra-polite, distant tone of his.

He turned then to address her grandmother. "Mrs. Osborne, I don't believe you attacked my uncle."

Octavia was completely nonplussed by Brett's words. She stared at him mutely.

"Why don't you?" Mab challenged. "Because I'm a sweet little old lady?"

Brett smiled. It was the first time Octavia had seen him smile. The rigid features of his face relaxed, the dark, forbidding angles and planes seeming to just dissolve. The silver in his eyes melted into a warm liquid pool.

Octavia caught her breath at the sudden transformation—and the sudden wild beat of her heart. The formidable legal Magician had just metamorphosed right before her eyes into an incredibly attractive man.

And all it had taken was a smile.

"No, I don't think you're a sweet little old lady, Mab," he said. "I think you're a hell-bent-for-leather rabble-rouser. And I also think you're too straight to attack someone from behind and too smart to throw your own gardening gloves and a weapon with your fingerprints all over it into a trash Dumpster where it's bound to be found."

"And I think I'm beginning to like you, Brett Merlin," Mab said as she walked over to him and slipped her arm into his. She smiled up into his face. "So now what?"

"Now you'd best get ready for the worst. Sergeant Patterson doesn't agree with my assessment of this situation. He's going to try to prove you did it."

"So it's up to us to find out who really did. Who do you think was upset enough at your uncle to attack him?"

"That may be the wrong question, Mab," Octavia said, recovering from her initial stupefying surprise at seeing this new side of Brett.

"Why the wrong question?" Mab asked her.

"Sergeant Patterson said Scroogen's wound was superficial. It seems to me that if someone really wanted to do Scroogen an injury, he would have inflicted a far more serious blow."

"Octavia is right," Brett said. "This attack was far more likely an attempt to injure you, Mab, than my uncle."

"Because it was made to look as though I had done it," Mab said. "Yes, I see."

"So maybe, Mab, what we should be asking is who dislikes you enough to try to cause you this kind of trouble?"

"That can't be right. Other than the Scrooge . . . sorry, I mean your uncle, I can't imagine anyone disliking me enough to give me this kind of grief."

"Well then, let's start with the basics," Octavia said. "Who has keys to the greenhouse and this storeroom?"

"The greenhouse is never locked. We want our members to feel they can come and go as they please to tend their gardens or just to sit on one of the corner benches and enjoy the plants and the controlled temperature and full-spectrum fluorescents that Douglas installed."

"This Douglas, is he a member of the Silver Power League?" Brett asked.

"Yes. He engineered the climatic controls in our greenhouse, which are monitored through that computer over there. The greenhouse simulates bright spring daytime light twelve hours straight during the fall and winter. It can get so gloomy here in Washington during this time of year, what with so many overcast days. Many of our members find the greenhouse's simulated light not only keeps the plants growing all year long, but also brightens their spirits."

"So anyone might enter the greenhouse," Octavia said, getting back to the subject. "But you used a key to get into this storeroom."

"Yes. As I said before, the expensive computer system that controls our greenhouse's climate is kept here, along with our stationery, office supplies and an extension telephone in case of emergencies." Mab paused to point at the telephone instrument sitting on the desk next to the computer keyboard.

"I can see putting the computer here, but wouldn't your supplies be more accessible in the community center?" Brett said.

"Constance, our designer, was quite adamant that the center's open architecture would have been ruined by the addition of a storage room," Mab replied. "Since we had to lock up the computer, anyway, it seemed to make sense to put everything needing security in this one room."

"Who has keys to this room?" Octavia asked.

"Only members of the Silver Power League's executive committee."

"So that's you, John, Constance and Douglas, right?"

"Right."

Brett crouched until he was eye level with the doorknob. He scrutinized it carefully.

"Doesn't look like it's been tampered with to me. But to be certain, we'd better ask an expert."

Octavia moved over to the door and bent down to see for herself. "You going to ask Coltrane to come by?"

"Unless you want to give A.J. a call."

Octavia read a solid professional respect in his silver eyes and a fluid personal amusement playing around his mouth.

A sudden delicious tingling began in her fingertips and spread throughout her body as the realization hit her on a whole new level that her formidable adversary had become her ally.

"You two can't really think someone broke in here just to steal my gardening supplies out of this cabinet?" Mab asked.

Her grandmother's question had Octavia straightening up and facing her.

"Broke in or let themselves in," she answered. "How else could they have gotten them?"

"But, Octavia, that doesn't make any sense. No one knew my gloves or gardening tool were in here. I didn't even tell the woman who asked me to look after her flower bed."

"You're sure you told no one? Not even a word in passing?"

"I'm sure. It was a favor I was doing for a friend. There was no reason to broadcast it."

"What about when you brought your gloves and the cultivator into the storeroom. Did someone see you then?"

"No."

"Have you used your cultivator since you brought it down?"

Mab shook her head. "I checked on the flower bed earlier this week and everything was fine."

"I saw some dirt on the gloves and cultivator."

"That's because I had weeded my backyard berry bushes the morning I brought the tools to the center."

"Then that narrows down our immediate suspects to three people," Brett said, "providing this lock wasn't jimmied."

"Now, wait a minute," Mab said. "You're not going to convince me that John or Constance or Douglas used my gloves and gardening tool to attack the Scrooge."

"Mab, they've all been pretty angry at the guy," Octavia reminded her. "Maybe when one of them opened this supply cabinet and just happened to see your gardening tool and gloves, he or she didn't realize who they belonged to. Maybe there was no intent for you to be blamed."

"Octavia, my initials are carved on the handle of that gardening tool. Whoever took it had to know it was mine."

"Unless whoever took it didn't have his or her glasses handy. Constance is the only one who wears her glasses all the time. I've never even seen you put yours on unless you have to read or study something up close."

Mab shook her head. "We both know even if the person who took my gardening tool didn't immediately see my initials, he still had to have known it and the gloves belonged to one of the members of the executive committee. No, none of them would have attacked the Scrooge like that, and none of them would have implicated another in the act. And that is the end to that."

"Mab, here you are," Constance said as she stepped into the storeroom. "Douglas said he thought he saw you come in here. Is everything all right?"

"Fine," Mab said, turning to her.

Constance was eyeing Brett suspiciously.

"It's all right, Constance," Mab said. "Mr. Merlin is trying to help."

"You've been gone for such a long time, I thought—"

"Sergeant Patterson just had a lot of questions," Mab interjected quickly. "How is the cleanup coming?"

"Douglas's boys are finished with the pumping. It's disinfectant time. Before we get started, we're going to eat. There's quite a spread set up. Plenty for all who are willing to work," Constance added as she looked meaningfully at Octavia.

"Octavia is hardly dressed for a cleanup job. My sweats are in the trunk of my car. Come, you can help me get them."

"What do you think?" Brett asked Octavia a few minutes later as they strolled together down the greenhouse path.

He watched her glide over to a cushioned bench in the corner opposite the storeroom and slip onto its seat. He sat beside her, resting his elbows on the back of the bench.

"A lot of the greenery is decorated with Christmas ornaments," she said, pointing to the tiny golden balls and silver bells and the two miniature fir trees with lights looped around their branches. "They are distracting enough that someone might sit here unobserved."

"Still, even if someone sat here and watched Mab enter the storeroom carrying her cultivator and gloves, that person would still have needed a key to get in."

"Yes, it still comes back to who has a key, doesn't it."

"What do you know about the other members of this executive committee of the Silver Power League?"

"Not a lot, really. Except that they're Mab's friends. Which presents a major problem. Mab is loyal to the end. She's not going to be much help in fingering one of them."

"Then it's going to be up to us to find out which one attacked Scroogen."

She turned to look at him directly. "Are you really willing to help?"

Brett found himself suddenly responding not just to Octavia's question but to the accompanying warmth in her eyes. His palms began to perspire and the muscles at the back of his neck began to tighten.

"He was my uncle. Of course I want to find out who attacked him."

She laid her hand on his arm. He felt his muscles immediately and involuntarily tensing beneath her light touch.

"I'm sorry for the pain that his passing must have caused you and his family."

"Dole and I didn't really know each other," he heard himself admitting.

"You were helping him for your aunt's sake, is that it?"

"Yes."

"How is she holding up?"

"She's been a lot better."

Her hand squeezed his arm. Then she released the pressure on his arm, removed her hand and looked away.

"I can't get over what an engineering marvel this greenhouse is. Did you notice the temperature and humidity gradations as you walked through? Douglas's computer system must alter the heat and humidity for individual sections so that diverse plants can exist in a kind of blended harmony. Amazing."

He knew she had changed the subject to relieve any awkwardness he might be feeling. She had a highly developed and exceptionally appealing sense of tact. Exceptionally appealing.

More and more he was becoming confused as to just who she was. And more and more he was becoming alarmed at how much he wanted to know.

"So do I call A.J. or do you call Coltrane?" she asked after a moment's silence.

"Let me call Coltrane," Brett decided immediately. "I pulled him off the case last night and it irritated him. He'll be delighted to be given the go-ahead again."

"Why did you pull him off the case?"

"After the sewage spilling incident at the community center, Dole fired me."

"Really? What a foolish move."

"Why do you assume it was a foolish move? How do you know he didn't have cause?"

"Brett, please, what cause could there possibly be to fire *you?*"

Her remark had been made in an off-hand way with, obviously, no intent to praise. Brett found himself quite pleased by it, anyway.

"Why would Coltrane be irritated at being called off the case?" Octavia wanted to know.

"He hates to leave things hanging, questions unanswered," Brett said. "Actually, I wish I hadn't called him off last night. If he had had someone still following your grandmother, he would have been able to give her an alibi this morning."

"Thanks for believing in her innocence. And for telling her. It means a great deal to both of us."

She leaned over then and kissed him, full on the lips, taking him once again completely by surprise.

Brett's body responded before a single thought could register in his brain. His lips pressed eagerly, hungrily, against hers.

She melted against him, her scent mixing with her pleasurable sighs in an intoxicating brew.

And he drank her in, thirstily, encircling her in his arms, his muscles taut from his neck to his waist as desire coiled tight and deep inside him.

She tasted meltingly hot and sweet, like a marshmallow suddenly thrust over a leaping flame. His lips moved over the soft fullness of hers again and again, unable to get enough of her feel and flavor.

Her arms circled his waist. He could feel her breasts against his chest, as soft and yielding as the sighs escaping from her lips.

Another total surprise. The woman who had warred with him so valiantly was answering his offensive with complete surrender.

A heat burgeoned within him . . . and a need like none he had ever known.

He pulled back, reeling at the roaring demand of it. His breath came out in ragged gasps. His muscles were so coiled in readiness, his want of her so deep, he ached.

He knew he should get up and leave now. He didn't even know why he had come. All he promised Nancy was that he'd find out how Dole had died. The autopsy being conducted right this moment would give him that answer soon enough. So what in the hell was he doing here?

It was a stupid question. *She* was why he was here. He couldn't get her out of his mind, not from the first, no matter how much he had tried to deny it. He wanted her so damn much—too damn much.

And her? What about her? What did she want?

She was sitting there staring at him with a flush on her face and an unfathomable expression in her deep blue eyes. She had responded to him totally. Yet now she seemed perfectly content just to sit there, one of those damn secretive smiles on her face, neither encouraging nor discouraging.

It was maddening.

He pulled her to him, breast to breast. He buried his head in the silk of her hair, drinking in the perfume of it and the feel of her until he felt drunk with them.

"I never know what you're going to say or do next," he said. "Does everyone have this trouble with you?"

"It depends on what kind of trouble they want to have with me," she said. "So, what's our first move?"

"First move?" he repeated. By his figuring, they were way past first moves.

"Yes," Octavia said, looking and sounding perfectly serious as she leaned out of his arms. "There must be a logical starting place to begin to prove my grandmother innocent."

"Oh, yes, of course," he answered like a man without a mind.

Naturally, she was talking about business since he had assumed she was referring to their personal relationship. He should know by now that when it came to Octavia, the opposite of what he expected would always be what he got.

For one crazy, impossible moment he found that thought tremendously exciting.

His beeper went off. He dug it out of his pocket.

"It's Sergeant Patterson's number. I can call him back on the car phone."

He rose and offered her his hand. She slipped both her hands into his as she stood, something else that he found tremendously exciting.

At that moment he had no idea what he was doing or where he was heading. He only knew that with Octavia Osborne by his side, the answers would be nothing he expected.

ZANE COLTRANE BENT DOWN to eye the lock on the storeroom door, a small intense flashlight in his clublike hand. He was a dark, mammoth man, dressed in black, with an expressionless face and eyes like shadows. Octavia could picture him on the trail of an unsuspecting quarry, effectively fading into the background whenever anyone looked his way. She did not find the image comfortable.

After a long moment of scrutiny, Zane rose to a standing position and addressed Brett.

"No scratches or lateral grooves. It hasn't been picked."

"Well, that answers that question," Brett said. "So now we have just those three suspects I told you about earlier."

"And you want background checks on them all as soon as possible," Zane said, his big, clumsy-looking hands deftly slipping the tiny flashlight back into his breast pocket. "I'll put my people on it right away."

Zane turned to walk up the greenhouse path. A second later, he had disappeared out of sight, without a sound.

"A.J. might take offense if I call her off the scent on this case," Octavia said to Brett.

"Dole was my uncle."

She nodded at the implication in his words. They left the locked storeroom door, walking along the path bisecting the plants. Octavia stole a look at Brett's face.

"Something disturbed you about that telephone conversation you had with Sergeant Patterson earlier. What was it?"

"The autopsy this afternoon was inconclusive."

"I see. So it wasn't a standard medical problem, like a heart attack, that killed your uncle. Do they have any ideas?"

"Not a clue. If the Seattle toxicology lab is backed up, there's no telling when they'll know. I had to call my aunt."

Octavia understood now why Brett had seemed so solemn since that call. He may not have been close to his uncle, but she suspected he had deep feelings for his aunt.

"The most difficult thing sometimes is the waiting," she said, trying to let him know she understood. "Even hard answers relieve the tension of not knowing."

She checked her watch as her stomach registered a growling complaint. "Just as I thought. I'm way overdue for lunch. Come on. I'll treat."

"No one will be serving lunch this late, Octavia. Restaurants are preparing for dinner."

"Not to worry. I know just the place."

Octavia gave Brett directions to a tiny health food store in the back of a small neighborhood shopping center. When he stopped the car in front of it, he glanced over at Octavia with a wonderful look of disbelief on his face.

"You're not serious."

"They have a refreshment counter at the back."

Brett was still shaking his head when he came around to open the passenger door and take her hand to help her out of the car. She liked how automatic these courteous gestures were to him. In some ways, he struck her as a man out of his time. She liked that, too.

"I never would have picked you to be a health nut," he said as he closed the car door behind her.

"Actually, I eat all kinds of foods. I've always found that what's on the menu is far less important than what's in the mind of the cook, haven't you?"

"I might if I had any idea what that means."

She laughed at the confusion in his voice.

Once inside the store, Octavia threaded her way through the haphazard shelves, full of herbs and vitamins and minerals in every size and shape, to the small white Formica refreshment counter in the back. It was quarter-moon-shaped with just two bar stools. Behind the counter, a mural had been painted of a giant Santa sleigh, the racks of herbs made to appear like wrapped packages within it. Octavia found the effect charming.

She took one of the bar stools and gestured Brett to the other. It had been a couple of years since she had been here. She hoped things hadn't changed. As soon as she saw the round face bob around the partition that led into the kitchen and Phoebe's Christmas-elf-clad body appear, she was reassured they hadn't.

"Octavia!" the hefty, seventyish lady shouted as she threw her stout body over the counter and her arms around Octavia, nearly choking her.

"Phoebe, please," Octavia said, laughing with the little breath that remained in her body. "I'm glad to see you, too, but I'm out of practice on breaking your wrestling holds."

"You haven't been keeping up your swimming, have you," Phoebe asked as she released her death hold and stepped back.

"You know chlorine was never my favorite fragrance."

Phoebe planted her hands on her hips, her green felt hat cocked to one side, her green-slippered feet askew. "I had hopes for you, Octavia. Best breaststroke I ever saw. You had both the wind and a natural athletic ability."

Octavia laughed. "And the prune skin. So, how have you been?"

"Hale and hearty as always. I heard you were in town. Word gets around at the community center. I was going to come by to say hello, but mother hasn't been feeling well and I didn't want to leave her."

"Nothing serious, I hope?"

"Another case of a broken heart, I'm afraid. You know how chaotic her love life has always been."

Phoebe paused to address Brett, obviously feeling this last comment needed explaining. "Mother's ninety-two, but she keeps insisting on going after younger men. Last one was barely eighty. I told her it wouldn't last, but, of course, some people just won't listen when you warn them about their actions courting disaster, will they?"

Brett flashed Octavia a meaningful glance as he gave a small smile. "Couldn't have said it better myself."

"Octavia, introduce this obviously intelligent man to me right away," Phoebe demanded.

Octavia chuckled. "Brett Merlin, Phoebe Winkle, Christmas elf, as well as proprietor of this establishment."

Phoebe extended a hefty hand over the counter. As they shook, Phoebe continued to regard him closely.

"Brett Merlin. Your name sounds familiar for some reason. Wait a minute. Aren't you the Scrooge's attorney?"

"Was," Brett amended, drawing back his hand. "He's...not in need of one anymore."

"So I heard. I'm not crying," Phoebe informed Brett quickly and most pointedly as her hands returned to her hips.

"It's okay, Phoebe," Octavia said. "Brett's on our side."

"Oh?"

"You just said he was intelligent," Octavia reminded her. "How about something to eat? We're starving."

"Coming right up. You want the usual to drink?"

"Absolutely."

Phoebe turned to Brett. Her tone wasn't exactly warm and friendly as it was when she spoke to Octavia, but at least it had lost its earlier sharp edge. "How about you?"

"I'll have whatever Octavia is having."

"Two Christmas carrot juices coming up," Phoebe said as she turned to fetch them.

"Christmas carrot juice?" Brett repeated with a distinct lack of enthusiasm as soon as Phoebe had left.

"Very good Christmas carrot juice," Octavia assured him.

When Phoebe returned a moment later with two tall glasses, Octavia picked up hers and offered a toast.

"To Santas everywhere."

Brett shook his head as he clicked his glass with hers.

He eyed the contents of his glass suspiciously, but after his first tentative taste, he seemed to reassess his initial reaction and took a good healthy swig. And then another. When he finally put the tall glass down on the counter, it was empty.

Phoebe almost smiled at him before once again disappearing into the kitchen.

"That wasn't just carrot juice," Brett said. "It couldn't have been."

Octavia moved closer to his ear. "Nothing served here is just anything. Wait and see."

They didn't have to wait long. Phoebe soon reemerged with two plates in her chubby hands. The wonderful aroma of whatever was sitting in the centers of those plates set Octavia's mouth to watering immediately. She asked no questions as Phoebe set the dish in front of her. She just picked up her fork and dug in.

"What is it?" Brett wanted to know.

"Christmas casserole," Phoebe answered. Before Brett could ask any more questions, Phoebe had disappeared once again into the kitchen.

Out of the corner of her eye, Octavia could feel Brett watching her slip the first forkful into her mouth. She sighed in appreciation as the wonderful flavors exploded onto her tastebuds. Finally, he picked up his fork and tried a small taste. The look of absolute surprise that stole over his face made Octavia smile. Then she gave absolutely not another thought to him as she concentrated all her senses on enjoying the perfect lunch that had been set before her.

When she next looked up, she noticed that not only was her plate empty, but Brett's was, too.

Phoebe returned with dessert and something that looked like coffee, but smelled so much better.

"This appears to be some kind of fruit pie," Brett said as she set the brown-crusted wedge in front of him.

"Right. Christmas fruit pie," Phoebe confirmed before walking up to the front of the store to wait on a couple who had been browsing for a few minutes and now appeared ready to pay for their choices.

Octavia watched Brett take his first bite of dessert, not nearly so hesitantly this time. They both made the pie quickly disappear from their plates and then sat back to sip the rich, hot beverage that tasted like Bavarian chocolate cream.

Phoebe had rung up the couple's purchases and returned to the tiny lunch counter.

"The food was fabulous as always," Octavia said. "Now, I'd like to pick that brain of yours if you have a few minutes."

"Sure. What can I help you with?"

As succinctly as possible, Octavia told Phoebe about the attack on Scroogen and the fact that it looked like Mab's gardening tool had been used.

"And the police are convinced your grandmother did it?"

"Yes. Only the other members of the executive committee of the Silver Power League have keys to that storeroom where Mab put her gardening gloves and cultivator. Logically, it must be one of them. Mab is too close to these people. I thought you might be a bit more objective."

Phoebe scratched her scalp beneath her green felt hat. "You've put me in a hard position, Octavia. I know and like Constance, John and Douglas, too. Of course, I realize nearly anyone can be provoked under the right set of circumstances. And the Scrooge set up some pretty provoking circumstances."

"If you had to choose from among the three, who would it be?" Octavia pressed.

Phoebe munched on her lips a bit before coming out with her answer. "John."

"Why John?"

"Douglas is crude and rough, and he's been known to fight at the drop of a hat, but he'd come at you face first, never from behind. And as for Constance, well she's such a fussy little thing. She might employ a sneak attack, but never with such demanding physical requirements."

"So you're saying John gets your vote by default?"

"That, and the fact that I don't know him as well as the others. He moved his ophthalmologist practice here from California only about thirty years ago, when his wife died."

"Thirty years isn't long enough to get to know someone?" Brett asked.

"With some people it might be. But John refuses to speak about how his wife died or why he left California so soon afterward. And he never has remarried. These things naturally make a person wonder."

"I can understand how his refusal to speak about his wife's death would raise questions in your mind," Brett said, "but why would his not remarrying cause you concern?"

"A man whose wife dies in his sixties might remain single afterward. But a man whose wife dies when he's in his forties is a man who will marry again—for companionship if not for love. So why hasn't John married? What is it about him that he doesn't want a woman to get too close to see?"

"WHAT DO YOU THINK about her picking John?" Brett asked a few minutes later as he opened the passenger door of his Bentley.

Octavia leaned her elbow on the open car door as she answered the question. "I think maybe we should go talk to John and decide for ourselves."

"You don't like the idea of it being him?"

"And it shows, I know. Both John and Mab have been alone a long time. I suppose I've always expected them to get together one of these days."

"As in marriage?"

"Well, neither is the type to just move in together. Mab is too traditional for that. Come on, I'm sure we'll find John at the community center helping out."

She slipped into the passenger seat then and Brett closed the door behind her and circled to the other side. When they were on their way, he asked the question prompted by her last comment.

"You say Mab is too traditional to live with John out of wedlock, and yet your mother never married."

"I see Coltrane got around to giving you that report on me."

"A few items, yes. Care to elaborate?"

"Mom and Dad got together in the sixties, when attitudes were quite different. They were married, but in a ceremony conducted by a tribal chief in Africa."

"That's not a legal marriage here."

"They were looking for a way to show their commitment without the formality of a legal certificate. They've been together more than thirty-five years. And every one of those years they've renewed their vows to each other in a private ceremony."

"If your mother is committed to your father, why didn't she take his last name?"

"The tradition of a woman taking a man's name stems from the days when she went from the property of her father to the property of her husband, with virtually no identity outside of the man who currently 'owned' her. Neither my mother nor father believed in perpetuating the trappings of such a tradition."

"In light of the historical reference, I can understand why a woman wouldn't wish to change her last name when she marries. But I don't understand why you carry only your mother's surname and not your father's."

"Those hyphenated last names can become pretty cumbersome. Mom and Dad simply agreed that if I were a boy, I would carry my father's surname, and if I were a girl, I would carry my mother's. It's a perfectly logical and eminently reasonable approach to assigning a surname to a child. The females follow the mother's line, the males follow the father's."

"I suppose there is no reason why a female line should have any less significance or carrying power than a male's," Brett said, finding the idea rather intriguing. "So are you a believer in marriage, like your grandmother, or in commitment without it like your parents?"

"I think that will depend on the man with whom I eventually enrich my life."

"Enrich your life? You mean live with?"

"Live with definitely doesn't say it for me."

"You mean you're going to let this man with whom you enrich your life decide whether you marry or not?"

"No, we're going to decide together. It isn't the kind of a decision that only one person in a relationship can make."

Brett couldn't figure her out, and every conversation they had just seemed to confuse him more.

She was thoroughly modern in some respects. Yet in other ways, she was contrastingly old-fashioned—like the fact she seemed to thoroughly appreciate his opening doors for her and didn't mistake the act of courtesy for condescension. And the way she always appeared so beautifully groomed and wearing high heels and suits with skirts, never slacks, all of which was definitely against the current fashion trends.

He was beginning to think it would be a full-time job just trying to understand all the different pieces that somehow combined to make her such a confusing and intriguing woman.

"So how did you like your lunch?" she asked.

"It was delicious, but I have no idea what I ate. Do you?"

"No."

"But you didn't ask."

"No point to it. Phoebe couldn't have told us, either."

"Now, that's a reassuring image. Perhaps our first stop should be the emergency room to have our stomachs pumped."

Octavia laughed. "Phoebe views every dish as an experiment to combine good taste and good health. She doesn't use recipes. She used to be my phys ed teacher in high school, as you may have surmised. Her love was swimming. Because of her, our team made it to the state championships."

"And because of your breaststroke."

Octavia laughed. "My muscles still ache thinking about it. That was the year I learned about the reserves of strength we all have in us, just waiting to be tapped."

"I learned that lesson with the first mountain I climbed."

"You're into mountain climbing? Well, well. Who would have thought. You're a risk-taker."

"I don't consider mountain climbing risky. I prepare mentally and physically for every ascent."

"A mountain climber who insists he doesn't take risks. I love it. I suppose next you'll tell me the only reason you climb these mountains is because they're in the way?"

How did she manage that wonderfully sweet sarcasm without one iota of change in her voice inflection?

Brett smiled. "You enjoyed the time you spent here with your grandmother while you were growing up, didn't you," he asked, deliberately changing the subject.

"Very. I was blossoming into the typical obnoxious teenager and my parents were pulling their hair out. Then, out of the blue, this wonderful offer came through for them to go traipsing off into the interior of the Brazilian rain forest through mud and muck to study a tribe of primitive people. They jumped at the opportunity.''

''It's hard for me to picture you as the daughter of two intrepid cultural anthropologists who like to rough it.''

''Hard for me to picture, too. At first they tried to take me on some of their forays into the primitive places, but even at five and six, I was insisting on a daily bath. After a while they just gave up.''

''And left you with your grandmother?''

''Happily, yes. Mab and I have always been close, and I enjoyed not having to move all the time. Not that I don't recognize that my parents are doing important work. I'm very proud of them. They're on a South Seas island now, studying another primitive culture.''

''You didn't miss them when they left you while you were growing up?''

''Very much, particularly the five years they spent in Brazil. But I'm not sure I would have such fond feelings for them now if we had been forced to try to survive under the same roof then. I'm a firm believer that the teenage years are a great time for parents to leave the country. Or the kids.''

''Yes, I remember only too well my own struggles with my parents during those years. But as difficult as it was, I think that it would have been more difficult not to see them for five full years.''

''Oh, my parents came home every Christmas for a week. Christmas Eve we'd all sit around the wood stove in my grandmother's home, drinking cider and eating Mab's amazing Christmas cookies while my parents would regale us with all their experiences. Maybe that's why Christmas has always been my favorite time of the year. I could hardly wait for Christmas morning and the unusual, surprising presents they had brought back. Those kind of presents are always the best, aren't they.''

''I wouldn't know. We didn't exchange Christmas presents. My parents didn't believe in perpetuating fantasies for which I would later be disappointed.''

"Are you telling me you *never* believed in Santa Claus?"

"You obviously consider me to have had a deprived childhood. I assure you, I was quite content."

"What were you read during storybook time?"

"There was no storybook time. My parents both came from very poor families. They didn't want to give me the false impression that things could be had by the wave of some storybook wand. They wanted me to understand from the first that I would have to work—and work hard—for whatever I got. They didn't fill my head with fantasies of any kind."

"Amazing. Here you are this wonderful magician of law, and yet you've missed out on the magic of a fantasy life."

"What's so magical about fantasies?"

"How good they make us feel, of course. Like the world is a place full of sparkle."

"I'll take the sparkle of a multifaceted diamond over a multiflawed fantasy any day."

"I find it very interesting that you're drawn to the sparkle of diamonds, Brett."

"Why? They're a good investment."

"So are stocks and bonds, but they don't sparkle, do they? Can it be that you're drawn to diamonds because they represent all that beautiful Christmas sparkle you missed out on when you were a child?"

"I'm surprised that your grandmother didn't become the authority ogre when your parents were gone," Brett said, deliberately changing the subject again.

"Mab has always had a unique outlook on life. She believes the best rules and regulations come from within us. She told me that whenever I was faced with any moral decision, I should follow my intuition, because intuition is a whisper from the heart. I've used that advice all my life and found it to be excellent."

"Sounds like you still believe in Santa Claus."

"Maybe a part of me does," Octavia admitted. "But I realize that doesn't mean anything to a man who doesn't even acknowledge the existence of a heart."

"I acknowledge the existence of a heart. Even mine."

"Why, because a doctor showed you an X ray of it?"

He had to smile at how sweetly she had managed to say that. "No, because I admit that I come with the standard set of emotions, just like everyone else. But I don't believe they can be relied on to live one's life."

"Have you ever tried?"

"Yes."

"Another surprise. First mountain climbing and now a confession that you've actually let your emotions be your guide. I must know, when was this?"

"When I was young and foolish and fell in love."

"Who was she?"

"A dangerous fantasy, all sparkle and glitter and nothing more. We're here," he said as he parked the car in front of the community center.

"Something's wrong," Octavia said, quickly exiting the passenger side, not waiting for Brett to open the door for her this time.

Brett understood her haste the moment he caught sight of John, racing toward them from the community center. Everything about the quickness of his stride and the look on his face told Brett that whatever news he brought, it wasn't going to be good.

John's words were breathy from his exertion.

"They took Mab, Octavia. Just now. I've been looking for your number to call you, but I couldn't find it."

"Took Mab? Who took Mab?" Octavia asked, surprising Brett as always with her clear, calm voice in a crisis.

"The police. They had a warrant. She's been arrested."

Chapter Nine

"Save your breath, Ms. Osborne," Sergeant Patterson said as Octavia and Brett faced him at the station. "We have her cold. We don't even need to wait for Seattle to get back to us now on the forensics. A witness has come forward."

Octavia knew she couldn't have heard right. "A witness?"

"Ronald Scroogen saw Mab Osborne sneaking up behind his father, pushing him to the ground, striking him on the shoulder and then throwing the cultivator and gloves into the open trash bin before running away."

"I find that very hard to believe, Sergeant," Brett said.

"I find it impossible to believe," Octavia added. "If Scroogen's son saw the whole thing, why didn't he come to his father's aid?"

"When Ronald reached the parking lot, he suddenly remembered he was supposed to meet an employee on the other side of town. He was exiting the parking lot when he saw the attack. By the time he turned the car around again, Mab had run off and his father was back on his feet. Ronald decided his father could take care of it, so he drove off to his meeting."

"Why didn't Ronald tell you this before?"

"Because when he got back to the office after checking on the job, the medics told him his father had just died. Needless to say, the young man had that other matter on his mind."

"I still can't believe he—"

"Ms. Osborne, we have your grandmother on assault. They're booking her now."

Octavia didn't phrase her words into a question. She made them a statement. "You're *not* putting her in jail."

"We're not monsters, Ms. Osborne," Patterson said, "just the police trying to do our jobs. And, no, we're not putting a seventy-six-year-old woman in jail. We'll be fitting her with an electronic monitor and restricting her to her home. You can wait and drive her if you like."

"Her home sustained structural damage, remember? It's not fit for her to return to."

"What do you suggest, Ms. Osborne?"

"She's staying with a friend, Constance Kope. Let her continue to stay there."

"All right."

"When is the arraignment?"

"Nine tomorrow morning. Judge Kuppsen's courtroom. You should have taken my deal, Ms. Osborne," Patterson said as he turned away. "Now it's too late."

"MY CLIENT PLEADS not guilty, Your Honor," Octavia said the next morning in the courtroom of Judge Roberta Kuppsen, a trim, fortyish brunette with a short cap of hair and an alert look.

Deputy prosecutor Edwin Glapp slowly rose to his feet. He was a thin, dark man whose droopy eyes on his youngish face made him look like he had just come out of a really sad movie.

"Your Honor, the people ask for five-thousand bail."

"Your Honor," Octavia began, "Mab Osborne has lived in Bremerton all her life. She is a co-owner of the local senior's radio station and is on the executive committee of their Silver Power League. With such substantial ties to the community, she is hardly a flight risk. She should be released on her own recognizance."

"I see no need for the formality of bail in this situation," Judge Kuppsen said. "The defendant will be released on her own recognizance. Preliminary hearing is set for December 22, ten o'clock. Next case.''

"So, that's it?'' Mab asked as she turned to Octavia.

"Yes. We'll be back in court on the twenty-second.''

"That's the day I'm helping to cook and coordinate the Christmas meals for the nonambulatory seniors. Then there's seeing to the repairs to the community center. I can't waste time here, answering these foolish charges.''

"Mab, this isn't an optional appearance,'' Brett reminded her as he stood beside her on the other side of the defense table.

Octavia rested her hand on Mab's shoulder. "We're going to do our best to try to clear this up quickly, Mab. As soon as they take that electronic monitoring device off your leg, we'll take you over to the community center and let you get back to work while we go check out this eyewitness.''

"Ronald Scroogen is lying,'' Mab said, her mouth tight.

"Or possibly mistaken. What Brett and I have to find out is whether he made this up for some reason or he honestly mistook you for someone else.''

Mab turned to Brett. "Do you believe me? Even over the word of your cousin?''

Octavia liked the small smile that drew back Brett's lips as he answered her grandmother. "Yes.''

Mab rose on her tiptoes to give his cheek a quick kiss.

Brett's smile got a little bigger. "You Osborne women certainly have a way with a thank you,'' he said, somehow managing to maintain that deep, solemn voice of his.

Mab grinned first at him and then at Octavia. "I'm really beginning to like this magician of yours.''

"Me, too,'' Octavia said. "Let's get that electronic monitor off you. It's definitely not your style of ankle jewelry.''

"I SAW WHAT I SAW,'' Ronald said defiantly, clearly upset with being challenged by Brett.

Brett leaned forward in his chair in the living room of the Scroogen home and looked Ronald straight in the eye. The young man tried to maintain his ramrod-straight poise, despite the soft undulating folds of the comfortable couch on which he perched.

"I read the statement you gave Sergeant Patterson, Ronald. I went to your father's office building and studied the area in which the assault took place. I even drove my car in and out of the parking lot trying to mimic the movements you described."

"So?"

"So, from my attempt to re-create the scenario you described, I think it would have been exceptionally difficult for you to have even seen the attack on your father. And once the police try to imitate your movements as I did, they most certainly will begin to doubt your story, also."

Ronald said nothing, just sat there glaring at Brett and trying to maintain his stiff posture.

"Giving false testimony to the police is a prosecutable offense," Brett warned.

Nancy sat forward, clearly alarmed. "If Ronald was simply mistaken, surely they wouldn't prosecute him for that?"

"Nancy, Ronald told the police he saw Mab Osborne attack Dole. He made a positive eyewitness identification. It was based on his identification and statement that Mab was arrested. If he is mistaken, they will go a lot easier on him if he comes forward now and admits to his mistake."

"I didn't make a mistake," Ronald said. "She did it. And she's going to pay for it. It's what my father would have insisted on if he hadn't died."

"I know your father assumed it was Mab who struck him," Octavia said in her rich, even voice from the other side of the room. "But even he wasn't sure. Remember he told his secretary that he didn't see his attacker?"

"I did," Ronald insisted stubbornly.

Brett had tried reasoning. It was time to try another approach. He rose and stood in front of the couch where Ronald and Nancy sat. He spread his legs and crossed his arms over his chest. He let his voice boom over them.

"How far away were you from the site of the assault?"

"I don't know."

"Estimate."

"Fifty feet."

"I measured the distance. The closest you could have been was two hundred feet. How long did the attack take?"

"The whole thing?"

"Yes."

"I think half a minute."

"You think or you're sure?"

"I'm sure."

"Were you watching the attack in your rearview mirror or your side mirror?"

"Neither. I was turned and looking out the back window."

"While driving forward you were looking out the back window for half a minute?"

Ronald's hands moved from his sides to circle his knees. "Well, no. I mean not the whole time."

"So you did turn your eyes forward some of the time?"

"Of course. Otherwise I would have crashed into something."

"If you looked away, you didn't see everything, did you?"

"Yes, I did."

"Even while you were focused ahead concentrating on not hitting anything, you saw everything that happened behind you?"

Ronald clasped his knees more tightly. "You're trying to confuse me."

"Your answers are doing that, Ronald. What was your father wearing?"

"A suit, I guess. He always wore a suit with suspenders."

"So you don't know, you're just guessing?"

"I'm not guessing. It was a suit. With suspenders."

"Was his jacket on or off?"

"I don't remember."

"What was Mab Osborne wearing?"

"I don't remember. Who do you think you are, questioning me like this?"

"Whether you believe it or not, I'm trying to be your friend. When you take the stand in court, it will be Octavia who will cross-examine you. She will ask a thousand questions, much harder than those I've just asked you. She will pin you down in a thousand different ways. And after she's finished, the jury will see quite clearly that in your grief over your father's death, in your desperate need to avenge an attack made on him in his final hours, you have perjured yourself."

Brett looked at Nancy. He changed the harsh note in his voice to one of gentle concern.

"Perhaps the saddest part about this misguided attempt to avenge his father is that Dole's real attacker might never be brought to justice, and it will be Ronald who goes to jail."

Brett once again let his eyes focus on Ronald's face. His tone remained gentle this time.

"Do you think your father would have wanted that, Ronald? What good will you be to Nancy and Katlyn behind bars? How will you take care of them from there?"

Ronald's hands were gripping his knees so hard now, his knuckles were white.

Brett turned away from him and nodded to Octavia that it was time to leave. She rose immediately and came to his side, a definite light of approval in her eyes.

Nancy also quickly rose, but the look in her dark eyes was troubled. She walked them to the door. Before Brett could exit, she laid a hand on his arm.

"I'll talk to him, Brett. He's just trying to do what he thinks Dole would have wanted him to."

She turned hesitantly to Octavia. "He doesn't mean to falsely accuse your grandmother, Ms. Osborne. He believes she really did it."

"I can see that, Mrs. Scroogen," Octavia said, extending her hand as well as her voice. "In his eagerness to see his father avenged, he's just gotten carried away."

Nancy took Octavia's offered hand, a grateful look on her face. "Thank you for understanding, Ms. Osborne."

Nancy turned back to Brett. "You've learned nothing about how Dole died?"

"It's up to the toxicologist in Seattle now. They'll send word as soon as they have anything, Nancy. I'm keeping in close touch with Sergeant Patterson. I realize it's difficult waiting. I'll let you know the moment I know."

Nancy nodded mutely as she let them out and closed the door behind them.

They were halfway to Brett's car when Octavia asked the same question foremost in Brett's mind.

"Do you think your aunt will be able to convince Ronald to recant his statement to the police?"

"I hope so, for his sake, as well as Mab's."

"You handled the situation well, Brett. You alternated between stern and understanding like a vocalist with perfect pitch. Needless to say, I am inordinately pleased we are on the same side in this matter."

Brett remembered his father often saying that the only reward a man needed was knowing inside himself that he had done his best. He had found that his father spoke the truth. Brett felt that success inside himself. The money that had followed meant little. The fame even less. Whether others acknowledged his success had not mattered at all.

Which was why he didn't know why it felt so good—so very good—that she acknowledged it.

"So, where were we before we were so rudely interrupted by this turn of affairs?" she asked as he opened the car door for her.

"We were on our way to see John and talk to him about his possible involvement in the attack. Hopefully, this sidetrack has been taken care of, and we can get on with our investigation and find out who really attacked Scroogen."

"JOHN'S NOT HERE," Mab informed them as she greeted them at the entrance to the center. Inside, Octavia could see the seniors in their old sweats, wearing rubber gloves and surgical masks, many down on hands and knees scrubbing with disinfectant. The masks made sense. Even with all the windows open, the disinfectant odor was quite pervasive.

"Where is he?" Octavia asked.

"His son, Lloyd, called to ask him to drop by. Lloyd is an ophthalmologist just as John was before he retired. Every so often, John consults with him on a case. You can see John at Lloyd's East Bremerton office if you like. I have his card here in my purse."

Mab moved her apronlike wrap to dig inside her fanny pouch purse. She pulled out the card and handed it to Octavia.

"It's not far from here. Probably only take you ten or fifteen minutes."

"We'll see him there, thanks."

"Why do you want to talk to John?" Mab asked.

"Just want to get his views on things. I know you're busy so we won't keep you from your work."

Octavia took Brett's arm and left quickly before Mab asked any more questions. She knew her grandmother would not be pleased to learn she and Brett were about to interrogate John about his possible involvement in the attack on Scroogen.

They arrived at the offices of John Lloyd Winslow, Ophthalmologist, exactly twelve minutes later. Octavia was just about to approach the receptionist sitting behind a large plastic nativity scene, when John came walking out of the inner offices. A look of surprise stole over his face.

"Octavia, Mr. Merlin, what are you two doing here?"

"We came to see you," Octavia said. "Is there some place we can talk?"

"There's a vacant examining room right back here. I'm sure Lloyd won't mind our using it. This way."

John led them down the hall and saw them inside before shutting the door and gesturing them to two side chairs. He remained standing in front of the door, underneath a red banner with white sequins that flashed Season's Greetings.

"Mab told me you're trying to help," he said to Brett.

Brett acknowledged John's comment with a nod.

"So, something you wanted to ask, Octavia?"

"We're trying to understand just how much animosity existed among the seniors collectively and individually toward Scroogen."

"A lot existed, both collectively and individually," John said. "I know it isn't proper to speak ill of the dead, but the man had absolutely no concern for anyone but himself. I'm sorry to have to say this to you, Mr. Merlin."

"No need to be sorry," Brett said. "We want your honest views."

"John, have you ever let the key to the storeroom door at the back of the greenhouse out of your sight?" Octavia asked.

John pulled his key chain out of his suit slacks. He pointed to the distinctive silver-plated key. "It's with me always."

"Was there anyone among the seniors who hated Scroogen enough to wish him harm?" Octavia asked.

John repocketed his keys. "You mean besides me?"

Octavia leaned forward in her chair. "You felt that strongly that you wished him harm?"

"Let's just say that occasional visions of him being hit by a truck did not cause me distress."

"John, where were you when Scroogen was attacked?"

"You think I might have done it?" John said, a mild surprise clearly peppering his tone.

"In view of your deep animosity toward the man, I thought that perhaps—"

"I was at the community center with Constance and Douglas when the Scrooge was attacked, Octavia. Still, it came as no surprise. The unscrupulous way he tried to force us out was only one of his nasty faults—and not even his worst one at that."

"What do you mean, John?"

John looked from Octavia to Brett and back again. He shifted uncomfortably on his feet. "I shouldn't have said anything. Forget it."

"I can't forget it, John. You did say something."

"I can't tell you, Octavia. Doctor-patient privilege."

"You were Dole Scroogen's eye doctor?" Octavia asked.

"No, nothing like that."

"Well then, how can you be bound by the doctor-patient privilege?"

"I became privy to the information I hold because of my close association with another ophthalmologist."

"Your son?"

"Yes," John admitted. "It's Lloyd's doctor-patient privilege that would be compromised were I to speak. I'm sure you understand why I cannot."

"Could you use some legal advice on the matter?"

"Legal advice? I don't follow you, Octavia."

"John, do you have two dollars on you?"

"Yes. Why?"

"Give me one and Brett one and, for the next five minutes, consider yourself our client. That way, anything you tell us will fall under the attorney-client privilege, and if there are any legal steps you should be taking, we can advise you."

"Octavia, I'm not sure—"

"John, if we don't know everything, we can't help Mab. What you could tell us might be crucial. Please."

"This is legal?"

"As long as we are told this information while we're acting as your attorneys, we can never repeat what you tell us on pain of disbarment. Plus which, if we did reveal what you tell us, it would be inadmissible evidence in any court of law. And I promise that Brett and I will turn around and donate the dollar you give us to the fund to save the community center."

John looked uncertainly from Octavia to Brett. "Even under this privilege umbrella, I'm not sure I'm comfortable discussing this with you, Mr. Merlin."

"I'm after the truth, John. Whatever it is."

"Are you sure you can handle it?"

"I'm sure I can handle nothing less," Brett replied without hesitation.

John studied Brett's face for a moment before nodding and reaching into his pocket.

"All right. It will feel good getting this off my chest, if nothing else. Here's the money."

As soon as Octavia and Brett pocketed their respective dollar bills, Octavia looked up at the clock. "The five minutes begins now."

John leaned his back against the closed door and adjusted the white silk ascot around his clean-shaven neck.

"Two days before Scroogen's death, his wife brought their daughter, Katlyn, in to see my son. The child had multiple retinal hemorrhages in both eyes."

"What is the significance of that?" Octavia asked.

"Ophthalmologists can recognize certain patterns in blood vessel breakage in the eyes of children. There was only one explanation for the pattern in that child's eyes. This girl had been shaken hard, viciously hard. She had ugly bruises on both her forearms where someone had grasped her."

"Who?" Brett asked, coming instantly to his feet, his hands balling into fists by his side. Octavia could feel the room suddenly heating with his anger.

"Nancy Scroogen gave Lloyd this story about how she looked into the backyard that morning where Katlyn was playing just in time to see a big kid she didn't recognize running away. She went out to check on Katlyn and found her crying. Nancy said Katlyn told her the boy roughed her up and smashed her toys."

"But you don't think Nancy Scroogen was telling the truth?" Octavia asked.

"Once Nancy learned the injury to her daughter's eyes was not permanent, her biggest concern became that Lloyd not ask Katlyn any questions. She said the incident had already been too upsetting for her child. Lloyd had the feeling that the only reason Nancy didn't want him asking Katlyn any questions was because the girl would have given him a different story. Lloyd didn't believe the bruises on Katlyn's arms were made by any kid.''

"When a doctor suspects child abuse he's supposed to report it,'' Octavia said. "Why didn't your son contact the police?''

"Because no matter what Lloyd suspected, he couldn't prove it. There were no documented previous episodes of injury. Contacting the authorities would have been futile.''

"Who does Lloyd suspect really injured Katlyn?'' Brett asked.

"Nancy could have fabricated that story to protect any family member—even herself,'' John said. "But from the temper I saw Dole display, I say the most likely suspect was Katlyn's father. Personally, I'm glad Mab whacked him. I only wished she'd done it harder.''

"THERE IS NOTHING MORE despicable than someone who abuses a child,'' Octavia said as soon as they were back in Brett's car, unable to keep the heat of anger out of her tone. "You didn't notice her bloodshot eyes?''

"I haven't seen Katlyn for several days,'' Brett said. "I've been too busy working for that father of hers.''

"Where are you heading?''

"To talk to Nancy. To find out who did it.''

"Brett, you know you can't mention anything about this to your aunt. The attorney-client privilege prevents you. I'm surprised—no shocked—that you would even consider it.''

He found a chuckle at the scold in her voice.

"I have no intention of mentioning John or anything I learned in his privileged communication.''

"Then how are you going to question Nancy?''

"I'm about to buy my little cousin a pretty party dress for Christmas. One with no sleeves. You can help me pick it out. Then when she puts it on to show me, I'll have a perfect opening to ask why she has bruises on her arms.''

"Very devious. I'm impressed.''

Brett smiled.

The car phone rang and Brett picked up the line.

"Brett, it's Ned Nordix from the Archaeology and Historical Preservation Department."

Brett lost his smile. He had forgotten all about the stone carving until this very moment—and all about its eventual tie-in to Octavia.

"Yes, Ned," he said, his mouth suddenly dry.

"I'm at the excavation site. Can you swing by? I think you're going to want to see and hear this firsthand."

Brett was sure he didn't. His eyes darted over to Octavia. "I suppose I could be there in a few minutes."

"Good. I'll be waiting."

Brett hung up the phone. "I'm detouring to the construction site next to the community center. Ned Nordix has something he wants to discuss with me. Octavia..."

The words stalled on his lips.

She was looking at him. Directly. "Yes?"

Brett took a deep breath and let it out, very slowly, very carefully. His hands wrapped tightly around the steering wheel. He returned his eyes to the road.

"Earlier you said you were glad we were on the same side. Just because I don't believe your grandmother attacked my uncle, that doesn't change our other...differences. I must abide by the law. And you must be held accountable for your actions."

He waited. She said nothing. Damn it, he needed her to say something.

He took the next corner so fast the tires squealed.

"Octavia, I can't protect you."

"You mean you won't. Why don't you drop me at the body shop on your way to the excavation site," she said. "They've agreed to provide me with a vehicle with a phone while I'm waiting for them to fix my car."

Brett's teeth were clenched. For some reason he couldn't seem to unclench them.

"Are you afraid of my driving or afraid of being confronted with what they've found at that site?"

"Running from fear only gives it time to grow."

"Then why did you suggest I drop you off?"

Her voice was perfectly mellow, maddeningly calm. "Because they said the loner car would be ready about now."

Brett pulled the Bentley over to the curb, shoved on the break and swiveled to face her.

"Damn it, Octavia. Don't you understand? I'm afraid for you."

She smiled as she stroked his cheek lightly with the tips of her fingers.

"Thank you for that."

He captured her hand in his and drew her into his arms, kissing those fingertips, then her hair, her forehead, her nose and finally her lips. As always she sighed and melted into him.

He could feel the hunger growing inside him—so wild, so witless. She was so much the exciting woman he wanted and so much the reckless woman he knew he must never have.

When he finally forced himself to pull back, he was breathing far too hard and she was smiling far too much.

"Something to remember me by when I'm in stripes breaking rocks?" she had the nerve to ask.

He rested his forehead against hers and groaned. "I don't know what to do with you."

She laughed, a full-bodied, happy laugh that danced down his spine.

He pulled back, exhaling in total frustration as he swiveled to face front.

"I'll drop you off at the body shop," he said through clenched teeth. "Then when they slap the handcuffs on, at least I won't have to be there to see it."

"Chicken," she said all too sweetly as she settled back, perfectly poised and self-possessed.

Brett's foot punched down on the accelerator. She was crazy—totally crazy. And he was crazy wanting her like this. And so damn close to taking her that his hands were shaking.

But he was not going to do it. He was not going to fall for a felon. Not as long as there was one ounce of sense still inside his skull.

"BRETT, OVER HERE," Ned Nordix called as he waved Brett to another part of the excavation site.

"You moved the stone," Brett said as he walked up.

"Yes. That's what I wanted to show you. Dr. Watson Pacer finally gave us the okay this morning to lift it out."

The icy rain that had begun as a mere drizzle only moments before started to slice down on them in earnest. Brett and Ned stood beneath it, Brett staring at the large stone slab as the ice crystals branded its face, and his.

"There's the bottom portion that was obscured by the dirt," Ned pointed out. "See? It contains two more full lines of images, all different from the ones above it."

"And as unreadable as the others?"

"So far. But progress has been made. That's why I called. Dr. Pacer and the team said that the stone definitely had been moved to the construction site recently."

Brett took a deep breath and shuddered, but not from the freezing air.

"Unfortunately, the construction crew wasn't too careful when they lifted the stone," Ned explained, "so the team will never really know for certain when it was brought here. They can only make a guess."

"Where is the team now?"

"Left. Not much more they can do now. I'm just waiting for a security guard to arrive. I'd better get a tarp and cover it."

"Yes, best to keep the evidence dry," Brett muttered.

"What?" Ned asked.

"Nothing."

Ned led the way to a makeshift tent that had been erected on the construction site and slipped inside. He was out a moment later with a folded blue plastic tarp in his hands. Together they spread it over the stone.

The rain was coming down in stabbing sheets now. As soon as the stone was covered, Ned beckoned Brett back into the shelter of the tent.

"Damn, it's freezing," Ned said once they had scurried inside. "There's coffee left. Want a cup?"

Brett nodded. He cradled the hot mug in his hands, wishing there was a way to melt the icy-cold certainty of impending disaster that had settled in his stomach.

He forced a lightness into his tone he definitely wasn't feeling. "So, Ned, what did the team find, a Made in Taiwan stamp on the back of the thing?"

Ned laughed. "Would have made determining who carved it a lot easier, that's for certain."

"They didn't find anything beneath it, did they?"

Ned swallowed a sip of coffee. "They don't know yet. Whoever moved the stone to this site might have buried something beneath it. The team plans to be back in the morning and start excavating, unless the weatherman is right and this ice storm changes into snow. If that happens, I'm afraid we won't be getting answers anytime soon."

"Why are they even bothering now that they know the stone was planted here?" Brett asked.

"Why are they even bothering? Brett, they have to have all the answers if they expect to make a decent report."

And prolong the agony of the inevitable, Brett thought.

"So how long will it take for them to make this decent report?" he said aloud.

"Weeks, hell, maybe even months. These people are sticklers for uncovering every fact."

"Weeks? Months? Ned, it was planted here. That's all they need to report."

"But I told you, Brett. They don't know when. Or by whom."

"I know."

"You know? How can you know? Four different scientists—the top in their field—don't agree on its antiquity or origin, and you're standing there telling me *you* know?"

Brett shook his head in confusion at Ned's words, certain the rain must have frozen his brain.

"What do you mean they don't agree on its antiquity or origin?"

"Some think it was carved twenty-eight thousand years ago. Others, only eighteen thousand years ago. That's a pretty wide spread. Of course, they still haven't the faintest idea who brought it here or when. That's why Dr. Pacer approved moving the stone. The team will now sift through the dirt beneath to see what they might find. Although no one has been able to read the markings, they hope that the sun sign does mean a grave is below."

"Wait a minute," Brett interrupted. "Am I hearing you right? Are you saying this stone carving is 'real'—as in, really made by ancient Indians?"

"Well, of course it's real. At least the experts have been able to agree on that. Brett, you look surprised. Did I forget to mention that?"

Chapter Ten

"I have some preliminary information that ties one of your three suspects to Scroogen," A.J.'s voice said on the other end of the telephone line.

Octavia took off an enormous, Christmas-tree-shaped rhinestone earring in order to position the car-phone's receiver closer to her ear. "Which one, A.J.?"

"Constance Kope owned one of the small houses on the same block as the community center. Scroogen bought it from her six months ago way below market rate. It was right after Constance's husband died. It seems Constance had to sell quickly in order to pay the doctor and hospital bills that had accumulated while her husband was ill. Scroogen took advantage."

Octavia's windshield wipers were having a hard time keeping up with the icy rain that stuck like sludge to the glass. The twinkling lights, twisted tinsel and silver bells of the Christmas decorations strewn across the traffic lights were swaying in the wind, blurred by the wetness. She kept a careful watch at the slick street in front of her as she considered A.J.'s words.

"Does Constance know Scroogen took advantage of her?" she asked after a moment.

"She couldn't help but know. Even the real estate agent told her to hold out for a better offer, but she was desperate to pay off those bills to retain her good credit rating. Definitely an old-fashioned lady. She's living in a tiny rented apartment now, trying to make ends meet on social security. Since your grandmother is staying with her, I assume you have the address.''

"Yes. Matter of fact, I'm on my way there now. Anything on John Winslow or Douglas Twitch?''

"Douglas seems clean. I have one of my people down in California looking into John's past. His wife died of an overdose of a pain reliever. She had terminal cancer. The police suspected John assisted in her demise. I really don't think it has anything to do with current events, but we'll keep digging. Zane Coltrane and his people are crossing our tracks a lot. You don't mind that we're duplicating effort?''

"Coltrane works for Merlin, and his concern is to find out who attacked his uncle. My concern is to clear my grandmother. Our intents are different and so could be the interpretation of our information.''

"I hear you. By the way, Coltrane's best female operatives have cozied up to every man you've ever dated or even known. They're after a connection between you and that stone carving.''

"How did you find this out, A.J.?''

"I put people on Coltrane's people.''

Octavia chuckled at the image of one P.I. shadowing another. "Now, why would you do that?'' she asked.

"Christmas time is always our off season. Most of my team are loners by profession and preference. With no family to spend the holidays with, they prefer to be working. Watching Coltrane and his team without getting caught keeps them on their toes.''

"Do me a favor, A.J. There's someone I would just as soon your competition doesn't find.''

"Who is it?''

"Gordon Twobrook.''

"I thought I knew all the men in your past, and that name doesn't sound familiar.''

"I'm glad it doesn't. There are only two other people who know about him. One won't talk because she's my grandmother, and Adam can't talk without violating the attorney-client privilege. But if by some fluke Coltrane's operatives—''

"Get anywhere near someone named Gordon Two-brook, I'll let you know," A.J. said, accurately finishing Octavia's sentence. "By the way, I figured turnabout was fair play and assigned someone to check out Merlin's personal affairs."

"Learn anything yet?"

"He's made a lot of money and has recently sunk most of it into a four million dollar, fifty-carat blue-white diamond called Midnight Magic. He outbid a lot of other people to get it."

"Hmm, that's interesting. How about women?"

"He's ultrasecretive about that part of his life. There must be a reason for it. I'll let you know when I find out what it is. By the way, are you aware his Bentley has been following you since you left the body shop a few minutes ago?"

Octavia glanced over at her rearview mirror to see the trailing headlights. "No, I wasn't. How did *you* know?"

"It's why I get the big bucks. Talk to you soon."

Octavia smiled as she hung up the phone. As familiar as she was with A.J.'s abilities, the lady still continued to impress her. Octavia turned up the next street and pulled over to the curb in front of Constance Kope's apartment house. She got out of the car and waited on the sidewalk, her umbrella shielding her against the sleet as Brett made his way over to her.

"Ned Nordix tells me that stone carving is real," he said immediately upon reaching her.

"Is it?" she said, using her sweetest tone. "How nice."

The driving rain formed rivulets down his furrowed brow. He looked like an angry thundercloud himself, one about to burst.

She decided to give him a break and led the way into the lobby of Constance's modest apartment house. Pinecones tied to red ribbons added a touch of holiday cheer to the faded walls. Once out of the wind and rain, Octavia folded her umbrella, and her arms, and then faced Brett.

"So what's the problem?" she asked.

"You deliberately led me to believe that stone carving was a fake."

"If you think back, I'm sure you will remember that not once did I ever venture an opinion as to whether that stone carving was real."

"You told me you would risk your license, even your freedom, for your grandmother. You can't deny that."

"And you took my words to mean what? That I stayed up all night to chisel that stone carving? You should be happy to discover I didn't."

"Octavia, I'm no fool. There was nothing coincidental about that stone carving suddenly appearing at that construction site."

She smiled. "Wasn't there?"

"The only possible explanation is that you secured that stone carving from somewhere and planted it there."

She stepped closer and gazed up into his scowl. He had such a wonderfully dangerous look in his quicksilver eyes.

She was playing with fire and she knew it. Fire could burn. But it could also generate a hell of a lot of heat. And she loved the feel of this man's heat.

"So that's why you're upset, Brett. I'm not behind bars yet. Are you so afraid of my being free? Am I that much of a threat to society? Or am I that much of a threat to you?"

For a moment she waited breathlessly as she watched the silver sparks igniting within his black-rimmed eyes.

Then he groaned and pulled her into his arms. His skin was icy wet from the rain, but his mouth was very hot and very hard and so was the rest of his body pressed suddenly so closely against hers.

His touch shot through her like a lightning bolt. She shook and tingled, a sweet ache opening deep inside her. His smoky scent surrounded her and held her captive in a velvet fog.

There was no mistaking his want of her. Or her want of him. She had never felt this aroused by a man before.

Was it the continuing risk he represented? She didn't know. She didn't care. She wanted and that was enough.

When he finally released her lips, she rested her cheek against the racing pulse in his throat and sighed as its heated throb beat inside her blood.

He held her strongly to him while he swore very softly in her ear, expertly enunciating every expletive. He even cursed like a gentleman.

She chuckled, happy to find this continuing evidence of that refined core inside him that appealed to her so much. What a waste it was for such a man as this to be so out of touch with his heart!

It seemed like a very long time before she felt her pulse and his slowing to anything approaching normal.

She leaned back, out of his arms, and reached for one of his hands, slipping both of hers into it.

"I was just heading up to Constance's place to have dinner with her and Mab. There'll be plenty for you, too. And I've found out something about Constance that is worth investigating."

"That business about her selling her home to Scroogen way below market price?"

"Zane Coltrane strikes again, I see. Come on. Since you know, too, you can help me ask her the right questions."

They climbed two flights to reach apartment 340. Constance answered Octavia's knock and greeted them both with a big smile. Octavia performed the formal introductions, although Brett and Constance had seen each other before.

"I've heard a lot of good things about you lately, Mr. Merlin," Constance said as she took Octavia's rain cape and umbrella and Brett's overcoat to deposit in the hall closet. "Mab very much appreciates your help."

"You don't mind my dropping in unannounced?" Brett asked.

"No, not at all. Mab has been preparing enough loin of veal with roasted garlic and Dijon mushroom gravy to feed the neighborhood."

"Hmm. Smells heavenly," Octavia said as she followed her nose into the kitchen where Mab stood over the stove stirring something in a gravy pan.

"Hi, Mab. I brought Brett for dinner, too."

"Good. Now, get out of here, I need to concentrate. This is at a very critical stage."

Octavia obediently left, closing the kitchen door behind her. She joined Brett seated on the small couch. His imposing size made it look like it had been designed for Munchkins. She brushed up against him as she made herself comfortable, her body tingling at the touch.

As she leaned back, she decided that Constance Kope's apartment was much like the little lady herself—tiny and tidy.

But despite the smallness of the place and its furniture, it was warm and bright with the glistening bulbs of a corner Christmas tree reflecting its bubbling lights. From the old-fashioned radio on a corner table, Nat King Cole's voice rung out, singing about Jack Frost nipping at a nose. It was a cozy, comfortable room and a welcome respite from the freezing air and rain outside.

Constance was seated in what looked like her favorite chair—swaying back and forward on its well-worn rockers, her hands busy knitting Christmas squares.

"Mab won't even let you in your own kitchen, will she?" Octavia asked.

Constance smiled. "No."

"She's that way with me, too, when she comes to my place," Octavia admitted.

"She accused me of trying to poison her the first night when I opened a can of hash," Constance said. "Since then, she's been buying and cooking all the food. But I can't say I've minded. She's wonderful in the kitchen, as you must know. I've never been much of a cook. I loved to clean, my husband loved to cook, we both loved to design. We were never blessed with children, but we were blessed with each other."

"How long ago did your husband pass away?" Brett asked.

Constance's eyes veered to the picture sitting on the table next to the radio. It was of a young smiling couple, clearly her and her husband in their early years of marriage. It was a moment before she looked back at Brett and answered.

"Several months ago. It was a blessing. He was sick for many years."

Octavia shifted her position on the couch to more fully face their hostess. Brett had gotten the conversation steered into the right direction. It was time for her to zero in on what they needed to know.

"Long illnesses like that have a way of eating up savings, don't they?"

Constance answered as she continued to rock and knit. "So many of the newer procedures aren't covered. Most are still considered experimental. They're so expensive. Of course, you feel the need to try everything, even though there is a part of you that knows nothing will work."

"I understand that after your husband passed on, you were forced to sell your home to Scroogen at below market rate," Octavia said as gently as she was able.

Constance suddenly stopped rocking and knitting and leaned forward until she was on the edge of her chair. Her glasses slipped on her tiny nose. She pushed them back.

"How did you know that?"

"The real estate agent spoke of it, Constance."

"He had no right."

"He was upset for you. He didn't appreciate the fact that Scroogen took advantage of your position. You knew Scroogen did, didn't you?"

"Please, don't tell Mab."

"Why, Constance? This is not your shame. It's Scroogen's."

Constance looked uneasily at the closed door to the kitchen. She grasped her knitting needles tightly.

"It is my shame."

"Are you embarrassed because of your financial diffi-culties? You must know that at least half of the members of the Silver Power League are relying solely on their social se-curity checks to make ends meet?"

"I paid off the bills. My credit rating is good. I'm proud I've managed within my means."

"Then what concerns you?"

Constance's eyes once again darted to the kitchen door. She lowered her voice, remaining on the edge of her seat.

"When I had to put my home on the market to meet my bills six months ago, I was very sensitive about it."

"I'm sure that was only natural."

"Listen to what I'm saying, Octavia. *Six months ago* I found out what kind of a man Scroogen was. I knew he was our new landlord at the community center. I knew I should warn Mab and the others what he was like. If they had known sooner—"

"It probably wouldn't have made any difference, Con-stance," Octavia said. "The building was already under-way. They couldn't stop in the middle. Besides, you couldn't have been sure what Scroogen had in mind for the commu-nity center. He might have lived up to his great aunt's wishes and let the seniors stay."

"No, I knew he wasn't going to. You would have known it, too, if you had seen his eyes the day he took my house from me."

"What do you mean?"

Constance's right hand suddenly grasped her knitting needle like it was a knife.

"He liked doing it, Octavia. He liked trading in on my distress. He was an evil man. I'm glad he's dead. Very glad."

Octavia was chilled at the tiny woman's suddenly stiff posture, at how she held that knitting needle, at how she said those words with such relief and such relish.

"Were you the one who attacked him?" Brett asked.

Constance slowly released her tight hold on the knitting needle. Her body relaxed back into her chair. She rocked.

"Attacked him? Me? Heavens, no. What a thought."

"Have you ever let your key to the greenhouse store-room out of your sight?"

"Never. It's right here in my purse."

Constance leaned over, picked up her purse and produced the distinctive silver-plated key for Octavia and Brett to see.

"Where were you when Scroogen was attacked?"

"At the community center."

"Did anyone see you?"

"I think John was there then. Or maybe Douglas. One of them came later."

"Who do you think attacked Scroogen?"

"Mab's the only one of us with that kind of courage."

The doorbell rang and Constance rose to get it. She returned to the dining room with Sergeant Patterson on her heels.

"Good evening, Mr. Merlin," Patterson said. He then nodded at Octavia. "Ms. Osborne. I'm looking for your grandmother."

"I'm right here," Mab said as she stepped out of the kitchen with a large steaming serving dish in her hands. She headed toward the dining room table.

"Dinner is ready, everyone," she called.

"Ma'am, I'm afraid there isn't time for dinner," Patterson said. "I need you to accompany me downtown."

"Now, wait a minute," Octavia said, immediately rising to her feet. "What's this all about?"

Before Sergeant Patterson could answer, Mab moved into the living room and planted herself in front of the detective.

"Ronald Scroogen was lying about seeing me attack his father. If you question him closely, I know you'll find that out for yourself."

"That's not necessary, Mrs. Osborne," Patterson said. "Ronald Scroogen came into the office this afternoon and recanted his statement. He wasn't even near the parking lot when his father was attacked. He was miles away meeting with an employee at a job site. The assault charge against you has been dropped."

"Well, thank heavens," Mab said.

Octavia wasn't so sure heaven deserved that thanks yet. She didn't like the somber look on the detective's face.

"If the assault charge has been dropped as you say, why does my grandmother have to go downtown with you?"

"Because this time," Sergeant Patterson said, "I'm arresting her for murder."

Chapter Eleven

Brett walked up to Octavia in the hallway at the police station. Her face was composed, her posture poised, but there was an unusual quickness about her movements and an uncharacteristic pacing that spoke of her inner agitation.

She turned to greet him. "Did you find out about the evidence against her?"

Brett gestured toward the nearby wooden bench. Octavia refused the offer of a seat with a swift shake of her head.

Yes, she was worried all right. Very worried. Which didn't make what he had to tell her any easier.

"The toxicology results came in on cause of death, Octavia. Dole died from monkshood poisoning."

"Monkshood is a poisonous plant. Patterson can't think Mab fed him a poisonous plant?"

"The plant's poison got into his bloodstream when Dole was struck on the back of the shoulder with the cultivator. The Seattle lab found aconitine and aconine from monkshood on the prongs, along with some of Dole's blood. And the only fingerprints on that gardening tool are Mab's."

"So that seemingly superficial attack *was* the cause of his death. This is incredible."

"There's more. The threatening letters that Dole received over the last couple of weeks have definitely been determined to have been prepared on Silver Power League stationery."

"You can't tell me Mab's fingerprints are on that paper."

"No, just Dole's. The police have concluded that whoever prepared the letters wore gloves. Naturally, they also have concluded that person was Mab since the stationery was kept in the supply room at the back of the greenhouse and she had a key."

"And so did three other people."

"I told Patterson that. But he's not particularly interested in pursuing that lead."

Octavia tossed her head, her eyes flashing. Both actions belied the continuing mellowness of her tone.

"Of course not. Why should he ruin his case against my grandmother by trying to find the real culprit?"

Brett took her hands into his. "Octavia, we'll get to the bottom of this."

She gave his hands a quick squeeze, a signal to him that despite her distress, she was dealing with it.

"Thanks, Brett. It's obvious that the same person who sent those threatening letters has to be the same person who stole Mab's cultivator and struck Scroogen with it. That person couldn't get Mab's prints on the paper, but he or she knew Mab's prints would be on her gardening tool."

"Possibly, but how did this person know Mab would take the cultivator to the greenhouse and put it in the storeroom?"

"Maybe he or she didn't. Maybe the perpetrator just went in there to get the stationery, nosed around, found Mab's cultivator and decided to use it as the murder weapon."

"I suppose it could have happened that way."

"It's the only scenario that makes sense."

"There's something else you should know, Octavia."

"What?"

"Since those threatening letters promised harm to Dole if he didn't cease his takeover of the senior's community center, and since grievous harm was subsequently done, the prosecuting attorney is going for premeditation."

"You mean the charge will be murder in the *first* degree?"

"Yes."

Octavia released Brett's hands and sank to the bench. Her shoulders were too stiffly erect, her gaze too fixed. Brett understood she was benumbed by the blow of that last bit of news.

After a moment she sighed. "I had a hard-enough time believing one of her friends was setting her up for an assault charge. But now she's being framed for first degree murder."

Brett sat beside Octavia. He said nothing. Uttering empty assurances that things would be all right had never been his style. He was a man who went out and made things right—if they could be made right.

He pulled some photocopied sheets out of his pocket.

"Patterson gave me copies of the threatening letters Dole received. Maybe they can tell us something."

Octavia took the three photocopied letters from his hand, unfolded them and studied them critically.

"The words have been cut out of newspapers or magazines and pasted onto the sheet. Were the envelopes like this?"

"Photocopies of Dole's business card were pasted to them."

"*Give us the land or you will pay,*" Octavia read aloud, then shifted pages. "*Hand everything over to us or else.*" She flipped to the third note and read, "*You had your chance. Now we take our vengeance.*"

She folded the short notes and handed them back to Brett.

"They sound like bad dialogue from some B-rated Zorro movie. The seniors have never suggested they be given the land, to my knowledge. Only that they not be charged an exorbitant rent designed to force them out."

"Well, one of them obviously thought otherwise. The envelopes and stationery are those made especially for the Silver Power League. And the only people who had access to that stationery are the people who have access to that storage room at the back of the greenhouse.''

"So they had to have been prepared by one of the other members of the executive committee of the Silver Power League."

"The police are satisfied they have the guilty party in custody, Octavia. If we don't find the real person responsible, it will be tough to prove Mab innocent with the kind of evidence they have against her."

Octavia nodded but said nothing this time.

"Is Mab in there being booked?" Brett asked.

"Yes."

"Has Patterson told you what will happen to her after she's been processed?"

"A policewoman will be taking her directly to a nearby hotel room for the night. She'll be arraigned tomorrow at eleven."

"Then there's nothing more we can do for her here. Come on, Octavia. There's one member of the Silver Power League's executive committee we've yet to talk to. Let's go pay a call on Douglas Twitch."

DOUGLAS TWITCH'S HOME caught Octavia completely by surprise. It was a turn-of-the-century, tastefully restored, Victorian estate with a full-size orchard, an honest-to-goodness turret and an astonishing array of lovely antique Christmas angels flying off the walls in the entry hall and formal front parlor.

Douglas met them in that parlor a few moments after a housekeeper had shown them there. He was dressed as usual in scuffed boots, old jeans and a checkered shirt, the latter two hanging off his rawboned body.

Octavia saw him plop down in the middle of a beautiful brocade love seat, two ancient ceramic Christmas angels adorning the end tables on either side of him. The man looked as out of place in that Victorian parlor as a Jackson Pollock painting on a wall full of Rembrandt's.

"I heard about Mab," he said. "Constance called a few minutes ago. What can I do to help?"

"Talk to us about Scroogen," Octavia said. "What did you know about him?"

"What everyone knew. He was scum."

"Had you ever had any dealings with him before his attempt to take over the community center?"

"Never even met him until he became our landlord."

"But we knew of him," said a voice from the doorway.

Octavia swiveled around to see a very slender elderly woman with paper-thin white skin. She wore a high-neck, floor-length light blue dress with an old-fashioned fitted waist. Her light silver hair was drawn tightly into a tidy bun. This woman fit this home like Douglas Twitch never would.

Her eyes were strong and mobile, darting between Octavia and Brett. Their agility was far at odds with the bent condition of her elderly spine and the stiffness with which she grasped the cane in her right hand.

Douglas immediately jumped up and went over to her. Slowly, and with obvious care, he helped her to the couch. Once he had her propped up with pillows, he gestured toward them.

"This is Mab Osborne's granddaughter, Octavia. And this is Brett Merlin who is trying to help Mab fight the charges against her. This is my wife, Edith."

Octavia liked the proud quality that suddenly effused Douglas's gruff, grating voice as he introduced his wife. Despite the fact that the two seemed from different worlds, the warmth in Douglas's tone told Octavia of the feelings that had built the bridge between them.

"We don't get many guests," Edith Twitch said. "Douglas thinks they tire me too much. But now that I have difficulty getting to the center, I do so enjoy company coming by. Have you offered our guests refreshments?"

"Thank you, we don't care for anything," Octavia said quickly, speaking for them both. She didn't want the obviously frail Edith Twitch to feel the obligations of a hostess.

"But we could use some information, Mrs. Twitch," Brett immediately added. "A moment ago you said something about having heard of Dole Scroogen before meeting him. Would you explain what you meant?"

"Our sons told us, Mr. Merlin. They're in the septic system business, as was Scroogen, only they service customers in Mason County. But even from that distance, our boys heard how Scroogen cheated his competition here in Kitsap County."

"It's been going on for more than ten years now," Douglas said. "The guy was really underhanded about it, too."

"Can you give me an example?" Brett asked.

"Plenty," Douglas said. "When Scroogen knew another septic company was bidding on a job he wanted, he'd have his workmen call up the prospective customer and pretend to be previous dissatisfied customers of his competition. Or he'd call up the competition and pretend to be the customer, telling them not to come because he'd changed his mind."

"And when the septic company didn't show up, Scroogen's people would," Edith said.

"Yeah," Douglas said. "The guy played real dirty."

Octavia sat forward. "Douglas, if you knew this about Scroogen, why didn't you warn the other members of the Silver Power League when you found out he was your landlord?"

"I knew he was cutthroat in business. But that was business. I didn't know he would go against his great aunt's wishes concerning the community center."

"Why not?" Octavia asked.

"Some men are real bastards in business, but honorable to family and friends. I thought that was the story with Scroogen."

"But you did have other thoughts at first, dear," Edith reminded him.

"Yeah, when I first heard, I said something like we'd better watch out for him."

"Who did you say this to?" Brett asked.

"Just John, I think. But then the months went by and Scroogen never contacted us about increasing the rent so I stopped worrying. It threw me as much as anybody when he showed up at our open house with that damn appraiser."

"You must have been pretty angry," Brett said.

"I was steaming. Like everyone else. But that night he deliberately severed the sewer pipe and flooded the center, well, I've got to tell you that's the night I really wanted to kill him."

"Did you?" Octavia asked in an even, conversational tone.

Douglas shifted uneasily on the sofa. "No."

"You hesitated before saying no," Brett observed. "Why?"

"Maybe because I wish it had been me who smacked him in the face. And maybe because I wish it had been me to go after him the next day like Mab did."

Octavia and Brett exchanged glances. No use asking Douglas who he thought did it.

"Have you ever loaned your key to the greenhouse's storeroom to anyone?" Brett asked.

"Never. It's right here on my key chain." He pulled it out to show them the distinctive silver-plated key. "Hasn't left my pocket since the day I ordered the lock and had the keys made with the Do Not Duplicate caution on them several months ago."

"And the only members of the Silver Power League with a key are the executive committee?" Brett asked.

"Yeah."

"Where were you when Scroogen was being attacked in that parking lot?"

"At the community center waiting for my boys to arrive to pump it out."

"Did you see John and Constance there?"

"Like I told the police, I don't remember when they arrived. Look, I know things are looking bad for Mab. She was only trying to do us all a favor by getting rid of Scroogen. If there's anything I can do..."

"EVEN HER FRIENDS THINK she's guilty," Octavia lamented as soon as they had dashed up Mab's stairs through the heavy wind and downpour and stood within the protection of the back porch, shedding their rain gear.

"Remember, Octavia. One of these so-called friends is really the murderer. And a very clever liar."

"Which one do you think it is?"

"At the moment I'm leaning toward Constance."

"Really? Why?"

"Because of all of them she's the only one I can picture creeping up behind Scroogen, knocking him to the ground and whacking him on the back."

Octavia flipped on the light as she stepped inside the kitchen, setting her purse and gloves on the counter.

"And Constance's motive?" she asked.

"Scroogen cheated her when she had to sell her home. Then he tried to take the community center she'd designed away from her and the seniors. Constance has no home, no husband, no children. The center and the seniors are all she has left. And with the condo complex going up and the expected changes in the neighborhood, she may even be forced out of that small apartment she's tried to make a home."

The lights started to flicker. Octavia reached into a kitchen drawer and brought out a flashlight. She set it on the counter in easy reach as she picked up a teakettle. The rain pounded above them, the wind howled and the walls reverberated with the sound of tree branches beating at the house.

"So now you admit that Scroogen's condominium complex would ruin the seniors' neighborhood?"

Brett leaned against the counter. "The impact of the condominium complex wasn't the point of law at issue, Octavia."

She filled the kettle with water before turning back to him.

"But it was the real point, Brett."

"Not for an attorney."

She set the kettle on the stove and faced him. "It might interest you to know that after long years of study, my parents found the best gauge of happiness among primitive tribe members was *not* how closely those tribe members followed their laws, but how closely committed they were to their families."

"Yes, but how successful were these individual tribe members in modern terms?"

"Modern terms? Brett, if finding happiness in life is not success in any terms, what is?"

Damn, she used tricky arguments. Way too tricky.

Still, he wished he could believe what those words implied and what he saw in her eyes. He wished he could believe that acting on what he was feeling for her would not lead to disaster.

But he knew better than to believe in wishes.

"The house is a little chilly what with just the tarps strewn over the roof to keep out the elements," she said, "but if you'd care to stay, I can whip something up for us to eat to make up for that veal dinner we missed."

He wanted to stay. God, how he wanted to stay!

"No, it's getting late," he said, stepping backward, determined to resist the overwhelming temptation she represented.

He turned and started steadfastly for the door. He never made it.

Because just then, a sudden flash of lightning shot all around them, a thunderous roar shattered his eardrums, and the roof toppled onto his head.

Chapter Twelve

"Octavia, wake up."

Octavia opened her eyes to see Brett's face, faint and blurry, disembodied, wavering above her as though through a mist. An eerie whistling rushed in with the wind that cooled her cheeks. The floorboards groaned beneath her.

She was on the floor? She blinked, fighting disorientation as sights and sounds refused to make sense.

"Octavia, talk to me."

She tried to get his features into focus, wondering why his voice sounded worried, wondering why the light was so dim, wondering so many things and finding answers to none of them.

"Octavia? Are you all right?"

His tone had become most insistent. She moved her head, arms, legs. Her body felt bruised and battered, but responded. The faint light around her quivered. She began to realize that Brett's features were dark and blurry and disembodied because she was seeing them through the beam of a weak flashlight.

"I'm okay," she answered finally, her throat dry and scratchy.

She raised her head and shoulders only to find she was caught under a couple of heavy structural beams criss-crossed over her middle—forming a gigantic letter X over her body. Fortunately, they pinned her in place by position, not by weight. She wove her hands into the small space separating the beams from her shoulders and pushed up with all her strength. They didn't budge. Her effort disturbed some plaster dust. She sneezed.

"They're too heavy to lift," Brett said, indicating that he, too, had tried.

"What happened?" Octavia asked.

"The roof fell in. Maybe from the lightning strike. Or maybe from the heavy wind weakening the remaining supporting beams. You're sure you're not hurt?"

"Just shaken up a bit."

Octavia started at a crashing sound from somewhere in the house. "What was that?"

"The rest of the house falling down," Brett said. "We have to get you out of here—and quickly—before what's left of these walls go. "I'll call for help from the car. I'll leave you the flashlight."

"No, Brett. Don't go."

He reached through the small opening between the crossing beams and touched her shoulder in a gesture of comfort. "It's all right, Octavia. I promise I won't be long."

"Brett, I'm neither afraid to be left alone nor am I getting hysterical on you. What I meant was that you don't have to call for help. At least not yet. I'd like to see if I can get out of here by myself first."

He withdrew his hand.

"Octavia, I've already tried to lift those beams. I nearly brought the rest of the walls down in the process. What's left of the structure will need to be braced before it's tried again."

Octavia had already slipped her feet out of her shoes and was wiggling out of her skirt in the small space left for her to maneuver beneath the constricting beams.

"I was thinking of trying something different."

"Different?" Brett repeated, clearly sounding confused.

"Give me a moment and I'll show you."

She let her body go limp then and concentrated on her breathing and her focus. She closed her eyes, blotting out the vibrating floorboards beneath her, the whistling of the wind through the broken windowpanes all around her, even Brett's worried brow above her.

When she was ready, she opened her eyes and slowly wove her elbows onto the beams above her, using them for leverage. Then she began to lift herself up and through the small opening between them.

It was more than a tight fit. Without a trained body, it would have been no fit at all. As it was, it took several minutes of strict concentration and considerable sweat. But when it was all over, she rested triumphantly crosslegged on top of the beams, free of their confinement.

"What was that?" Brett asked in a voice full of surprise, the weak flashlight beam in his hand scanning her head to toe.

"Yoga," Octavia answered with a smile. "It's what I use to keep my muscles toned and flexible."

"Yoga," he repeated, shaking his head, but relief was replete in his tone. "Phoebe would not be disappointed."

Octavia chuckled. "Which way is out?"

"You'll never make it without your shoes. What's left of the floor is a land mine of glass. Here, hold the flashlight. I'll carry you."

Octavia took the flashlight and felt two very strong arms scoop her up as though she weighed nothing. Being a tall, full-bodied woman she found the sensation truly delightful. She circled one arm around Brett's neck for balance, leaned against his warm steel chest and concentrated on focusing the flashlight in front of them with her free hand.

He made his way carefully through the rubble toward the back door. But when they reached it, it was blocked by another enormous beam.

"I need to put you down for a minute."

Octavia took the hint and scanned the floor with the flashlight until she found a spot clear enough to stand on. Once Brett had set her there, Octavia watched as he easily lifted the heavy beam with his bare hands and shoved it aside. Then he kicked open the broken back door. Octavia directed the flashlight shaft into the gulf of darkness that lay beyond.

"The porch is gone and so are the stairs," Brett said. "Get ready for a rough landing."

Once again, he lifted her into his strong arms. She felt the power and solid weight of him as his body absorbed most of the impact of that rough landing. He nestled her snugly against the strong beat of his heart as he ran through the frigid rain to the car. He laid her gently on the passenger seat.

Octavia loved the strong, gentle feel of Brett's care and concern for her safety and comfort. She also loved the intensely feminine reactions erupting inside her in response to such treatment. This man had a lot more heart than he gave himself credit for.

As he circled to the driver's side, she pushed herself into a more erect sitting position in order to see out. The heavy rain beat down on the windshield, obscuring her vision. It took a sudden flash of lightning to illuminate what was left of her grandmother's home.

Her heart squeezed inside her chest.

"It's as flat as the proverbial pancake," she said with a sigh as Brett opened the driver's door.

"Still, I'm glad it's the house and not us," Brett said as he swung into the driver's seat.

The interior light gave her a clearer glimpse of their wet and muddy clothes and a nasty gash across Brett's right shoulder that had torn open his suit coat.

"You're hurt."

"Just a scratch. A little hydrogen peroxide from the first-aid kit in the glove compartment is all I need."

She quickly got it out for him. He took the bottle from her, pulled down his coat sleeve, dumped some of the solution right over his torn shirtsleeve and pulled his coat sleeve up again before she could even get a look at the wound. He was ultracareful with her, ultracasual with himself.

"There are available rooms in my hotel," he said as he handed her back the bottle.

"Check into a hotel without any money or identification?"

"Your purse is back there in that rubble, isn't it? Well, no matter. I'll take care of the hotel."

"I appreciate the offer, but checking into a hotel looking like this without shoes, a toothbrush or a change of clothes for tomorrow is definitely not an option."

"So where do you want me to take you?" Brett asked.

"Only one place left to go. Home."

ALL THE WAY THERE, reaction shivers snaked through Brett as he kept reliving the sight of the roof falling in on Octavia and kept seeing her trapped beneath those beams.

Once, he'd lost his footing at ten thousand feet and had dangled for hours from a lifeline with nothing but thin air around him. Another time, he'd been trapped on a glacier for four days without food or fuel. But those minor inconveniences paled into insignificance when compared to the torture of watching her lying hurt and knowing he was powerless to do anything about it.

He forcibly pushed the nightmarish memories aside and concentrated instead on imagining what her home would be like. His mind went through several possibilities. He could see her standing on a graceful balcony of a Seattle high rise, her face turned to the wind as she surveyed the lights of the city below.

Her sophisticated air and sense of style also lent itself to the image of her descending a circular staircase in a stately English Tudor in the Queen Anne district.

And with very little effort, he could also see that beautifully disciplined, yoga-taught body walking through a state-of-the-art exclusive retreat on Mercer Island, full of eccentric artistic angles and mysterious hidden rooms.

With all of these divergent concepts in his mind, Brett was certain he had covered all the contingencies. Until she directed him to park at the edge of Lake Union, just north of

Seattle, and gestured for him to follow her barefoot lead across the gangplank and into the structure she called home.

Even he could hear the reverberating incredulity in his tone over the beat of the driving wind and rain. "You can't live on a ferryboat."

She slipped a key from beneath an old-fashioned lantern lighting the entrance and turned to flash him a smile. "Come on, you're getting wet."

He followed her inside, once again shaking his head to realize that no matter how hard he tried to anticipate her, she continued to surprise him.

Once the door was closed on the storm outside, she switched on the lights and Brett found himself in one large room, supercharged with incredible color. Every inch of deck and wall panel had been splashed with a different, bold, luminous paint—orchid pink, cool mint, hot lemon, verdant turquoise, wet orange, ribald red, plush purple and a dozen more shades and hues too numerous to take in.

The portholes were covered in striped silk venetian blinds. The deeply pillowed sofa, chairs and ottoman were vivid limes and puce and gorgeous green plaid. He had the distinct feeling he had just stepped into a rainbow.

And completing the fanciful impression—there, in the middle of the deck rising to the ceiling—sat a fifteen-foot natural pine Christmas tree, completely decked out in gold.

From the dozen wrapped presents beneath its thick branches, to its tinsel, shining ornaments, lights and glistening crown of a star at the top, the tree sparkled with the Midas touch—a fitting pot of Christmas gold at the center of this riotous rainbow.

"Have you changed a leprechaun into a Christmas elf?" Brett asked.

She laughed as she took his damp suit jacket and hung it next to hers on wrought-iron hooks affixed to the wall next to the door. She opened a small closet door and disappeared inside for a moment. When she reappeared, her blouse and slip had been exchanged for a red-and-white Christmas robe with reindeer prancing on it, and she had a pair of red velvet slippers on her feet. She flipped a switch and a group of happy voices began to sing "Deck the Halls" through hidden speakers.

She surveyed the twinkling lights of the Christmas tree with a smile. "It's impossible not to love this season, isn't it?"

"Is it?"

"Come on into the galley, Mr. Humbug, and we'll explore that lamentable attitude while I fix us something to eat."

The "galley" turned out to be a very modern maritime-green-colored kitchen, the counters of which were embedded with colorful sand and shells and gave the impression of the shallow bottom of a clear sea pool. Above the center island, between the fragrant wreaths of fresh pine and holly, hung copper pots so shiny, Brett could see his reflection in them.

He sat on one of the burnt orange bar stools as he watched her take a bottle of chilled white wine out of the refrigerator door and a corkscrew out of the drawer. She set them in front of him along with a terra-cotta bowl full of fresh-smelling nuts.

Brett popped a few of the nuts into his mouth and began to twist the corkscrew into the wine bottle.

"Mr. Humbug, you can't tell me that as a kid you didn't sometimes hanker for the kind of Christmas all your friends were celebrating?"

"Maybe, when I was very young, I might have wished that one Christmas morning I'd walk into the living room and find a decorated tree with a present underneath it for me."

"Aha! I knew it. What kind of a present did you want?"

"Something different, special."

"Like that expensive diamond you now own?"

"So, A.J. told you about Midnight Magic. Yes, I suppose it qualifies. But my parents were right, Octavia. Things don't come by wishing. They come by working hard for them, as I worked hard to get that diamond."

"Why that diamond? What makes it so special?"

"Its blue sparkle is dazzling. It's truly a rare beauty. Tell me how you came to live on a ferryboat."

She pulled some eggs and cream out of the refrigerator and lifted a large sherbet-colored mixing bowl off a shelf before returning to the counter.

"I was looking for a place on the lake when I drove by this sign that read For Sale—My Broken Heart. I simply had to take a look."

"Yes, I can imagine you would. *Heart* is the name of this ship, I take it?"

She whisked the eggs as she answered.

"Actually, it was christened *Full of Heart* when it served as a foot ferry between some of the small islands in the Sound several decades ago. It was given that name because no matter what the weather, this little ship carried its commuters faithfully back and forth. I fell in love with it at first sight, although the sign had told the truth. It was quite broken, from stem to stern. Still, the best rewards come from tackling the greatest challenges, don't you think?"

"Yes, and that should worry me."

"Why?"

"Because I'm finding myself agreeing with you lately on things, and that has to be a bad sign."

She laughed again. He really liked hearing that deep, robust, full-of-life laugh.

He popped the cork on the wine bottle and got up to get a couple of glasses that sat atop one of her cabinets. It felt good to be here with her on this rocking, rainbow ferry. Entirely too good.

"What is your home like?" she asked as she reached for a fresh orange sitting in a bowl and began to grate off some rind.

"It sits on the top of a hill in Bellevue, with windows everywhere and a one-hundred-and-eighty-degree view."

"Mountain climbing and a home on a hill. You obviously like being on top of things. I bet this house of yours is all no-nonsense slate floors and stainless-steel cabinets and sinks."

"Was that an astute guess or have you sneaked over there and taken a look?"

"With you having me watched every second? Now, you know the answer to that one."

He smiled as he poured them both some wine. He set her glass next to her as she added Grand Marnier, cream, sugar, vanilla and some grated orange rind to the whisked eggs.

He raised his wineglass for a toast. "To humbugs everywhere."

She chuckled as she clicked her glass to his before taking a sip. Then she set the wineglass aside and resumed mixing the ingredients she had placed into the bowl.

Brett appreciated the refreshing, delicate wine, a light pinot chardonnay.

"I've been thinking about who attacked Scroogen," she said, surprising him with her sudden return to business.

"The more I learn about John and Constance and Douglas, the more I like them," she continued. "Imagining any one of them could do this thing is very difficult."

"But you do imagine one of them doing it?"

"Douglas."

"Why Douglas? Of the three, I would have thought him the least likely."

"On the contrary. He's obviously the most likely."

Brett helped himself to a few more nuts and took another sip of wine. "How do you figure that?"

"Because Douglas strikes me as the kind of man who would not back down from a fight."

"All right. I admit I see that in him. So?"

"So think about what happened. Douglas was the one who raced out of the flooding community center to find out what was going on. He was the one who rushed up to us later with the news that Scroogen's sewer line had been opened and that the firemen had declared it to be deliberate sabotage."

"So?"

"So then Scroogen comes barging into the midst of the seniors and spouts off about fining them for something he did."

"Careful, Octavia. We still don't have any evidence that Scroogen was the one who opened that sewer line."

"Still, you have to agree he was the mostly likely suspect in the minds of the seniors there that night. So here in their midst is suddenly the man they believe to have caused this terrible blight on their beautiful center. And the only one who strikes a blow back is Mab."

"Probably only because I got Scroogen out of there fast."

Octavia began to dip both sides of some sliced French bread into the liquid she had mixed in her bowl and was transferring the soaked pieces to a dish. She wiped her hands on a paper towel before turning back to Brett.

"You may have saved Scroogen more smacks. But the point is, Mab's the only one who retaliated. Now, how do you think that makes a big hulking man like Douglas Twitch feel?"

"Like maybe he should have been the one to do it."

"Right. And I think he did do it the next day. It would have taken a big man to push Scroogen to the ground."

"Not necessarily. If Dole were walking and someone pushed him even lightly, it could have been enough to cause him to lose his balance and fall. Besides, you said Douglas is strong and you're right. If he had knocked Scroogen to the ground, he would have struck a much harder blow to his shoulder."

"Unless he had known it was only necessary to scrape the skin to get the monkshood poisoning into Scroogen's system."

"Deliberate premeditation with something as unlikely as monkshood?"

Octavia paused as she set the counter with lemon linen napkins and real silverware.

"Why do you say 'as unlikely'?" she asked.

"Well, can you really see Douglas in some field, carefully collecting the poisonous leaves and roots of some monkshood and spreading its aconitine and aconine on your grandmother's gardening tool so he can slash Scroogen's shoulder with it?''

"Granted, he does seem more the type to punch someone in the jaw than to poison them. So, you still think it was Constance?"

"Yes. But I agree with what you said earlier. It's hard to suspect any one of these people, particularly now that I've had a chance to talk with them. Maybe part of the problem is because all our suspects are over seventy, so we're working with a bias."

Octavia's lips pursed in thought as she leaned down to get some Canadian bacon out of the refrigerator. She placed it into a skillet to heat and put a container of maple syrup on the side of the stove to warm before turning back to Brett.

"I think my biggest problem is believing one of them intended to frame Mab for the crime."

"Yes, Zane's background checks on all the seniors, Mab included, show they've been good friends for many years. The only slightly shady part of any of their pasts is that thing with John and his wife. I'm sure A.J. told you the police had their suspicions that he performed a mercy killing."

"Even if it were true, that hardly seems to have relevance here. If one is harboring resentment toward Mab for some reason, that reason has been well hidden. So why the frame?"

"If we had the answer to that, Octavia, maybe we'd have the answer to everything."

"Well, if the guilty party won't come forward, we're just going to have to find out who it is and expose him or her."

"Any ideas on how to do that?"

"Something will occur to me. It always does."

He chuckled at the assurance in her tone. "Always?"

"Why, yes. Don't you find that as long as you believe in something hard enough, it's bound to come true?"

"On the contrary. I know if I work hard enough for something, I can make it happen."

"Same philosophy."

"Is it?"

"Certainly. You believe your hard work will pay off so it does. I believe my intuition will give me a trail to follow to our killer and so it will. Hard work is the phraseology you use. Belief is what I use. They both define our expectations that, in turn, determine what we will both receive."

"That sounds a little like the philosophy I heard Mab expound upon when she did that radio program on sex for seniors."

"Well, she was the one who taught me that our attitude and expectations are what have the capacity to make our lives either magnificent or mundane."

She placed the soaked bread into a skillet she had heated. In minutes she had cooked them to a golden brown. She slipped them onto two plates, dusted them with confectioners' sugar and garnished each with a fresh slice of orange. Then she served the Grand Marnier French toast right there on the kitchen counter with the cooked Canadian bacon and warm maple syrup.

Brett had never tasted a better meal. And she seemed to have prepared it so effortlessly. Like she seemed to do most everything. As he was finishing his wine, she slipped the dishes into the dishwasher and wiped the counters clean.

"Would you like a tour of the rest of my *Heart?*"

He smiled at the phraseology of her invitation, set his wineglass down and slipped off his bar stool.

He followed her up a spiral staircase off the kitchen to the top deck and another room, one end of which was curved into a series of bow-shaped windows.

Brett recognized this room had once been the observation deck and probably offered a view of water and land during the day. Now night lay like a black curtain behind the windows, turning the icy rain beating down on the panes into flickering crystal lights as the ferry rocked gently in the wind.

The walls behind the riotous-colored casual furniture were filled with books. Brett read the jackets of a few.

"These are mostly romances and mysteries."

"Naturally. The law books are at work where they belong."

Brett smiled as he turned away from the shelves. A double set of doors led toward the stern. He pointed toward them.

"And behind there?"

She preceded him to the door, one of those special smiles drawing back her lips. "Come see."

He expected another room of riotous color. Of course, since that was what he expected, it wasn't what he got.

Suddenly he was stepping into a room of pure white. From the plush carpet at his feet, to the delicate wallpaper, to the dresser in the corner, to the sheer curtains on either side of the portholes, to the strings of twinkling lights shaped like a Christmas tree that draped from the ceiling over the swinging bed—everything was pure white.

Brett headed directly toward that swinging bed within the streamers of twinkling lights. He studied the chains holding it in place as a climber would, to see how well they were embedded in the ceiling. He gave one a tug to test its tensile strength. He ran his fingers over the pure white comforter that was obviously synthetic and yet felt as soft as a snow rabbit's fur. He pressed fingers into the mattress and knew it had to be filled with down to be so light.

She had moved beside him. He could feel her. Smell her. Sense her in every excited cell of his being. Tantalizing. Tempting. Tormenting.

He knew he should leave now. He knew he would not.

"Why a suspended bed?" he asked.

"A suspended bed is the only practical kind on a small ship. Particularly on a night like this when the wind is up."

She circled around him, stepped through the strings of twinkling lights, sat on the bed, slipped off her slippers and tucked her legs beneath her. The bed swung ever so slightly as the ship tipped back and forth. Her smooth, liquid-rich voice vibrated against his eardrums like a siren's song.

"A suspended bed acts like a pendulum, seeking balance and keeping you level. A fixed bed couldn't adjust to the movement of the water beneath you, and you might find yourself rolling onto the floor if the vessel lists too far to one side.''

He was listening to her explanation. But mostly he was just enjoying the vision of her lying on this soft bed of white, surrounded by the twinkling lights, her flame-red hair afire around her face, her eyes a sparkling promise of a different kind of blue midnight magic beneath the stars.

Brett had always thought nothing could match the sparkle of his blue-white diamond. But looking into this woman's eyes tonight, he knew he'd been wrong.

She was so damn stunning she took his breath away. His heart beats had begun to accelerate like piston strokes gathering speed. He wanted her so much his muscles had tightened into iron cords throughout his body. His words sounded raw and husky through his throat.

''So this bed that swings from the ceiling is *practical?*''

''Try it out,'' she taunted in that damn liquid brandy voice of hers, her eyes staring boldly, beautifully, straight into his.

This time Brett had no battle to wage—only need that vibrated through his veins, hot and heady. If she believed herself to be safe from him now, she was wrong.

He shed his shirt, tie and shoes in less than a second. Then he lowered himself to her. He heard the sharp intake of her breath as their bodies touched and blended. Hers was as soft and giving as the bed. His was as hard and ungiving as the chains that held it in place.

He stared deeply into her eyes and let her clearly read the intent in his. Then he took her lips as he took his mountains, as a conqueror must.

HIS KISS THIS TIME was the taste of wine and warm maple syrup. The hard possessive pressure of his lips sent shivers right down to the soles of Octavia's feet.

She knew instantly that this wasn't going to be like anything she had experienced before.

There was a dangerous demand in this man's eyes that was echoed in his kiss and in the firm, strong hands that now very deliberately and competently were untying her robe.

What was it? What was making his touch feel so different? What was it that was igniting her senses and making her nerve endings sizzle?

The answer quivered through her in a wave of want so strong it left her dizzy. Brett Merlin wasn't just about to make love to her. He was about to possess her.

She should have understood immediately what that gleam in those silver-black eyes had represented.

But she hadn't seen it. She had only sensed it on some primitive, intuitive level that was only now making itself clear. This was the true risk that Brett Merlin represented.

His mouth and hands had already hypnotized her body to his will. Even if she had been able to stop him, it was way too late to stop herself.

Desire, hotter than she had ever known, flared through her as he devoured her lips and then her neck, the heat of his tongue a lash that whipped her skin, his every breath and touch spinning a spell of possession. A shooting ache of need erupted between her thighs as his strong fingers snapped her nylons out of her garter belt and slid them down her legs.

And suddenly she knew that anything this man wanted with her he could have—would have. Her will, once so strong, now trickled away, weak as water.

The rain rapped hard on the roof above them, matching the beat of her blood. The smoky incense of his skin and hair mesmerized her like a drug. She was blind to all but the feel of his hands and mouth.

Octavia dropped her head back with a sigh of surrender as his tongue licked a hot trail down her throat and his fingers spread open her robe.

The cool brush of his hair on her bared chest tickled tantalizingly as his mouth seared the top of her breasts swelling out of her bra. She arched her back to greet his touch, wanting more, so much more.

He pulled her bra straps down and his tongue licked her swelling nipples. She cried out as shimmers of sweet aching heat spread into her deepest core.

His hand returned to her leg to make its way up her thigh. Deliberately, torturously, slow it slid across her flesh as he licked and sucked, and her body throbbed with pleasure and growing need. She wanted him to touch her everywhere; she ached for him to touch her everywhere.

She could feel the heaviness of her breaths as she dragged air through her lungs. She couldn't seem to move, not while he touched her like this, not while he commanded her body like this.

He anchored her body with his. His palm pressed lightly between her thighs and her body quaked anew with need. And then, as he took her nipple deep into his mouth to suckle, he slipped his fingers under her silk panties to stroke her wet heat.

A bolt of intense pleasure broke through her. She cried out.

She pressed against him, wantonly, eagerly, knowing that she would give this magician anything—everything—if he would just continue to work his magic on her.

He took her other nipple into his mouth to suckle as the pressure and pace of his fingers increased. She moaned and arched against him, again and again. Then suddenly he had her shouting and soaring toward the ceiling as the power of the bursting climax broke through her.

She floated there light and free, suspended by the magic of his ministrations, weightless and totally empty.

Then she felt the feather-light feel of his lips against her cheek. She sighed in contentment as she drifted down, back onto the bed, at this soft summons.

Dazed, she opened her eyes to see him above her. His chest was bare, full of powerful, rippling layers of corded muscle. He looked magnificent, the quicksilver in his eyes alive with the knowledge of the pleasure his possession had brought her body. And full of the promise of more pleasure yet to come.

She tried to shake her head to tell him that for her it was over, but she didn't have the energy.

He took her hands in his and drew her slowly into a sitting position. Gently, so very gently, he removed her bra. Then he planted firm, sweet kisses across her shoulders that sent new tingles down the nerve endings of her spine.

He laid her back on the bed and slipped off her panties.

As he stood over her, consuming her naked body with his eyes, he stripped off his slacks and shorts. Chills began to break out all over Octavia's skin as he stood before her naked, aroused, magnificent in the power of raw, elemental masculinity.

He continued to mesmerize her with those silver-black eyes as he grasped her feet.

His hands were firm; his mouth was hot. She had never had her toes licked and sucked before. The total eroticism of it shivered up her legs. A mere moment before she had been achy with contentment. Now she was once again quivering with need, like a leaf in the wind torn from its supporting branch.

He nibbled at her ankles next, then her calves, then munched on her knees. He was conquering her all over again, bottom to top this time. By the time he had reached her thighs she was spreading them once again for him, hot and wet and eager.

He teased her swollen folds with his tongue and then made his way to her belly and then her breasts. She withered and moaned impatiently beneath his magical ministrations, wanting more, so much more. He took her hands in his and stretched her arms over her head and held them there. For an instant, he locked eyes with hers, breast to breast, breath to breath.

Then his mouth claimed hers with a fierce possession as he buried himself deep inside her heat.

She wrapped herself around him as he filled her, all of her with all of him. She cried out with the intensity of the contractions leaping within her, tightening her womb as she met every one of his thrusts into her giving, enveloping heat.

He erupted inside her with a final powerful plunge that seemed to pierce her heart as the force of her name exploded from his lips to sear her soul.

She was captured. Claimed. Possessed by the spell of the magician who held her in his arms.

BRETT WOKE TO A FAINT light filtering in through the portholes, a shade darker than the pure white veil of snowflakes that now replaced the rain. "Winter Wonderland" played softly through the stereo speakers hidden somewhere in the room.

He was caught in a winter wonderland, all right, the stuff of storybooks and dreams and fairy-tale fantasies.

He turned to look at her—the biggest fantasy of all—asleep on this soft white bed surrounded by strings of twinkling lights, the beautiful sparkling present that he had never found beneath his Christmas tree.

She was naked, the flame of her long thick hair spread like a deep fan behind the light gold of her skin. A matching flame triangle nestled between her satin thighs.

He hadn't realized until he had undressed her last night just how lovely she was. He had only a glimpse or two to guide him. Because despite the stylish and beautiful clothes she wore, her skirts and blouses had never been tight, and her hem always hung at the knee. Even her silk bra and panties, now lying on the floor where he had thrown them the night before, were white and modestly cut.

Modestly cut. Dear God, she was modest. This newest revelation hit him on a whole new level. Deep down, this bold, brainy and beautiful woman, who lived inside a rainbow ferry and slept suspended in this white fantasy of a bedroom, was modest!

Modesty didn't fit her at all. The perfection of her form could put a Cellini statue to shame.

And yet, when he thought about it again, he realized modesty fit her perfectly. It explained why she had never sought the notoriety of trials but preferred to arrange better settlements behind the scenes. She didn't care at all about all the pomp and ceremony that went with celebrity status. He doubted status was even a word in her vocabulary.

Because she was modest. Such an unexpectedly beautiful trait to add to her others. Smart. Fierce. Loyal. Loving. God, how she was loving!

Not that the image reconciled with what Zane had told him. His P.I.'s report said Octavia dated lots of men very casually, and most of them thought her beautiful and fun, but distant.

Distant? She had never been distant. Not with him. He smiled with the remembered pleasure of their night together. Each time he had awakened her, she had melted into his arms. Each time he had touched her, she had opened for him. He was very glad she was distant with other men. All other men.

He wanted her to himself.

He was in love with her.

God help him.

Now what?

Now the fantasy would end. No man could serve two mistresses. And his first mistress—the law—was all-demanding and possessive and would allow no rivals.

Brett gathered Octavia into his arms, craving the warmth of her body to hold back the chill that had suddenly begun to circle his heart.

She stirred and deep blue eyes squinted sleepily into his. Her hands wound automatically around his neck.

"Good morning," she said, her voice a salient sigh, her body an armful of sultry silk.

His heart stilled inside his chest at the sparkle in her eyes. He couldn't seem to catch his breath at the beauty of her smile. He crushed her to him fiercely, possessively.

He took her then, not like a magician at all but like a madman, and all the while cursing that other mistress's prior claim.

"How did the arraignment go?" A.J. asked.

"About as expected," Octavia said into one of the Port

Orchard Courthouse phones. "Because of the seriousness of the charge, bail's been set at seventy-five thousand dollars."

"You able to raise it okay?"

"Yes. Mab'll be out soon, although she's got another electronic ankle monitor and she'll be restricted to Constance's place. They're not even going to let her do her broadcasts or help with the meals for seniors or with getting the community center ready."

"Scroogen's widow was interviewed by a Seattle TV station this morning. She said she's lost all respect for the seniors and their cause and is going ahead with the condominium complex in memory of her dead husband."

Octavia sighed. "Yes. The story is front-page news here. Support for the seniors and their cause has dried up over night. No one is buying their Scrooge dolls. They're not going to be able to raise the money for their rent."

"How is she holding up?"

In her mind's eye, Octavia once again could see her grandmother as she had stood beside her at the arraignment. Mab's once-bouncy curls had been matted, her normally erect shoulders slumping, her hands nervously fingering the edges of her suit jacket.

Octavia's heart swelled and ached at the memory.

"She's lost her home, half her radio station and all her hope for helping the nonambulatory seniors and keeping the community center going. Plus which, she's being accused of a murder that all her friends believe she committed. She's always been a strong woman, A.J., but it's taking its toll."

"You know everyone here will do whatever they can."

"Yes. Thanks."

"What's your next move?"

Octavia's eyes glanced over at Brett, looking so wonderfully calm and confident, as he spoke with Patterson. She fingered the velvety poinsettia she had pinned to her lapel. For the first time in hours, a smile found her lips.

"Brett and I are going to Scroogen's funeral soon. After that, we plan to pour over the evidence that Brett has obtained on a discovery motion to see what we can learn from it."

"Oh, I'm glad you mentioned Merlin. I have some news about his personal life, specifically his wife."

The smile slid off Octavia's face. "His *what?*"

"His wife, Danette Merlin. You must have seen her. She was an up-and-coming fashion model eight years ago—made the cover of *Vogue, Mademoiselle,* several of the big ones."

Octavia's mouth suddenly felt very dry. She tried to swallow but couldn't. "They're still married?"

"No. He dumped her after she was caught smuggling dope."

Octavia sighed in some relief as she absorbed the information, let it sift through her mind and heart. She remembered his words about being young, a fool, falling in love.

"I have no respect for anyone who smuggles dope, A.J. I can't say as I blame Brett for ending the relationship."

"Still, you have to admit, it was kind of cold, inasmuch as he dumped her right after they returned from their honeymoon."

Octavia frowned. "It happened right after their honeymoon?"

"They combined their honeymoon with one of her overseas fashion tours. She brought the stuff back in her luggage. When her case came to trial, she was convicted primarily because of Brett's testimony."

Octavia shifted uneasily in front of the phone. "He testified against her, too?"

"Not only did he testify against her, he was the one who turned her in."

Octavia's heart skipped several beats as the breath stilled in her lungs.

"Octavia, did you hear me? I said Brett Merlin turned in his own wife when he caught her smuggling dope. She was lucky she was a first offender. She served a minimal senence. Still, her modeling career ended up in the Dumpster.''

Octavia stared at Brett as A.J.'s words revolved around in her brain. She kept remembering how completely he had possessed her the night before, how fiercely he had claimed her that morning through a furious flurry of curses—like he would never, ever, let her go.

But would he?

If he had the proof that tied her to that stone carving, would he see that there was a difference between what she had done for her grandmother and what Danette had done?

Or would he only see the law?

"Don't trust him, Octavia," A.J. was saying in her ear. "This guy has ice water in his veins."

But Octavia could only remember the heat of his hands, his lips. He had captured her heart, claimed her soul.

She swallowed, hard. "A.J., there's something I want you to do for me."

After she told the private investigator what it was she wanted, A.J.'s voice exploded in her ear.

"Octavia, you've got to be out of your mind! You can't want me to do that."

"I do, A.J."

"No, Octavia. Get someone else to—"

"No one else can do it. Not effectively. You know that. A.J., please, do this for me."

A.J. exhaled heavily in her ear. "All right. It's your funeral. God, I hope to hell you know what kind of a risk you're taking."

"I know," Octavia said. "But when your heart whispers, you have to listen."

Chapter Thirteen

Nancy leaned on Brett's arm as they walked away from the burial site beneath the light snowfall.

"Nancy, are you sure you understand the difficulties you'll be facing by going ahead with the condominium complex?" he asked.

"The complex was what Dole wanted."

"It's a major project. How will you coordinate it?"

"Ronald worked with his father. He knows the particulars."

Nancy paused to flash Ronald a smile as he took her other arm. "I'm sure the three of us can make Dole's dream come true."

Making Dole's dream come true was not top on Brett's list of priorities. Besides, he knew Nancy had been a journalist, not a businesswoman. He doubted she had any idea how difficult the undertaking would be.

"What about the seniors and their community center, Nancy? I thought the fact that Dole was pushing them out bothered you?"

"They can keep their buildings if they move them elsewhere."

"They may not have the funds to do that, even if they could find a suitable place."

"You said the study of the ground beneath the stone carving will cause a few more weeks' delay. That should give them time to get the funds and to find another place."

Nancy's casual dismissal of the enormous difficulties of such an undertaking told Brett just how naive she was being.

Ronald spoke up suddenly from Nancy's other side.

"We should keep the buildings. Serve them right for what they did. Merlin, how could you bring that Osborne woman to my father's funeral, knowing her grandmother killed my father."

Brett turned his attention to the black limousines where Octavia waited.

On the lapel of her deep blue cape, she wore the large poinsettia he had impulsively bought for her that morning when he swung by his place for a change of clothes.

She had surprised him totally and pleased him enormously by pinning it on as though it were an orchid. Now he watched her full flame hair blowing lightly off her face, the snowflakes sparkling on its straying strands like diamond facets.

"I don't believe Mab Osborne did it, Ronald," he said.

"The police do," Ronald said.

"The police also once believed your eyewitness account of her attack on Dole. I will find out who really is responsible for your father's death. Now, if you'll excuse us, Ronald, I'd like to talk privately with Nancy."

Ronald looked ready to object until Nancy laid a hand on his arm. "Ronald, would you sit in the car with Katlyn? She shouldn't be left alone. You know she doesn't understand about Dole's death, yet. She needs her big brother to comfort her."

Ronald looked from Nancy's face to Brett's and back to Nancy's before nodding and leaving to do as she asked.

"He's really been a comfort these last few days, Brett," Nancy said as she watched her stepson leave. "And so good with Katlyn. I don't know what I would have done without him."

"I'm glad, Nancy."

"Oh, I know he still gets a bit belligerent. But his father's death has changed him. Really. Strange how tragedy can bring out the best in some people."

"Nancy, I need to ask you something and I need you to be completely truthful in your answer."

She stopped and turned to face him, alarm sifting in her eyes and voice. "Brett, what's wrong?"

"When I hugged Katlyn today, she said I hurt her. I took off her coat and rolled up her sleeves. She has the remnants of nasty bruises on her upper arms. How did they get there?"

Nancy's face turned quickly away. She dropped her hand from where it had rested in the crook of Brett's arm.

"Kids are always bumping into—"

"The truth, Nancy," Brett said, deliberately firm.

Nancy exhaled into a heavy sigh. "It was an accident."

"Tell me about this accident."

Nancy said nothing for a moment, just stood with head averted, biting her lower lip. She did not meet his eyes. When she began to speak, her tone sounded strained.

"I told Katlyn never to disturb her father when his study door was closed. I explained to her it meant he was trying to concentrate and it would make him very angry to be interrupted. But kids being kids..."

"Go on."

Nancy's gloved hands began to twist around each other as though their cloth protection wasn't enough to keep them warm.

"I thought she was playing with her dolls in her room. I took the time to retreat to our bedroom to wrap her Christmas toys. Suddenly, I heard her screaming. I ran out of the bedroom. The door to Dole's study was open. She was inside. Dole had her by the arms and was shaking her."

Nancy choked on a small sob. Brett took her shaking hands into his and held firm until she continued.

"I was so shocked, so scared, I stood there frozen. It was Ronald who came running and pulled Katlyn away from his father. He handed her to me, and I carried her back to the bedroom to pack. All I could think of was leaving with my baby."

"What changed your mind?"

"Dole came in a moment later. He said he was sorry that he'd lost his temper. He explained that he had looked up suddenly to see Katlyn sitting on the floor in his study, playing with some very sharp scissors. He thought she was going to poke herself in the eye with them. He grabbed them out of her hands. Yelled at her to never pick them up again. He didn't mean to shake her so hard. He didn't mean to hurt her, Brett."

"Had he ever laid hands on her before? The truth, Nancy."

His aunt's eyes rose to his. "No. Never. That's why this was so surprising to me."

"Nancy, are you sure?"

"Do you think I would have stayed with him if he had? This was an accident, a one-time thing. His fear for how she could have hurt herself caused him to overreact. He hadn't meant to hurt her. I tell you, it would never have happened again."

Brett was not nearly so sure. He was bothered by the scene his aunt had described. Very bothered.

"Nancy, why did you marry Dole?"

"Why? Well, what a question. Because he asked me. Because I wanted to."

"You could have done so much better."

Nancy laughed without any mirth. "Brett, I was a big, gawky woman going on forty. Believe me, men weren't sending me candy and flowers. Dole offered me marriage and a home. Okay, he wasn't Prince Charming; but, remember, I wasn't Cinderella. We accepted who we were. We understood we had to make do."

Make do. The very same words he had used when he described his own relationships with women less than two weeks before. Hard to find fault with his aunt when he, too, had set up his expectations to accept *make-do* relationships. No, not just to accept them, to seek them out.

His eyes once again went to Octavia. Had it really been less than two weeks since that outrageous redhead had come into his life?

"It's only fair I get to ask now," Nancy said. "You were so in love with Danette. What happened, Brett?"

Brett faced his aunt. "I found out her beauty was only surface, only a fantasy."

"I know she did wrong in smuggling that dope. But how could you turn her in, loving her like you did?"

"When I caught her, she admitted she'd been smuggling dope for years. Not because she was an addict or really needed the money. She was just greedy. When I tried to talk to her about the terrible impact of dope on its victims, she laughed at me. That's when I realized I had married a stranger—an ugly stranger—and the only way I could stop her was to turn her in."

Nancy rested her hand on Brett's arm, in a gesture of both understanding and comfort.

A hefty young woman with an anxious look ambled up to Brett and his aunt. She stopped hesitantly in front of Nancy.

"Mrs. Scroogen, I'm sorry to bring this up now but will . . . will anything change about the job?"

"I don't know, Tami. Ronald and I will need to discuss it. Brett, have you met Tami Lammock, Dole's secretary?"

When Brett indicated he hadn't, Nancy performed the introductions. Brett motioned for Octavia to join them.

When she reached them, Brett introduced her to Tami, all the while noticing that Nancy barely looked at Octavia. Despite his assurances to the contrary, he could tell that Nancy, like everyone else, was convinced Mab was guilty.

"I need to join Ronald and Katlyn," Nancy said. "I'll see you later, Brett?"

"I'll be by," he promised.

"Are you working for Ronald now?" Octavia asked Tami as soon as Nancy had walked off in the direction of a waiting limousine.

"It's hard to tell what's going on. Dole never really let his son do much. I think Ronald is kind of lost. He may not want me to stay. Dole only hired me a month ago as a temporary, part-time secretary. I was lucky to get the job.''

"Why do you say that, Mrs. Lammock?" Brett asked.

"My husband is in the navy, temporarily assigned to the Bremerton Shipyard. He could be reassigned at any time. We have a girl in first grade and a boy in third. Dole was the only employer willing to let me work just the mornings so I could be home in time to be with my kids.''

And Dole got an employee he didn't have to offer a medical plan, vacation or holiday pay, Brett added mentally to himself.

"What do you remember about the threatening letters that Dole received, Tami?" Octavia asked.

"There were three of them. All in the same silver envelopes. All with a photocopy of Dole's business card glued on the front. They were delivered by the post office carrier. Dole showed me and his son what was inside the first two after he opened them. Ronald thought they were a joke, but Dole took them seriously right away. He had me get the police on the phone to report them and the telephone threat he had received earlier.''

"When did he receive the telephone threat?" Octavia asked.

"The afternoon before the first letter. He received another threatening call at home, as well as two more at work.''

"Tell us what you remember about the voice behind the threatening telephone calls, Tami," Octavia urged.

"Oh, I never heard it myself. The calls at work came in the afternoon when I was home. But Dole did tell me about each one of them the next day.''

"What did he say?"

"That it was the same person, always warning him to hand over the center to the seniors, or else. He said the voice sounded like Mab Osborne's, only a little muffled as though she were trying to disguise who she was.''

"Had he heard Mab's voice over the phone?" Brett asked.

"She called the first week I came to work for Dole. She was quite pleasant to me. Identified herself as Dole's tenant. Said she had business to discuss with him. I put her through.

"A few moments later, Dole came charging out of his office to tell me that I was never to put a call through from her or anyone else again without first asking him. He was very angry."

"He said nothing about Mab making any threats to him on that call?" Brett asked.

"No. But it was pretty clear whatever she had to say hadn't pleased him. I'm sorry about your grandmother, Ms. Osborne. I have a grandmother her age, and it's still hard for me to believe such an elderly lady would commit such a violent crime."

"Me, too, Tami," Octavia said.

"Mrs. Lammock, something has been puzzling me," Brett said. "According to the police report, my uncle was struck on his shoulder, the wound tearing his shirt. Why wasn't he wearing his suit coat? It was a very cold December morning."

"Oh, he never wore his suit coat while he drove, Mr. Merlin. Said it was too restricting."

"Didn't he normally put his coat on before coming into the office?"

"Yes, but he wasn't wearing it that . . . morning. He must have taken it off after being attacked."

"Tami, do you know of anyone who was angry enough at your boss to want to cause him harm?" Octavia asked.

Tami turned her attention toward the limousine that was just pulling away from the curb in back of them. An intent look drew her eyebrows together as she looked at the three people in the back of the limousine—Nancy, Ronald and Katlyn Scroogen.

"Dole wasn't very nice to his son. I always felt kind of bad about that. I understand Ronald is going to end up owning half the business."

"Do you think Dole's own son might have—"

"Of course I really don't know anything, Ms. Osborne," Tami interrupted quickly. "I have to go now."

And with that, she all but ran to her small gray Tercel parked at the far end of the curb.

"So she suspects Ronald," Octavia said.

Before Brett could comment, he heard his name being called. He turned to find Detective Sergeant Patterson approaching. The detective nodded in Octavia's direction before addressing Brett.

"I see I just missed your aunt again. I'd hoped to catch her this morning. We've played an exhausting round of telephone tag the last couple of days. I've been trying to return her husband's effects to her. Why don't you take these off my hands and see that she gets them."

Patterson pulled a manila envelope out of his breast pocket and an itemized, typed list of its contents on a piece of paper. He handed both to Brett. Brett read through the short list.

"This is all?" Brett asked.

"Yes. Just his keys and some loose change. His driver's license, money and credit cards were all in his wallet."

"Which was where?"

"In his suit coat pocket, locked in the car."

"Had the coat been torn?"

"No. Apparently he wasn't wearing it when he was attacked. If you'll sign this for me, we can make the transfer official."

"Do you know why he left his suit coat in the car that morning?" Brett asked.

"He probably just forgot to take it with him when he got out of the car."

Brett glanced inside the envelope. Something immediately caught his eye. He pulled out the keychain, separating the distinctive silver-plated key from the rest.

"Sergeant Patterson, do you know what this key fits?"

"No. We had no reason to check his keys."

"It's identical to Mab's key to the storeroom at the back of the greenhouse," Octavia said. "It even has the Do Not

Duplicate warning on it. Scroogen had a key to the store-room!''

"So?" Patterson asked.

"How did he get it?" Brett asked.

"Does it matter?" Patterson asked.

"Yes. If Scroogen had a key, then someone other than Mab and the seniors could have used his key to gain access to the storeroom and take her gardening gloves and tool, as well as the Silver Power League stationery."

"Douglas ordered the keys, Sergeant," Octavia said. "Can't you at least have a talk with him?"

"All right," Patterson said, sounding clearly coerced. "Never let it be said that I didn't follow up a lead."

"YES, OF COURSE I KNEW Scroogen had a key," Douglas said as they all stood in the hallway of the Twitches' home. "He was our landlord. When we had the new buildings constructed, naturally we had to give him one."

"Why didn't you tell us this before when we asked you who had a key to the storeroom?" Octavia asked.

"Because you didn't ask me that question," Douglas replied. "You asked me if the members of the executive committee were the only members of the Silver Power League to have a key, and I told you yes. I just naturally assumed you knew that Scroogen had one, too. Why is this key he had such a big deal?"

"Because it means the person who took the stationery to send Scroogen those threats and Mab's cultivator to attack him needn't be anyone associated with the League at all," Brett said.

"You're saying someone else wrote those letters demanding Scroogen give us the center?" Douglas asked. "Someone other than Mab attacked him? But who would do that? And why?"

"DOUGLAS'S QUESTIONS ARE good ones, Octavia," Brett said. "If someone else did write those notes to Dole and then later struck him with Mab's cultivator, what was the motive?''

"It had to be to throw the blame on the seniors," Octavia said, walking between Brett and Sergeant Patterson as they headed back to their cars in front of the Twitches' home.

"We know that Scroogen wasn't an ethical man. Maybe this was someone who was trying to get back at him and using your uncle's feud with the seniors as cover to do it."

"You're forgetting that whoever did this had to have had access to Dole's key to the center. What I do know about my uncle does not lead me to believe that he would willingly let anyone have access to his keys."

"Look, folks," Sergeant Patterson said. "This has all been interesting. But just because Scroogen had a key, that doesn't mean someone used it."

"Sergeant," Octavia said, "when Ronald recanted his seeing my grandmother strike his father, he said he was meeting an employee at a job site, right?"

"Right."

"Were you able to verify he was at that site?"

"Well, no. The employee he was supposed to talk to didn't arrive."

"So you don't know where Ronald really was when his father was attacked."

"What are you suggesting, Ms. Osborne?"

"I'm suggesting Ronald could have gained access to his father's keys, inasmuch as he lived in the same household."

"It's a point to consider," Brett added.

"All right," Patterson said. "For the sake of argument, let's say that Ronald did somehow get the key to the storeroom off his father's key chain. I'll even go a step further and say he could have stolen the Silver Power League stationery and used it to send his father threatening letters, pretending they were from the seniors. Why?''

"So later he could kill his father and blame it on the seniors," Octavia said. "Tami Lammock told us this morning that Dole didn't treat Ronald well."

"It's true," Brett said. "I saw evidence of that myself."

"Tami Lammock also told us Ronald is inheriting half the business now that Dole is gone," Octavia added.

Sergeant Patterson frowned. "You're saying Ronald killed his father because he was mistreated and wanted to inherit?"

"He had opportunity, means, and yes, I think the motive is there."

"If it is Ronald, he's been very clever about it, Sergeant," Brett added. "From the first he's made it appear as though the seniors—and specifically Mab—were behind both the calls and threatening letters. So when something did finally happen to his father, everyone would look to them to blame."

"I'm not saying I'm buying any of this," Patterson said, rubbing his mustache. "But I suppose it wouldn't hurt to ask Ronald some questions."

"We'll come with you," Brett said.

"RONALD'S NOT HERE," Nancy said as she stepped aside for them to enter her home.

"Where is he, Mrs. Scroogen?" Sergeant Patterson asked.

"He's running a few errands. What is it? Is something wrong?"

Brett took his aunt's arm and led her into the living room where Katlyn sat on the carpet cutting out paper dolls with a pair of blunt scissors.

"Hi, Brett," his little cousin said as she flashed him a smile.

"Hi, Katlyn," he responded before turning back to Nancy.

"Sergeant Patterson wants to ask Ronald about Dole's key to the storeroom in back of the Silver Power League's greenhouse."

"What key?" Nancy asked as she sat across from Brett.

Brett nodded toward Katlyn. "You may want her to play elsewhere for a while, Nancy," he suggested softly.

"There is something wrong, isn't there?" Nancy asked, immediately shooting forward in her seat. "Brett, you must tell me what's going on."

Out of the corner of his eye, Brett could see his cousin's head rise at the sound of her mother's worried tone. He also saw Octavia immediately move over to the little girl and sit down on the carpet next to her.

"Hi, Katlyn, I'm Octavia. What is it you're cutting out here?"

"I'm making Santa a helper so he can answer all the letters he gets."

"That's a very good idea. But is one helper enough?"

"Oh, no. There are too many letters from boys and girls. I've made lots of Santa helpers. Some of them are in my room answering letters. Do you want to see?"

"I'd love to."

Octavia winked at Brett as she accompanied Katlyn to her bedroom, getting the little girl out of earshot. Brett eased Nancy back onto the couch and sat beside her.

"You think Ronald did it, don't you?" Nancy asked in a tone filled with the same kind of panic that had entered her eyes.

"Mrs. Scroogen," Sergeant Patterson began, "we are just trying to get the facts. Now, I understand that the relationship between Ronald and his father was not always an easy one, is that correct?"

Nancy began to rub her hands together nervously. Her voice picked up a defensive note. "Like all fathers and sons, they had their disagreements."

"Did Ronald know he would inherit half the business on the death of his father?"

"Well, yes. Of course he knew. Just as I knew I would inherit the other half. Brett, it means nothing."

"Tami says Dole never let Ronald do anything around the office. Maybe Ronald thought it was time he was given a chance."

"No, no. Ronald wouldn't... I know it hurt him when his father ignored him so much and belittled his efforts. But it was just Dole's way. He wasn't a very...sensitive man. Ronald still admired his father. He still tried to please him."

"Was he successful?"

Nancy shook her head vehemently. "No, no. What you're suggesting can't be true. He never would have hurt his father, Brett. Not his own father."

"Are you sure, Nancy?" Brett asked, making his voice as gentle as possible.

Nancy rolled into a ball and began to rock back and forth. "No, please. No. Don't take Ronald away from me, too."

"It may be out of our hands, Nancy," Brett said.

"Then again, it may be within our hands," Octavia said suddenly from the other side of the room.

Brett looked over to see an unusual expression on her face. He immediately got to his feet.

"Octavia, what is it?"

"Brett, Mrs. Scroogen, Sergeant Patterson, I wonder if you would join me in Katlyn's room for a moment."

A moment later, they stood at the entry to Katlyn's room. The little girl was sitting on her bed, looking very guilty, obviously hiding something underneath her rumpled bedspread.

"Katlyn," Octavia said, "tell your mommy and your cousin and Sergeant Patterson how you learned to prepare your letters to Santa that special way you showed me."

"I don't want to get into trouble," Katlyn moaned.

"You won't get into trouble, sweetie. Just tell the truth."

"I just wanted to help daddy," Katlyn said. "Only he got real mad at me. He shook me so hard I dropped my scissors."

"Your scissors?" Brett said. "Katlyn, when your daddy shook you that day, you were using your scissors?"

"Yes. I'm not allowed to use sharp scissors."

Nancy walked over to Katlyn's bed and threw the bed-spread back. Beneath was an assortment of letters cut out from the headlines of newspapers and magazines. Some had been pasted onto a sheet of paper.

"Mommy, I'm sorry."

Nancy sat on the bed and took her daughter into her arms. "You've nothing to be sorry for, dear. Everything's all right."

Brett exchanged a glance with Octavia before turning to his aunt. "Nancy, have you been in Dole's study since he died?"

"No. I couldn't bring myself to."

"Which room is it?"

"Down the hall. First one on the right. But I don't—"

Brett didn't hear any more. He was already halfway down the hall. The door to the study was closed. He turned the knob and entered.

The room was small, cluttered, dark, the windows tightly closed, the blinds drawn. A taste of dust lingered in the stale air. Brett flipped the light switch. The overhead fixture came to life, but the room remained a dark cubbyhole.

Octavia stepped from behind him. "Over there. On the desk," she said, pointing.

Brett made for the stack of newspapers and magazines gathered at its edge. He was leafing through them when Sergeant Patterson entered the room. Brett held up one of the newspaper pages with several cutout headlines for the detective to see.

"Exhibit A," he said.

"You can't mean—" Sergeant Patterson began.

"All we have to find now is the stationery," Octavia said, interrupting the detective as she circled the desk and began to rifle the drawers. She lifted several items out of the bottom drawer and held them high.

"Exhibits B, C, D and E, Sergeant."

Patterson circled around the desk to take the blank sheets of Silver Power League stationery and envelopes, several photocopies of Dole's business card and paper paste out of Octavia's hands.

"Well, I'll be damned," Patterson said as he sunk into the desk's chair. "Scroogen sent the threatening letters to himself. But why?"

Brett rested a leg against the desk. "To discredit Mab and the seniors, of course. He was very angry at Mab for thwarting his plans to become president of the Chamber of Commerce. So he pretended to get threatening calls from her. He sent himself threatening letters. He did everything he could to put her fight against his condominium complex, and her, in a bad light."

"But when he reported the calls," Patterson said, "he was careful to say it only sounded like Mab disguising her voice. Why didn't he just say it was her?"

"My guess would be because he was afraid Mab might have an alibi for one of those times he claimed to be getting a call from her. By saying it just sounded like Mab, he still could have claimed it was one of the other seniors who made the call if Mab could produce an alibi."

"All right. I admit that what you're suggesting makes sense. But if Dole Scroogen stole the stationery and orchestrated this threat campaign against himself, who struck him with the prongs dipped in monkshood poisoning and killed him?"

"There's only one person it could have been, Sergeant," Brett said.

"Yes," Octavia agreed. "Just one person."

"Who?" Patterson asked.

Chapter Fourteen

"Dole's coat was the giveaway," Brett said. "It was a cold morning. Even if he didn't drive with it on, he would have put it on the moment he stepped out of the car."

"Unless he was planning something that made wearing it that morning inconvenient," Octavia said.

"Like rolling on the ground in the mud and striking himself on the shoulder with Mab's gardening tool," Brett finished.

"Wait a minute," Patterson said. "Are you two saying that Dole Scroogen killed himself?"

"Not intentionally, I'm sure," Octavia said. "When he unlocked the greenhouse storeroom to steal the stationery, he must have found Mab's gardening tool and gloves and decided to use them to implicate her further in this fabricated campaign against himself."

"Only he didn't realize that before putting her cultivator in the greenhouse's storage room, Mab had done some weeding in her own garden," Brett said. "The first time I went by her house I noticed the area she had cleared around some Christmas berry bushes. I didn't think much about it at the time. But now I'm sure she must have dug up some wild monkshood without even realizing it."

"The forensic people did find soil on the prongs of the cultivator and on her gloves," Patterson said.

"Dole was trying to make it appear as though Mab had attacked him," Octavia said.

"While being careful to only say it sounded like Mab just in case she had an alibi," Brett said.

"He never realized," Octavia continued, "that by inflicting even those minor wounds on himself with her cultivator, he would be introducing poison into his system."

Patterson stroked his mustache. "I admit it's plausible. But before I'm convinced, I'm going to have to see some evidence that points to Scroogen striking himself with that cultivator."

"Dole sent the letters? He struck himself?"

Brett turned at Nancy's voice and saw her standing in the doorway, her face white, her body quivering.

He went to her and cupped her shoulders with his hands. "I'm sorry, Nancy. It looks like that's what happened."

Tears started to fall from her eyes, silent tears that streaked down her cheeks. Octavia moved to Brett's side and spoke to Nancy in a gentle voice.

"Mrs. Scroogen, I know this is extremely difficult, but will you try to help us find the truth?"

"What can I do?" she asked.

"Where is your husband's car?"

"It's in the garage, has been there since one of Sergeant Patterson's men returned it to the house a few days ago. Why?"

Brett found himself interested in the answer to that question, too.

"If your husband had Mab's gardening tool and gloves with him when he drove into work that morning," Octavia explained, "some of the dirt from them could have gotten onto the seat. If such dirt were found inside the car, that would prove he took the cultivator and used it on himself."

Brett nodded as he turned to Sergeant Patterson. "It's worth a forensic check of the car."

Patterson nodded. "Let's take a look."

Nancy led the single-file procession out to the garage. Brett spied the specks of dirt against the beige upholstery first. "There," he pointed through the open window. "On the passenger seat."

Patterson nodded. "I'll get it sampled right away."

"Dear God, it's true! He did it all himself!" Nancy cried on a sob.

"Hey, what's happening?" Ronald asked as he stepped into the garage. When he saw Nancy crying, an angry look descended on his face.

"What are you doing to her?" he demanded as he rushed to his stepmother's side.

Ronald pulled Nancy out of Brett's hands and put his arm around her shoulders, drawing her to his side. "It's all right," he said as he rested her head on his chest. "I'm here."

And from the fiercely protective expression on Ronald's face, Brett knew that eventually it would be all right for Nancy. She had lost a husband in this tragedy. But she seemed to have gained a son.

His beeper went off. He checked the number. It was Zane. His timing was good. Brett was eager to give him the good news that the case was solved. He left Sergeant Patterson to fill Ronald in on the circumstances surrounding Dole's death as he went to use his car phone.

"We've got the goods on her, Brett," Zane said.

"The goods on who?" Brett asked, momentarily confused.

"We can tie Octavia Osborne to that stone carving through her relationship to a native American chief by the name of Gordon Twobrook. Frankly, we only found out because one of A.J.'s operatives let something slip. It seems Octavia and the chief were pretty chummy back in her law school days. And, get this, he is rumored to have a stash of uncatalogued, bona fide, early artifacts from an ancient people who once lived in Washington State. You've got what you need to get her disbarred and charged, Brett."

"So, SCROOGEN KILLED himself?" Adam's voice asked on the other end of the telephone.

"Yes," Octavia said. "The forensic evaluation of the dirt on the front seat of Scroogen's car definitely proved it was the same dirt contaminated with monkshood poisoning that came from Mab's cultivator and gloves. Sergeant Patterson is now convinced that Scroogen stole the gloves and cultivator when he stole the stationery. Patterson's drawing up the paperwork now to have Mab released.''

"Congratulations, Octavia. Now, let's discuss some of the more subtle aspects of this attorney-client relationship you insisted on being established between us."

Octavia recognized the scolding tone in Adam's voice. She had heard it often enough. She could guess what was coming.

"Octavia, would it surprise you to learn that two very young and attractive women have taken turns this past week literally throwing themselves at me?"

"Why, Adam, I didn't know you had it in you," Octavia said, trying to sound innocent.

"Curiously enough, both ladies proved more interested in you and ancient Indian stone carvings than they were in me."

"Oh, really?"

"Octavia, let's not play games. Those women were employed by Coltrane to get the goods on you. You got Gordon to plant that Indian artifact on the land adjacent to that community center your grandmother was trying to save, didn't you?"

"Yes."

"Octavia, you've always been unorthodox, but I've never known you to violate the law before. What's going on here?"

"She's my grandmother, Adam. Don't you see?"

"No, I don't see. Have you thought about what would happen if Merlin found out about your planting that artifact?"

"He has found out. Matter of fact, I made sure he did."

"What? My God, do you know what kind of jeopardy you've put yourself and the firm in? Have you gone mad?"

"Adam, have you forgotten that I was there six years ago when we were chasing after your wife and breaking every law in the book?"

"That's ancient history, Octavia."

Octavia's voice softened. "No, Adam. It's still very current history for you. It's why you refuse to talk about it. The scar that you carry on your neck is nothing compared to the scar that has been left on your heart. You are going to have to deal with that someday."

"That is my personal business, Octavia. We are discussing a very pressing professional problem that reflects on you and this firm. You deliberately let Merlin know that you violated the law. Now he has to turn you in."

"Maybe."

"Maybe? Octavia, he's bound, as we all are, by a strict code of ethics. I would have to turn you in if you hadn't maneuvered me into learning of this stuff while I'm your attorney. Damn it, you've taken one too many risks."

"Adam, the biggest risks in life are the ones that carry the biggest rewards."

"And the greatest chance for disaster."

"Yes. Disaster is always a possible consequence. But so is incredible joy. What kind of a life are we living if we never go for that joy? It's what makes us feel *alive*."

"MAB, YOU AND THE community center look absolutely beautiful tonight," Octavia said as she surveyed her grandmother's formal scarlet dress as they strolled in the midst of the beautifully dressed seniors at the Silver Power League's Christmas Eve party.

"Thanks to you, Octavia, I am free and among my friends with my very special granddaughter. I have much to be grateful for this holiday season. Our center shines for us all tonight."

"That it does," Octavia agreed as she looked around at the beautiful new tree at its entrance and all the lovely decorations and twinkling lights everywhere. John sat at a piano donated by a member for the evening and played

"White Christmas" as Constance, Douglas, Edith and other seniors stood around singing along.

"I'm sorry about the land, Mab. By the time I spoke to Nancy, she had already sold it along with the building plans to a holding company looking for development property. A.J.'s promised to trace the owners. I'm not giving up."

Mab sighed. "We have no money to offer them."

"There has to be a way, Mab."

Her grandmother patted her hand. "If there is, dear, I know you'll find it. Just listen to those whispers from your heart."

Octavia didn't tell Mab that those whispers had been curiously and sadly silent over the last few days.

John gestured at them from across the room to join the seniors singing around the piano. Mab waved back, a very young smile suddenly drawing back her lips.

"Why don't you marry that man," Octavia asked. "It's so obvious you love each other."

"We do, but John made a mistake I can't forgive."

"You mean when he assisted his wife to die?"

Mab turned to her. "You investigated my friends? Even after I told you they didn't do it?"

"I'm sorry," Octavia said. "I should have listened."

"It's all right, dear. I know you were thinking of me. Anyway, you got it wrong. John's mistake wasn't assisting his sick wife to die. It was refusing to assist her. He wouldn't go against his doctor's oath. She had to steal the drug to end her pain. You once said you wanted a man willing to give up everything for the woman he loves. Well, your old grandmother feels the same way."

"I . . . see."

Mab patted her hand. "Don't look so sad, dear. John and I are good friends. That's important, too. And speaking of friends, where is that magician of yours? Last time I saw him was at the arraignment, and that was days ago."

"I haven't seen him since he left the Scroogens' garage to answer a call that came in on his beeper. He just . . . disappeared. Perhaps it's best."

"He'll be back," Mab said confidently.

"I don't think so, Mab."

"Think again. Here comes your magician now."

Octavia turned her head in the direction of the entrance. Brett was coming toward them, all right, all six-foot-four of him in competent, quick strides. He looked magnificent and utterly foreboding, the shoulders of his custom tuxedo dusted with snow, that obdurate shine in his black-rimmed, silver eyes hard with determination.

Octavia's heart somersaulted in her chest as her hands and arms tingled in anticipation. God, it felt so good to see him again!

Brett stopped not two feet in front of her. Without taking his eyes from her, he spoke to Mab with that controlled tone of polite distance Octavia remembered so well.

"Would you excuse your granddaughter and me for a moment, Mab? We have something to discuss."

"Yes, I can see that," Mab said as she smiled at them both before turning to join the seniors singing at the piano.

Brett offered Octavia his arm and gestured toward the entry with perfect expectation that Octavia would accompany him. Octavia held her ground.

"We can talk here."

The silver sabers in his eyes sharpened as he kept his arm extended. "Believe me. You do not wish this conversation overheard."

She believed him, or, more accurately, she believed that very dangerous look lighting his eyes. She took his formally extended arm and walked to the entry with him.

"This will do," he said, suddenly pulling her into the cloakroom and closing the door behind them.

She faced him, feeling the danger and excitement he exuded jolt adrenaline into her bloodstream. She tried to sound cool and unconcerned. She was not.

"There's something you wanted to say?"

He pulled some folded papers out of his jacket and held them out. She stiffened as she realized they were legal papers.

She unfolded them with trembling hands and found to her annoyance that she had to read them twice before the words made any sense. When the message of them finally sunk in, she exhaled in a sudden whoosh of breath.

"This is a land deed for this property. It's made out to the Silver Power League."

"They own it now," he said. "Free and clear."

She looked up at his face, at his wonderfully solemn face.

"You were the one who bought all the land from Nancy using some dummy corporation. My God, it must have cost you a fortune. What an incredibly reckless thing to do!"

He smiled then, a marvelous smile. "Yes, wasn't it?"

She wrapped her arms around his neck, tears of relief and happiness stinging her eyes.

"Brett, this is the best Christmas present ever. And you're the best Santa Claus in 'bah humbug' disguise I've ever—"

He silenced her with an urgent kiss and with a painful groan at how good she tasted and felt after so many—far too many—days and nights apart. Octavia melted happily into his strong, warm arms, crushing her to him.

"Why did you buy the land, Brett?" she asked against his ear.

"Because if anyone else owned this land—even Nancy— I would have had to have turned you in for planting that Indian pictograph on it and interfering with their legal right to develop it."

"You found a legal way to protect me. But you had to sell your beautiful blue white diamond to buy all this property, didn't you?"

He drew back to look deep into her eyes, and smiled. "Yes, but I found another midnight magic sparkle I value more. By owning the land, I'm the only one financially disadvantaged, and I can choose not to press charges."

"I'm so glad you're letting this lawbreaker get away."

He held her to him closely, breast to breast. "No, Octavia, I'm not letting you get away. I'll be right next to you for the rest of your life to make sure you go straight from now on. Believe it.''

There was no arguing with the warm, liquid silver in those eyes. Octavia's heart swelled inside her chest as she wove her arms around his waist.

''It's a sentence I'll be happy to serve. I love you, my Magician.''

''And I love you, my multifaceted and flawless beauty. Although it did take a roof falling in on me to finally realize it. I have no idea what the future will bring. But with you by my side, I suddenly can't wait to find out.''

''What are you going to do with the rest of the land?''

A humorous smile circled back his lips. ''I could always build a museum for native American artifacts on it, I suppose.''

She laughed in his arms—that wonderful, musical laugh that vibrated in his bones and sent his pulse to soaring.

As they came together in a joyous kiss, they could hear the seniors' muted voices rising in a favorite holiday tune. *We wish you a Merry Christmas,* they sang, *and a Happy New Year.*

BRIDE'S
BAY RESORT

UNLOCK THE DOOR TO GREAT ROMANCE
AT BRIDE'S BAY RESORT

Join Harlequin's new across-the-lines series, set
in an exclusive hotel on an island off the coast of
South Carolina.

Seven of your favorite authors will bring you exciting stories
about fascinating heroes and heroines discovering love at
Bride's Bay Resort.

Look for these fabulous stories coming to a store near you
beginning in January 1996.

Harlequin American Romance #613 in January
Matchmaking Baby by Cathy Gillen Thacker

Harlequin Presents #1794 in February
Indiscretions by Robyn Donald

Harlequin Intrigue #362 in March
Love and Lies by Dawn Stewardson

Harlequin Romance #3404 in April
Make Believe Engagement by Day Leclaire

Harlequin Temptation #588 in May
Stranger in the Night by Roseanne Williams

Harlequin Superromance #695 in June
Married to a Stranger by Connie Bennett

Harlequin Historicals #324 in July
Dulcie's Gift by Ruth Langan

Visit Bride's Bay Resort each month wherever
Harlequin books are sold.

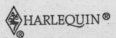

HARLEQUIN®

BBAYG

INTRODUCING...  WINNER'S CIRCLE

A collection of award-winning books by award-winning authors! From Harlequin and Silhouette.

Falling Angel
by Anne Stuart

WINNER OF THE RITA AWARD
FOR BEST ROMANCE!

Falling Angel by Anne Stuart is a RITA Award winner, voted Best Romance. A truly wonderful story, *Falling Angel* will transport you into a world of hidden identities, second chances and the magic of falling in love.

"Ms. Stuart's talent shines like the brightest of stars, making it very obvious that her ultimate destiny is to be the next romance author at the top of the best-seller charts."
— *Affaire de Coeur*

A heartwarming story for the holidays. You won't want to miss award-winning *Falling Angel*, available this January wherever Harlequin and Silhouette books are sold.

HARLEQUIN®

I N T R I G U E ®

Into a world where danger lurks around
every corner, and there's a fine line between trust
and betrayal, comes a tall, dark and handsome man.

Intuition draws you to him...but instinct keeps you
away. Is he really one of those...

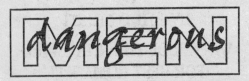

You made the dozen "Dangerous Men" from 1995 so
popular that there's a sextet of these sexy but
secretive men coming to you in 1996!

In January, look for:

#353 OUTLAWED!
by B. J. Daniels

**Take a walk on the wild side...with our
"DANGEROUS MEN"!**

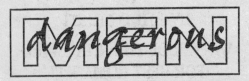

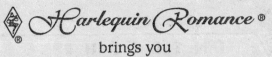

brings you

How the West Was Wooed!

Harlequin Romance would like to welcome you
Back to the Ranch again in 1996 with our new
miniseries, Hitched! We've rounded up twelve of our
most popular authors, and the result is a whole year
of romance, Western-style. Every month we'll be
bringing you a spirited, independent woman whose
heart is about to be lassoed by a rugged, handsome,
one-hundred-percent cowboy!

Watch for books branded **Hitched!** in the coming
months. We'll be featuring all your favorite
writers including, **Patricia Knoll, Ruth Jean Dale,
Rebecca Winters** and **Patricia Wilson**, to mention
a few!